WITCHLINGS

THE GOLDEN FROG GAMES

CLARIBEL A. ORTEGA

SCHOLASTIC PRESS

NEW YORK

All rights reserved. Published by Scholastic Press, an imprint of Scholastic
Inc., *Publishers since 1920*. SCHOLASTIC, SCHOLASTIC PRESS, and associated
logos are trademarks and/or registered trademarks of Scholastic Inc.

The publisher does not have any control over and does not assume any
responsibility for author or third-party websites or their content.

No part of this publication may be reproduced, stored in a retrieval system,
or transmitted in any form or by any means, electronic, mechanical,
photocopying, recording, or otherwise, without written permission of the
publisher. For information regarding permission, write to Scholastic Inc.,
Attention: Permissions Department, 557 Broadway, New York, NY 10012.

Library of Congress Cataloging-in-Publication Data available

ISBN 978-1-338-74579-5

10 9 8 7 6 5 4 3 2 1   23 24 25 26 27

Printed in the U.S.A.   37

First edition, May 2023

Book design by Christopher Stengel

TO DAVID, WHO BELIEVED IN ME
BEFORE I BELIEVED IN MYSELF
AND DID ALL THE LAUNDRY
AS I GALLIVANTED IN RAVENSKILL.
YOU WILL ALWAYS BE MY PUMPKIN.

TABLE OF CONTENTS

15th December 1789

It has been three months since the monstruos began speaking to me and there is nothing I can do to stop them.

—From the diary of Delphinium Larkspur, the Monstruo Uncle

CHAPTER ONE
SECRETS, SECRETS

DEEP IN THE SHADOWS of the Cursed Forest stood Seven Salazar and her secret.

It was a terrible secret and a dangerous one, but right now Seven had other things to worry about. Namely, the flock of skeleton birds with razor-sharp beaks and glowing red eyes that kept diving at her from the tippy tops of the Strangling Figs.

Cymric Rune, the Hastings-on-Pumpkins Uncle, cleared his throat. "Hmmm. This should not be that complicated."

"It should be *easy* to summon birds," Sybell the Oracle said, from where they were draped on a mossy log like some sort of model.

"Why don't you try again?" Cymric said softly, before shooting the Oracle a weary glance.

Seven nodded once, then raised her hands toward the

trees, which were bathed in the eerie purple light of the early morning, and spoke.

"Aves!"

A few seconds passed in tense silence, but then like every time before, instead of summoning normal birds, her magic brought the flock of skeleton creatures toward her. They pecked at her scalp and any exposed skin before spewing disgusting goo all over her. It burned like hex.

"Rats!" yelled Seven, waving her arms wildly to get the green slime off and stop the sting.

"The healing mushrooms, Seven, quickly!" cried Cymric.

"Surely she can pull off *this* simple spell," muttered the Oracle.

"Hongos!" said Seven, throwing her hands up and out. The earth rumbled slightly, and for a moment, Seven thought she might've gotten it right. Instead, a sound like a balloon deflating fizzled in the distance and her magic failed. Again.

"Hongos." The Oracle waved their hand lazily in Seven's direction as they flipped through an issue of *Teen Witch!* magazine. From a distance, the whispering of leaves approached. The whispers turned into violent rustles that shook the forest around them. A batch of multicolored cura-shrooms emerged from between the twisted trees and zoomed right at Seven. They hung suspended in the air around her, then each cura-shroom exploded like a firework, a chalky poof filling the air with rainbow smoke. Purple, green, and pink dust settled on Seven, and instantly her blistering skin was healed.

"See?" The Oracle licked their finger and turned another glossy page. "Easy."

Sometimes Seven Salazar wished the Nightbeast had never spoken to her. Right now, covered in dust and goo, in the middle of the Cursed Forest, her body weary with exhaustion, was one of those times.

"Is . . . something keeping you from focusing?" asked Cymric. His eyes, a vibrant green with slit pupils that were typical of a half fae, half witch, were kind, his demeanor patient, and yet Seven felt hot shame wash over her.

"She looks delicious," hissed a flor culebra as it slithered past Seven. She tried not to look at the petals sprouting from its skin—a beautiful monstrosity.

Yes, she wanted to say, *there are a million things keeping me from focusing.*

Instead she shook her head no, and Cymric nodded.

"All right. Let's try that one more time."

It had been four months since Seven learned she was meant to be the next Town Uncle, the second-most-powerful witch in her town, with the gift to speak to animals. And apparently monstruos. At first, she'd been so froggin' excited. It had been a welcome win after being declared a leftover witch, a Spare, and not having her coven circle close. She had been the first Witchling in many years to invoke the impossible task in order to make sure she and the rest of her coven didn't lose their powers. And Seven, Valley, and Thorn *had* beaten the impossible task, not by killing the Nightbeast but by stopping it. And then the Nightbeast had spoken to Seven. She had been blessed with the powers of the Uncle, given to her by nature. It was something that didn't happen to *Spare* witches. Not ever! And it had felt like a dream come true.

That was . . . until the voices of the monstruos didn't stop like they were supposed to. For most Uncles, after the first appearance of their powers, they could only hear animals— not monstruos. But for Seven, the monstruos were growing louder and louder, and one terrible voice in particular was growing loudest of all. But Seven hadn't told anyone that. Not even Valley and Thorn.

"Witchling, if nothing is keeping you from concentrating, then why is it you can't summon birds, of all things?" the Oracle asked. "It is a low-level Uncle task. One of the most basic."

"I have a name, you know," Seven said. "And technically I'm not a Witchling anymore."

Everyone kept calling Seven, Valley, and Thorn Witchlings. It was as if everything that had happened last year had left them marked for life. She had, in fact, grown half a toadstool since then.

"It's a term of endearment," said Sybell with a shrug.

Seven held in a laugh. Sybell liked to play at being tough on her in front of the Uncles and the Gran, but in reality, the two witches had something resembling a friendship.

"Nature has lost trust in our Uncle because of Barbatos and his coconspirators. The connection between animals and Uncles hinges on that trust. It will take time to build it up again," said Cymric.

"Agreed. But it is still strange," Sybell said.

They stretched and got up from their log, moss sticking to their holographic cape and metallic-dusted cheekbones like it was meant to be there. It was obvious Sybell came from House of Stars. If anyone lived up to their coven motto—beautiful, brilliant, generous to all—it was the Oracle. They were indeed gorgeous, and brilliant, an expert in their field. They were definitely generous with their time but also with their critiques. That was the thing about coven mottos, thought Seven—sometimes things that sounded positive could also be bad. She'd learned that much in the past few months.

"It is . . . a bit strange." Cymric mussed his soft auburn curls. "You're positively sure there's no interference with the communication from animals? No monstruos speaking to you still?"

Seven began to sweat.

"Would it really be that bad to talk to monstruos? Aren't some monstruos animals too?" Seven looked up into the trees, and ten pairs of beady black eyes blinked back at her.

Raccoons. A few of them smiled, their pointy little teeth glowing in the near darkness.

The Oracle scoffed. "Yes, it's bad. Remind me: What does section 17, paragraph 187 of your Uncle handbook say?"

Seven sighed and recited the section. "'The first Uncle communication is often the most powerful and can therefore manifest in unusual ways, such as hearing deepwater creatures, bacteria, fungi, or, in the rarest of cases, monstruos.'"

"Correct," said Cymric, holding Seven's gaze. "And after that first communication, it should never, ever happen again."

Except it is happening to me.

The Cursed Forest *should* have been the one place Seven could actually concentrate, because—with the exception of animals that were part monstruo, like raccoons for example— animals did not dwell here. They should've been far enough away that they wouldn't interfere with Seven's training, and indeed they were. But that did not stop her from hearing the Forest's culebras, mega-ratas, skeleton birds, and all the other monstruos. Being here and trying to practice magic was torturous. Seven wrung her hands, her head just about ready to split.

"What if an Uncle were to keep hearing monstruo voices?" Seven asked slowly.

Cymric and Sybell exchanged looks.

"We don't know. It has never, to our knowledge, happened before, but I imagine it would not be good," Cymric said.

Disappointment pressed on Seven's chest, making it hard for her to breathe.

They were lying.

There *had* been an Uncle who spoke to monstruos long, long ago. Her name was Delphinium Larkspur.

Seven's Uncle training required her to know about all the functions of Ravenskill, which meant lessons that had nothing to do with animals. This winter she had spent an entire month helping Alaric, the head archivist in the Hall of Elders (and a ghost), organize old, abandoned Uncle records. Deep in the Hall of Elders one snowy day, Seven had wiggled her way into a crawl space only big enough for a Witchling and found a dust- and cobweb-covered box, Delphinium's diary forgotten within. Seven tried not to look at her rucksack, where the pilfered diary now sat, buried beneath her schoolbooks. She had been making her way through the entries slowly, but the truth within those pages frightened her.

Seven shook her head and pushed her sleeves up. "Shall we try again?"

"Yes. At the very least, you need to be ready for your Uncle exhibition at the Golden Frog Games," Cymric said.

Seven raised her hands again, intoning the summoning spell and getting the same pitiful results. Again, the Oracle healed her and another layer of colorful dust settled onto her clothing, skin, and hair. This would be a nightmare to wash out.

"Somehow you are capable of spells high above your skill level, and you even helped defeat the Cursed Toads, but you cannot manage this level-one Uncle spell," Cymric said, before running his hands over his face in frustration.

Seven cringed.

The Cursed Toads had been the Ravenskill, Stormville, and Boggs Ferry Uncles, or at least everyone had thought they were. In reality, they had been the Spare witches of 1965, who used powerful and forbidden archaic magic to take on the forms of three Town Uncles. They had relegated the real Town Uncles to a punishment—living out the rest of their days as toads—that was meant for the Spares for not completing their own impossible task. The Uncles had watched from their tanks as their lives, their loved ones, and their powers were snatched away. The Cursed Toads had also done the unthinkable—they had hexed the entire Twelve Towns into forgetting. It wasn't until last year, thanks to Seven, Valley, and Thorn, that the truth had been uncovered.

"Could it have anything to do with the pace at which we're training her? We've been at this all morning. The Witchling must be tired," the Oracle said.

"No." Seven furrowed her brow. "No. I have to keep going. There's only a few months till the autumnal equinox."

If she could only train herself hard enough, maybe it would fix her magic. Maybe she could learn enough to quiet the monstruo voices and be a normal Uncle.

Cymric smiled. "That's not for six months! And if you don't pass your Uncle trials this fall, you can try again."

"You will be okay, Seven," the Oracle said.

Although Seven nodded, she knew that wasn't true.

The Town Grans and Uncles had been patient with Delphinium too. They had waited. Until one day when their patience ran dry and they decided she would have to die.

Because instead of getting her powers under control, Delphinium's connection to monstruos had grown stronger every day.

Just like Seven's was now.

They had grown afraid of what Delphinium might be capable of.

Just as they would with Seven.

And there was one voice, louder than all the rest, consuming her every thought, her every waking moment. Even now, it spoke to her. Crisp and clear as if it were whispering right in her ear. She could almost feel its hot breath on her skin, the brush of fur on her cheek.

"I'm *ever* so hungry," said the Nightbeast.

CHAPTER TWO
SPIN, STITCH, SEW

A BITTER BATTLE between House of Stars and Goose House had been going on for months. The covens, which were usually allies, had both set their sights on hosting the Frog Ball—the party that commemorated the near-end of the Golden Frog Games and was the highlight of many a Twelve Townian's tournament experience. Whichever house had the honor of hosting the ball also got something much more coveted than the party itself: bragging rights.

As the coven known for its parties, Goose House had hosted the Frog Ball for as far back as anyone in Ravenskill could remember. This year, however, House of Stars had begun campaigning early, citing highly suspicious and dangerous explosives magic that would make Goose House an unsafe fit for the festivities.

Goose House was incensed. There were a record number

of essays sent in to the *Squawking Crow*, denouncing the House of Stars claims and assuring Ravenskillian residents that Goose House was not only safe but the most capable coven to host the party. They had gone so far as to accuse House of Stars of having *bland* food. An outrage.

House of Stars had simply taken out a full page in the newspaper with a list of every explosion, fire, and catastrophe that had occurred in Goose House in the past three years. The list was 212 items long.

In retaliation, a few Goose House witches had schemed to plant explosives magic in their rival's basement and then alert the press that House of Stars was, in fact, the most unsafe option. However, their plan had backfired when two of the witches had gotten into an argument and accidentally set off an explosive spell right outside their own front door.

Caught red-handed, Goose House had no choice but to concede hosting the ball to House of Stars, with the caveat that the costura auditions would be held in Goose House.

"It was not our first choice, of course," said Mayhem Lilitoad, the Goose House witch ushering Seven, Valley, and Thorn to the ballroom. "But we made the most of what we were given. Besides, costura *is* the most popular sport. After toad racing." Mayhem was a tall, round witch with shining blond hair and a striking face. She walked briskly through the coven house.

"Graves said the explosions were so loud, she heard them all the way from her coven house," Valley said.

"Is that so?" Seven quirked an eyebrow at Thorn, who held in a giggle.

For months, Valley had been talking nonstop about Graves Shadowmend, a Moth House witch she'd met at the Monstruo Care Club after school. And Seven would bet her entire plant collection that Valley had a crush on her.

The hallways of Goose House were a pearly white and boasted elaborate molding adorned with golden geese along their borders. Enormous portraits of Goose House members of years past decorated the walls, and crystal vases with colorful flower arrangements sat on glass-and-gold side tables carved to look like delicate trees. Mayhem adjusted her special-occasion Goose House cloaks, which trailed behind her for many toadstools, as they rounded another corner.

"Must take a lot of scrubbing magic to keep this place clean," whispered Valley.

"You have no idea," said Mayhem as she opened the enormous double doors to the ballroom.

All three Witchlings gasped. Hundreds of iridescent stalactites seemed to grow from the ceiling itself, washing the ballroom in glittery light. A banquet of famous Ravenskillian food—including creamy mashed plantains, butter faeapple tarts, and crispy summer sausage cut into perfect little circles and drizzled with honey—blanketed the long table. Elaborate pastel flowers adorned every wall of the grand room, with vines snaking out to hug the corners and wrap around the closest stalactite-shaped lights, making it feel more like an enchanted cave than a room inside a coven house. The Witchlings stared in awe; every direction they looked, there was a new wonder to discover.

"Let's see House of Stars top this." Mayhem winked.

Onstage, a band played jaunty music while witches mingled on the ballroom floor. Some of them greeted Seven, Valley, and Thorn as they walked past, while just as many of them stared or whispered behind their hands and laughed. Valley shot them all annoyed looks and Seven rolled her eyes, but Thorn wrung her hands.

Thorn was doing something that had never been done before: attempting to enter the Golden Frog Games, the most important magical tournament of their world, as a Spare.

"You'll show them." Seven squeezed Thorn's hand.

"And if you don't, I will," Valley said, giving a cruelly smirking Moth House witch a death stare.

"That boil cleared up yet, Lapis?" Mayhem shouted.

The witch's face went bright red and he quickly turned away, but not before whispering nastily to a friend, "Thank goodness they're finally doing something about this Spare problem."

His friend nodded. "It's gotten quite out of hand."

What was that supposed to mean? thought Seven.

"Don't pay them any mind," Mayhem told Thorn as they walked farther into the glittering room.

They reached the backstage area where Thorn's dressing room was. "This is where I leave you," Mayhem said. "I've got to get ready to present my own creation."

"Oh," said Seven. "You're auditioning too?"

"Yep. Only Goose House witch from Ravenskill." Mayhem smiled proudly. "Good luck out there, Thorn. I'll be rooting for you."

"Thanks, Mayhem. I'll be rooting for you too." Thorn smiled, and the Goose House witch closed the door and left the Witchlings alone.

Valley immediately flopped onto the dark teal sofa. "Can't wait for you to make all those witches eat crow. Especially when you show them what we worked on. You practiced on your own, right?"

Thorn nodded. "I did the obstacle course twice a day for three weeks straight. That part I feel okay about." Thorn was already fussing over her entry: socks that wouldn't slip off, no matter what, even if you had boots on and your feet were sweating.

"Your idea is brilliant. And practical. And it works," Seven said. "You've always done a great job making clothes. Now just do what you normally do and try not to think too hard about the butt-toads out there."

"I should've maybe made a mirror pair of socks." Thorn bit her lip.

Costura, or fashion magic, was one of the oldest magic disciplines in the Twelve Towns. Historically, any enchanted fashion item was created in a pair to comply with the Rule of Mirrors. According to this rule, each garment or accessory in the pair was required to have an equal but juxtaposing power. Just like the covens and the Black Moon Ceremony, it was a way to keep balance in the magic world. Having a mirror kept any one creation from being too potent, which was especially important since the pieces were normally passed down within wealthy, influential families. If there was an item to counter another's power, it could always be tempered.

"So socks that never stay on?" Valley asked. "What good would that do anyone?"

"It wouldn't do any good, but it *would* be a show of my historical knowledge. It could've won me some points for presentation at the very least."

"It's probably too late to start working on those now though, right?" Seven nudged Thorn gently.

She knew her friend was looking for any possible excuse as to why she might not be named a champion. But this whole thing was hard enough as it was without Thorn beating herself up.

Thorn wiped sweat from her forehead and softly reinforced another grippy spell on the top of her socks. Her skin looked almost green with worry. Seven hadn't seen her friend this nervous since the night they fought the Nightbeast.

"You can do this, Thorn. If anyone can be a costura champion—the youngest one, and a Spare at that—it's you," Seven said.

Thorn nodded slowly. "I just . . . really want this. Things have been hard at home lately. My parents took the impossible task stuff hard last year . . . they were more worried about me than they let on, and I think they're just afraid of, well, afraid of losing the only kid they've got left."

Seven held Thorn's gaze.

"Ever since Petal died, nothing's been the same at home. My parents pretend they're okay, but the other night I found my dad in the kitchen crying alone, holding Petal's picture. My mom always has dark circles under her eyes because she can't sleep, and Grandma Lilou feels just as helpless as I do. But I know it would mean so much to them if I became a champion. It would, I dunno, give them all something to cheer for and look forward to. I want to live up to my mom's legacy and make my family proud and maybe give the Larouxs a win. We need it right now." Tears welled in Thorn's dark blue eyes, but she shook her head and bit them back.

"I can't speak for your mom," Valley said. "But if I had to take a bet, I'd say she was already proud of you. Leaf and Grandma Lilou too."

Seven nodded. "It's normal for your parents to miss Petal.

But don't put too much on your shoulders. I get wanting to give your family hope, but just having you around is enough," Seven said.

Thorn cracked a small smile, but Seven knew no matter what she or Valley said, there was a sadness deep inside her that they could not understand. If this was what Thorn needed to do to feel better, then it was their job to support her through that journey. That's what friends did.

Someone rapped on the door quickly, and a witch dressed in the tan-colored robes of the Golden Frog Games judges stuck his head in.

"Ten-minute warning! Might be a good idea for your two friends to head out." The judge smiled. "Thorn Laroux, right?"

Thorn nodded shyly.

"Ah, there are high hopes for you, Witchling. I watched your mother on the winning costura team many years ago— big shoes to fill. You'll need all the luck you can get, especially as a Spare."

Thorn's face went red and Seven opened her mouth to tell the judge off, but he was out the door before she could say butt-toad.

Valley got up from the sofa, shaking her head. "See you out there, Thorn. Remember, we've been through worse; this will be pumpkin pie." She squeezed Thorn's shoulders and stood at the door waiting for Seven.

"Good luck," Seven said. "But not to you, to those other

goats. Because I know you're going to knock their socks off." Seven grinned annoyingly and both Thorn and Valley groaned.

"Let's go before your jokes hex her socks," Valley said, and she and Seven made their way back into the ballroom.

"I'm getting some snacks," Seven said, and they walked over to one of the many banquet tables.

As they ate summer sausage, a cool-looking witch with dark teal hair sidled up to them and put her chin on Valley's shoulder.

"Hi," said the witch.

Seven opened her eyes wide and Valley started coughing.

"Oh goats, sorry, Valley!" the witch said, pouring a large glass of water.

Valley nodded and drank the whole glass quickly.

Seven smirked. This must be Graves Shadowmend. She had seen her around the Goody Garlick Academy for Magic, but had never officially met her or had any classes with her.

"You okay?" Graves asked, her sepia-brown skin reddening.

"Yup, A-okay, perfect, great!" Valley's voice squeaked.

"I'm Graves." Graves smiled at Seven. "Nice to meet you finally."

"Seven Salazar, nice to meet you too." Seven crossed her arms and smiled gleefully. "Valley's told me *a lot* about you."

Valley was about to start coughing again, when the band

stopped playing and the singer announced that the games host, Enve Lopes, would soon take the stage.

"Oh, they're starting! I better go back to my sister," Graves said.

"Saved by the drag witch," Seven muttered under her breath.

"See you later?" Graves whispered to Valley, squeezing her hand before going to join a group of Moth House witches on the other side of the room.

"The famous Graves, huh?" Seven asked.

"Mm-hm." Valley nodded, her cheeks bright pink.

"You . . . like her?" Seven asked.

"No, no, we're just friends. Gross, I don't like anyone," Valley said, but as she said it, her eyes found Graves in the crowd and she smiled softly.

No, my buns.

The Ravenskill fight song began to play and the two Witchlings hurried to take their seats next to Thorn's parents and Grandma Lilou. Moments later, a shadow of a witch appeared at the back of the stage. All around them, witches whispered excitedly. On beat, a spotlight illuminated Enve Lopes. Everyone cheered wildly as the drag witch smiled, her movements regal and confident. Enve sauntered to the front of the stage, taking her time to let the audience admire her spectacular ensemble. She was wearing a formfitting white gown that glittered in the ballroom lights. It had a long train trimmed in feathers, in honor of Goose House, Seven guessed. Her pink shoulder-length wig was styled in old-timey swoops, she wore long white gloves, and her elaborate makeup played up her sharp features. Everyone cheered as Enve flashed them a dazzling smile before grabbing the microphone from its stand. The crowd quieted down.

"Witches! Welcome to Ravenskill's costura auditions of the Golden Frog Games!" The witch threw her arms up dramatically and everyone applauded. "I am Enve Lopes, and I'll be your announcer for this year's tournament!"

"You know, I would've never pegged Jonafren as a drag witch, but Enve Lopes looks froggin' good," Seven said.

"She really does." Valley nodded.

"I will be traveling with you to Crones Cliff Manor for the champion unveiling and attending all the major events! Make sure you get my brand-new T-shirts *and* my album, *Done Licking Stamps*, at the back of the room!" Enve gestured behind the crowd, and they turned to see Alaric dressed in head-to-toe Enve Lopes merch, twirling to show it off. "And now for the moment we've all been waiting for: The champion audition! And we'll begin in alphabetical order!"

"This is gonna be a long day," Valley said as they settled in to watch witches from every coven, of all ages, present their costura creations. There were gloves that produced fire for a magic-weary witch in battle, followed by a cape that sprouted a giant green leaf for the rain, which didn't go over so well

("Isn't that just an umbrella?" asked Seven). They clapped supportively when Mayhem Lilitoad presented boots that absorbed sound and made your footfalls silent.

"Could've used those sneaking into the Nightbeast's cave," whispered Valley.

Almost as if it could sense the Witchlings talking about it, a low growl rumbled in Seven's ear.

"When will you come speak to me? I need your help," said the Nightbeast, but Seven just closed her eyes and willed the voice to go away. She couldn't do this, not now. She reminded herself that the Nightbeast was far from her, in some secret enchanted glade the Gran had created to keep it from hurting anyone else.

"A prison," said the beast. Seven clenched her fists tight, trying with all her might to push the voice out of her mind.

Mercifully, the creature went quiet after that, because at long last it was time for the youngest witch, and the only Spare, to present.

"Let's go, Thorn!" Valley yelled, and Seven whooped and screamed.

"Oh, I am so nervous," said Pixel Gibbons as Mrs. Laroux squeezed her hand. Pixel, a Spare witch who used to work for the Dimblewits, the awful family that had helped the Cursed Toads the year before, was now working with Mrs. Laroux. Seven was relieved to see that she had clothing that wasn't ripped and shoes that were free of holes. Mrs. Laroux was training her in costura, and paying her well enough to save up for a small house in downtown Ravenskill—a fact that made many Hill residents unhappy.

"Don't you worry, our Thorn is going to destroy them," Thimble Laroux said, an intense shine in her eyes.

"And if she doesn't, that is okay too," chuckled the very tall and muscular Leaf Laroux.

Thorn walked onto the stage and Seven's heart swelled to the size of the moon. She wanted so badly for her friend to do well. Seven wished there was something she could do to help, but unless her enchanted socks needed ten raccoons to model them, Thorn had to do this on her own.

"All right, Miss Laroux, let's see what you can do!" Enve Lopes said.

Thorn nodded and opened a bejeweled box that rested on a small table beside her, pulling out the socks she had been working on. She slipped her boots and normal socks off and placed the enchanted socks on her feet, before finally putting her boots back on.

"These socks will stay up even in the most extreme situations," said Thorn. "Saving you from the discomfort of having to take your boots off to adjust them."

Thorn raised her hands and, in just moments, the stage was covered in fake snow. Somehow, Enve Lopes suddenly had a faux fur coat on to match her ensemble.

"Incredible!" the drag witch said.

Thorn raised her hands again and her boots, which were a deep pink color, went completely transparent.

"The Laroux flair," whispered Mrs. Laroux excitedly.

A sort of obstacle course, including hoops, a pond, and a ramp, was pushed out by the stage crew.

"Not only that," Thorn continued, "but these socks will never get wet, and add an additional three levels of dexterity to your shoes."

There were plenty of shoes with added magical dexterity, but by applying that magic to socks, it gave a witch an extra level of protection against counterspells.

"Allow me to demonstrate," Thorn said, then took a running start and leapt through the first hoop, which was easily five feet off the ground, coming back to earth with the grace of a slowly falling leaf.

"Wow," said Valley, eyes wide.

"You trained her well," Seven said.

Thorn landed on the other side with a small thump, one knee down, before bolting through the glittering snow. She ran straight through the pond and, as promised, it was clear that water repelled right off the socks.

"Those socks would sell out in five seconds in the shop," said Pixel.

"Easily," said Mrs. Laroux in wonderment.

Finally, Thorn ran up the ramp and launched herself the

ten or so feet to the floor right in front of the stage, landing gingerly before taking a small bow.

The crowd exploded. There was no denying how incredible Thorn's presentation had been. Everything from the snow to the obstacle course to Thorn's showmanship, added a level of pizzazz that made her socks stand out.

"I'll admit," Enve said, "when you announced your entry was *socks*, I didn't expect much." The crowd chuckled and Thorn's cheeks went bright red. "But if your coven has proven anything, it's that only a fool would underestimate you. I won't make that mistake again." Enve gave Thorn a short curtsy and a smile. The audience cheered and Thorn looked dazed as she walked off the stage to join her family and friends.

Seven and Valley hugged Thorn at once, almost knocking her over.

"You did it!" Valley said.

"Thanks." Thorn smiled shyly. "Now we have to see what happens at the Unveiling of the Champions."

"I'm pretty sure I know what's going to happen," Seven said, and she meant it.

Because not for the first time, a Ravenskill Spare had just made history.

CHAPTER THREE
THE TWELVE TOWNS TRAIN

"MOVE YOUR BUNS, we're gonna miss the train!" Seven shouted as the Witchlings and their families ran to the Ravenskill train station a few days later. Ahead, a rainbow sea of cloaks streamed into the high-speed locomotive. It was so early, the sun was still resting behind Oso Mountain, but if they were going to make it to the Unveiling of the Champions in Crones Cliff Manor, they had to leave extra early.

Eyes followed the Witchlings as they arrived at the train just in time and climbed aboard to look for seats.

Seven's mom, Fox Salazar, gave a friendly "Hello" to anyone who looked their way, both familiar witches from Ravenskill and a few Seven didn't recognize who must've been from the four Twelve Towns to the north of Ravenskill. Some people greeted them back, while others turned away quickly.

Seven smiled awkwardly at people who caught her eye,

glad she had her parents with her. And, of course, her coven. Thorn was walking down the aisles like she was on a runway, and Valley was threatening horrifying hexes with every glance.

"The famous Spares," said the conductor, who had stepped in front of them. "Turnip Brightdash at your service. I've set aside a compartment just for you, although I am afraid it's only big enough for the three Spares." Turnip looked apologetically at Talis, Fox, Leaf, Thimble, and Quill.

Talis Salazar shook his head. "The price of having a famous daughter."

"Abandoned again," said Quill with a smile as she kissed the top of Valley's head gently.

"Is it okay if we go?" Seven asked, eyes wide.

"Of course!" Fox said. "Go live the luxurious life without us."

Seven groaned and Fox laughed.

"I'm kidding! I'm kidding. Go, go, we'll be fine," Fox said.

"Well, then, shall we?" Turnip asked, and led the Witchlings to the luxury cars at the center of the train.

Seven had taken the Triple T before, but only to nearby towns like Sleepy Hollow, and only in the normal cars. She had never been in one of the luxury cars, and walking in, she had to keep from yelling at how fancy it was. There were pink velvet seats with gold trim and retractable lunch tables and giant windows. It even smelled nicer in here, and the air felt more refreshing to breathe—all things that Seven had noticed about the Hill as well. It took a lot of magic to make something this pleasant. And though she wished it wasn't limited to those who paid extra, Seven all but melted into the comfy, cushioned seats, her exhaustion winning over any objections she might have.

"You're sleepy, aren't you? Serves you right for not helping poor Nightbeasty," said Edgar from Seven's bag. Thorn had fashioned her a rucksack with a clear mushroom-shaped compartment for him.

"I'm not in the mood, Edgar," Seven said, her eyes closed.

"What did he say?" asked Valley.

Seven's cheeks went red. "He's just being annoying about the run here being bumpy," she lied.

"I am NOT," Edgar said.

Seven hadn't told Valley or Thorn about any of the monstruo voices she was hearing, including the Nightbeast's. She was afraid of how they'd react, especially Thorn. Hexed or not, the Nightbeast had killed her twin brother, Petal, and Seven didn't expect Thorn to forgive that. But of all the witches she had to keep this a secret from, her coven sisters were the most painful.

The Witchlings took off their spring cloaks and settled in to do one of their favorite activities: gossip.

"I heard that a House Hyacinth witch *paid* to get on the toad-racing team," Valley whispered conspiratorially.

"Is that even allowed?" asked a scandalized Thorn.

Seven scoffed. "As if that ever stopped rich witches from being sneaky squirrels. No offense, Valley."

"None taken, Salazar." Valley smiled. Valley didn't live on the Hill anymore anyway. Not since her parents separated. They were in the middle of "a nasty divorce," the social pages of the *Squawking Crow* had said, but as far as Seven could tell, Quill, Valley's mom, wasn't the one making it difficult. No surprise there. Seven had tried to talk to Valley about it, but she kept dodging questions.

"Plus, Thorn's family is probably even richer than mine. They just don't live on the Hill," said Valley with a smirk.

"We aren't—we just look fancy because we know how to dress," Thorn said.

As Valley and Thorn kept chatting, Seven took her twenty-sided crystal out and began inspecting it. Each side had a sparkling number on its iridescent blue face, which popped out to be used as a tracker. Once Seven attached one of the tracking tiles to an animal, provided she had completed the enchantment correctly, the slot where its number had been would turn into the silhouette of said animal and the crystal would record the location and voice of the animal at set intervals throughout the day. The Gran had tasked Seven with tagging twenty animals in Crones Cliff Manor while she was there so that she could practice her long-distance care spells. She had tried practicing the tracker enchantment back in Ravenskill, but so far, the only silhouettes that had appeared were of the ten raccoons that followed her everywhere. Seven placed the rosebud speaker she had connected to the crystal in her ear and listened. She could hear the raccoons talking, mostly about food, or her, and wondered why she could get the tracker to work with the half-monstruos but not any animals.

Seven rubbed her face and put her crystal and rosebud speaker away. She'd barely gotten any rest last night, and the monstruo voices were becoming louder and more insistent every day. She knew she should tell someone, that this wasn't the kind of thing a young witch could handle on her own. What if she told Thorn and Valley? Surely, they'd be able to help, and it wasn't like they would be afraid of her like everyone had been of Delphinium. She sat up a bit straighter, testing the words out in her mind—*I can hear monstruos.*

Something screeched, loud and piercing like a dagger.

Seven nearly jumped out of her seat, but as she scrambled to compose herself and Valley and Thorn gave her curious looks, she realized she had been the only one to react. She'd been the only one to hear the sound. Seven was reminded of an entry from the diary in her bag:

My family thinks me mad. For hearing things that are not there, for hearing creatures that no witch had ever been meant to hear. They have stopped setting a place for me at dinner. I am only ever alone.

All thoughts of telling her coven vanished then. How could she when the mere knowledge of what she could do might be enough to put them in danger as well?

"Are you *sure* you're okay, Salazar?" asked Valley.

Seven sighed. "Yes, I'm just more tired than I realized. Haven't been sleeping much."

"Of course you haven't. The Gran has been working you to the bone. I really don't think it's fair how much they're expecting of you," Thorn said.

"Someone has to look after the animals," Seven said.

"There are nine Uncles besides you, let them take turns," Valley said.

"It's not that simple. Even one town being without an official Uncle is a catastrophe, and right now there are three. Until one of the other towns' Uncles is chosen and trained, I have to work as hard as I can."

Valley and Thorn exchanged looks.

"Don't start planning things behind my back. I'll find out from a winged wombat or something." Seven yawned and closed her eyes in hopes they'd drop the subject altogether.

Everything was mercifully quiet for a moment, and Seven began to slip into sleep, then the animal voices erupted again. Seven opened her eyes and gave up on getting any rest. Thorn and Valley were talking quietly, but Seven couldn't register a thing they said. Instead there was an insistent chorus of

"The beagles have invaded our food supply!" and "The rats are holding an illegal fighting ring in the Cursed Forest!" or "My baby bird's gone missing!" Each request from the Twelve Towns animals was more insistent than the next, but none more so than the Nightbeast, which reminded Seven, once again, that it wanted to see her.

"Seven?" Thorn asked. "Did you hear what I said?"

"Oh yeah, totally," Seven said.

Valley rolled her eyes. "Okay, what did Thorn say, then?"

"I . . . I'm sorry, goats. I wasn't listening." Seven's face went hot.

Valley shook her head. "She *said*, are you froggin' out about your Uncle exhibition for the games?"

Thorn nodded, eyes wide. She probably needed someone to share her nervous excitement with.

Seven winced. "I am frogging out. I'm a mess."

Seven rubbed her neck, her own words hitting her a bit too hard.

"At least the Uncles just do a demonstration." Thorn nodded. "So you can't lose like you can in one of the other sports."

"That is a relief," said Seven, though it really wasn't. She wasn't so much worried about winning as she was about completely failing in front of every Twelve Townian. What if she completely flopped, and skeleton birds started pecking people's eyeballs out or something? She didn't want to let her coven or her family or the Gran down. She didn't want to give everyone more of a reason to unfairly judge the Spares.

The games were the biggest deal in the Twelve Towns, and the worst place Seven could think of to show off her faulty Uncle magic. There were seventeen sports in all, with everything from ottersleighing to bear lifting to seahorse polo. Whichever town won the most sports would be the overall winner of the tournament, but the highest honor went to the MVW—Most Valuable Witch—of the games: the witch from the winning town who got the most overall points was granted the honor to touch the Golden Frog and see a crucial vision about their town.

In the past, the vision had helped towns avoid monstruo attacks, find a hoard of gold, and even win the next Golden Frog Games—and the glory of winning was the highest honor any town could hope to achieve. Ravenskill was hosting this year's games, and they hadn't clinched the coveted MVW win in over fifty years. Tensions were understandably high for them to bring the Golden Frog home, especially while hosting.

"I'm getting a drink. Want anything?" Seven asked.

"Water with a slice of lemon, please," said Thorn.

"Black cherry cola, extra ice, extra fizz," said Valley.

"I'll be right back," Seven said, and left their compartment.

She tried to ignore the stares of other witches as she made her way to the dining car and ordered their drinks.

"Hey, Seven," said a familiar voice from behind her.

"Poppy, hi." Seven turned around to see a smiling, rosy-cheeked blond witch in a lavish purple spring robe.

Poppy Mayweather had been best friends with Seven their whole lives. That is, until last year, when Poppy had been sorted into the powerful, popular House Hyacinth coven—something that had always been Seven's dream—while Seven had been designated a Spare. They had patched things up though, and were at least friendly again, if not the close friends they once were.

"You excited about the Unveiling of the Champions?" Poppy asked after she ordered a lemonade.

"Um, yeah. Rooting for Thorn," Seven said.

Poppy peered at her. "You doing okay? You look like that time we watched *River Clowns 2* and you couldn't sleep for a week."

Seven smiled. They might not have been as close as they once were, but Poppy knew her better than pretty much anyone.

"Just tired from training, and Pepperhorn won't stop talking," Seven said.

Poppy chuckled. "*Pepperhorn.* I remember when we were both afraid of Valley."

"Things have really changed, huh?"

Poppy glanced around and pulled in close to Seven. "Speaking of which, have you seen the latest *Squawking Crow*?"

Seven shook her head. Normally she was a faithful reader of the newspaper, especially Tiordan Whisperbrew's column, but she hadn't had much time for anything lately and had missed the last few issues.

"I need to show you something," Poppy said. She held her hand out, and Seven let Poppy lead her to a nearby compartment.

"Good, nobody's in here," Poppy said as they went inside. It felt weirdly like old times, except Seven was a completely different witch now and so was Poppy. Somehow though, things just fit together like they used to. In a new way, yes, but they still fit. Poppy closed the door to her train compartment with purple Hyacinth luggage and robes strewn about, and pulled a newspaper out from her suitcase.

Poppy held the newspaper to her chest. "It's . . . bad. I know you have a lot going on and this is the last thing you need, but. . . . Maybe it's better if you know."

"What?" Seven asked, her heart in her throat. "Just show me, I can take whatever it is."

Poppy looked conflicted.

"Poppy, I fought a Nightbeast, I can handle a newspaper article," Seven said.

"And when will you come see me?" the Nightbeast said.

"All right," Poppy said. She turned the paper around and gave it to Seven.

"An Attack on Spares" read the front page. Right beneath the headline there was a picture of a young witch with older, patched-up clothing, a sad expression on his face, and bruises along his arms. A Spare named Magpie Bitterfoot, according to the caption beneath the photo, victim of an attack in Castle Point. There was an article detailing the incident and the increasing unrest regarding Spares across the Twelve Towns in the past month. Seven skimmed the article until she spotted her name, then quickly folded the newspaper.

"Can I keep this? I want to read it later," she said, her stomach in knots.

"Of course," Poppy said. "I didn't mean to upset you, I just want you to keep safe."

Seven nodded. "I know, don't worry. You're right, it's important for me to know this is happening. Especially since it's probably happening because of us."

"Seven . . ."

"Witches are afraid of unfamiliar things, that's all. When they realize Thorn, Valley, and I aren't some evil, baby-eating warlocks, maybe they'll stop all this. I'm okay, really, but I've gotta find a way to help the other Spares. What's happening to them is not okay."

"I'll help too." Poppy smiled.

"Thanks, Poppy. I better bring my drinks back to the car."

"All right, see ya."

Seven grabbed their drinks and made her way back to their compartment, her head spinning the whole way. Initially, she had thought that maybe her Uncle-ship would help turn the tide for Spare rights. That Twelve Townians would see they were capable of anything witches in the five other covens were capable of. But maybe all it did was make things worse. There were a lot of witches who were unhappy about it. One thing was certain: If witches were this upset about the next Ravenskill Uncle being a Spare, there would be riots if they knew that she could also speak to monstruos. Seven had to keep her secret, even if it killed her.

Balancing the drinks carefully, she opened the door to their compartment to find Thorn and Valley in a heated conversation.

"Fashion is worth double most sports, third only to spaceball and toad racing. It *is* important," Thorn said.

"I never said it wasn't! Just that it's not as exciting *to me*," Valley said.

"Why do you let her troll you?" Seven asked Thorn as she sat down. "She just wants to get a rise out of you!"

Valley smirked as Seven handed over her cherry cola and a pouting Thorn her water.

"Aw, nuts, they gave me toad cola," Valley said, making a grossed-out face. "I'm gonna go get a new one."

"Want me to come with—" Thorn started, but Valley was already gone.

"Weirdo," murmured Seven as she watched the towns swoosh by outside the window. They made stops at Hastings-on-Pumpkins, Sleepy Hollow, and Faerytown, and with each town came more witches scrambling for seats or settling for standing-room-only areas. Each time they passed the Witchlings' compartment, whispers and stares passed with them.

"That's them!" squealed one witch around their age.

"They're smaller than I imagined."

"Where's the pink-haired one?"

"Where *is* Valley?" Seven asked Thorn.

Thorn looked up from her issue of *Cauldron Couture* magazine and shrugged. "She's been gone for a while."

"Almost an hour," Seven said, worry prickling her mind.

"She probably went to sit with her mom," Thorn offered.

"You're probably right," Seven said.

Seven eyed Thorn. She was lost in the magazine pages, taking notes and sketching in her fashion ideas notebook, so Seven reached for her rucksack.

She fished out the brown leather diary that had belonged to Delphinium and picked up at the last entry she'd read. She had spent the night before reading until she couldn't keep her eyes open, and she was anxious to see what the next entry said.

15th December 1789

*It has been three months since the monstruos began
speaking to me and there is nothing I can do to stop
them. I have searched for a cure or an answer to my
ailment, but it does not seem to exist. I have only
another month before they decide what to do with me
if I cannot make the monstruos stop. I wonder if I made
a mistake in telling the Gran. Another thought has
been plaguing me lately: If all the magic we know of
comes from stars and nature, perhaps there is magic
that can come from somewhere else. Perhaps my magic
is not tainted, just . . . different. There must be a way
to show them that though I speak to monstruos, I am
not one myself.*

"What's that?" Thorn asked.

Seven quickly closed the journal, her chest tightening.
"Just some Uncle reading."

"They're really putting a lot in your cauldron," Thorn said
softly. "Should be some sort of laws against making young
witches work this much."

"Mm-hm." Seven's heart was beating faster than a
hummingbird's wings.

"Hopefully once you pass your trials this autumn, things
will ease up." Thorn smiled.

"Yeah," Seven said softly as she turned to look out the window.

The next portion of the ride was quiet and peaceful as they passed wildflower meadows and ogre-sized trees, the lapping waves of the Boggy Crone River, and the Oso Mountain range that extended deep into the southern Twelve Towns. Beyond the mountains, Seven could see the curling smoke of the mist from the Enchanted Grim—a monstruo-infested expanse that separated the Twelve Towns from the wild lands and cities beyond. She was glad to not be closer, imagining how all-encompassing the monstruo voices would become if she ever was. As she watched the landscape whoosh past, sleep overtook Seven and she drifted off into a blissful nap.

She awoke hours later, right before they were set to arrive in Crones Cliff Manor. Seven yawned and looked around.

"Still no Valley?" Seven asked.

Thorn shook her head. "Nope. We're almost there though. Make sure you don't leave anything behind."

Seven and Thorn gathered their things as the train began slowing down to pull into the station.

"Valley better come back, I'm not carrying her suitcase," Seven said.

"I'm here, I'm here," said a breathless Valley, breezing back into the car. Her cheeks were bright red and she had a bracelet on that Seven didn't recognize.

"Where the hex were you?" Seven asked.

"Just hanging around," Valley said with a shrug.

"Did you get your cherry cola at least?" Thorn asked.

"Cola?" Valley asked.

"You said they gave you the wrong one," Seven said, narrowing her eyes.

"Oh, right. Nope, they had . . . run out."

"Sure," Seven said. "Well, better hurry up and get your stuff—we're almost there."

The Witchlings had made their way out of their compartment and onto the station platform when Graves ran up to them.

"I didn't get to say bye," Graves said. "I had a lot of fun today. Thanks for the bracelet." She held up a matching beaded bracelet to the one Valley had on. "See you tonight, pumpkin," Graves said shyly, then ran back to a group of witches who were looking on.

"Pumpkin!" Seven spluttered.

But Valley Pepperhorn just shrugged, lugging her black suitcase down the platform, her face still bright red. It looked like Seven wasn't the only one keeping secrets.

CHAPTER FOUR

MEETING MISS DEWEY'S BOYFRIEND (POSSIBLY. EW)

CRONES CLIFF MANOR was a wonder to behold. Every house was beautiful, giant yet cozy—with gardens filled with colorful vibrant flowers, perfect lawns, and streets that looked like they were crafted by artisan gnomes. Here, the Boggy Crone River met the Atlantis Ocean. Instead of being accessible like it was in Ravenskill, the water flowed below a giant majestic cliff, waves lapping against its jagged foundation. It was Seven's first time visiting the faraway town, and she couldn't take it all in fast enough. It was almost like a bigger, fancier version of the Hill in Ravenskill, except the whole town got to enjoy the flowers, the soft magical breeze infused with sweet-smelling tonics. They passed a cheese shop where a worker was using a glittering string to cut the purple cheese into thin slices, and a tavern that was already open, serving orange-and-cream drinks in frozen glasses.

"Suddenly I'm hungry again," Thorn said.

Seven nodded. "We'll get something soon, but we need to meet our guide in front of the Crones Cliff Museum of History and Curiosities now." They had been personally invited to the champion unveiling by the Crones Cliff Manor Gran, making them extra important guests who also got a guide. Not everything about being a famous Spare was great, but there were some perks.

They walked on, following the signs pointing to the museum. They were passing by a knickknack shop when Valley stopped abruptly, staring at something on the newsstand in front of the store. Her face went red and Valley clenched her fists before walking on.

"Valley, what is it?" Seven asked, before stopping to see for herself.

"Disgraced Heir to the Pepperhorn Dynasty" was splashed across the front page in big, bold letters. Beneath it, a picture of Mr. Pepperhorn, Quill, and Valley posing for a family portrait. Mr. Pepperhorn stood stiffly and his hand sat on Valley's shoulder. Valley's face held the blank expression it often had back when she still lived in Blood Rose Manor, and her mother, Quill, had a small smile. But there was a big red X over Mr. Pepperhorn's face. Seven quickly scanned the story: It connected him to the Cursed Toads and included lots of details about the divorce. Seven cringed. She understood the part about the Cursed Toads being news, but the divorce? And why did they have to put Valley and Quill on the front page too? It was embarrassing enough for Valley as it was. It seemed like all the big stories that day had to do with Spares. Most of the town knew Valley's father, butt-toad of the century, was fighting for full custody of Valley, while her mother, didn't want Valley to see her dad at all. But for their entire region to be talking about it was too much.

Thorn, who was standing beside Seven, shot her a worried look.

"Valley, wait," Seven said as they caught up to her. "Are you okay?"

Valley glanced back. "Why wouldn't I be?"

"Well . . ." Thorn wrung her hands.

"The newspaper," Seven said. "I would be mad too, if they were writing about my family that way."

"I'm fine." Valley kept walking.

"Are you sure?" Thorn asked. "You can tell us, Val."

"Yes. I don't want to talk about it anymore, okay?" Valley snapped, and Seven and Thorn asked no more questions after that.

They continued on the path to the museum, passing rows of neat little houses, weeping willows, and witches strolling hand in hand. The animals here were calmer than the Ravenskill ones—likely because they had an experienced Uncle to take care of them—and mercifully, there were no monstruo voices at all. A pang of guilt overtook Seven. She should be home, making sure the Ravenskill animals were okay.

But really, worryingly, her heart ached for the monstruo voices as well.

"I am here," the familiar voice growled, and Seven's heartbeat slowed to a normal rhythm.

What was happening to her?

Seven's mind whirled with questions as they made it to the museum, where witches were breaking off into tour groups led by guides—Crones Cliff Manor witches who were dressed in their finest spring robes. Minutes passed, and soon the Witchlings were the only three left.

"Where's our froggin' guide!" Seven threw her hands up.

"I suppose they're not coming," Thorn said.

"We should just go in ourselves; how hard can it be to navigate a museum?" Valley said.

But then a familiar voice called out to them and all three Witchlings swiveled toward a figure coming in their direction.

"Are those my Stupendous Spares I spy?!" A beautiful, elegant woman waved a silk scarf in the air, and all three of them smiled. A warm, happy feeling, one she hadn't felt in quite some time, bloomed in Seven's chest as the witch approached. It wasn't just *any* witch, it was Miss Dewey.

Their favorite librarian ran to them, her pencil skirt and heels making her take little steps. She always looked like a star from the olden-days movies, and this time she was with someone who looked like he could've been her leading man.

A witch with a bright smile and bouncy black curls that swooped to the side walked beside Miss Dewey, making sure she didn't trip on the cobblestones.

"Oh, I've missed you three." Miss Dewey leaned down, and the Witchlings opened their arms to welcome a hug. Miss Dewey had helped them throughout the impossible task when many other adult witches in Ravenskill had turned their backs on them. If it weren't for her, they might not have had the morale, or the much-needed information, they needed to go up against the Nightbeast.

"We've been busy." Seven rubbed her neck anxiously.

"Busy being too grown-up! Look at how tall you've gotten!"

All three Witchlings blushed.

"I want you to meet someone." Miss Dewey flourished a hand toward the man beside her. "This is Ambert. He's a fellow librarian!"

"Ambert Lophiifor?" Valley asked, wide-eyed.

Ambert laughed, showing dimples on his golden-tan skin as he did. "The very one, nice to meet you."

Ambert Lophiifor had famously won the MVW trophy for Crones Cliff Manor in the last Golden Frog Games. He had won the familiar agility trials with his squirrel, a sport only librarians could participate in. He was pretty much a celebrity, and Seven suddenly felt so shy she didn't know what to do with her limbs. Thorn literally covered her face with her hands.

"Nice to meet you, Mr. Lophiifor!" Valley said, shaking his hand.

"Please, call me Ambert, and welcome to Crones Cliff Manor. Shouldn't you be doing the museum tour right about now?" Ambert asked.

"We're supposed to, but our guide never came," Seven said indignantly.

"Whaddaya say, Ambert?" Miss Dewey nudged him playfully.

"I suppose I can do it," he said just as playfully.

Seven cringed. Were they flirting? *Gross.* Also, go Miss Dewey! Ambert was *famous.*

"Come on, you're going to love it. Ambert knows more about the history of the Twelve Towns than anyone I know," Miss Dewey said.

Seven wondered if Ambert knew anything about Delphinium. She would never ask, of course, but she could ask Miss Dewey, couldn't she? Her favorite adult aside from her parents would never tell—at least Seven was pretty sure she wouldn't. But pretty sure wasn't enough when it came to life or death, and that's exactly what her secret was.

Right at that moment a giant wave crashed on the cliff, spraying them with a cold, salty mist and startling the Witchlings.

Ambert flashed a mischievous smile. "Before we go in the museum, come. I'd like to show you something." He gestured at them to follow him toward the cliff's edge, and they did, stopping at the crystal-like barrier. Ambert looked over the barrier and Seven followed suit. She expected to see a straight drop down, but instead there was a well-paved path with trees and more of the crystal guardrail, leading to a row of houseboats along the shore. Seven wondered how the houses weren't destroyed by the waves.

"If you look down here, you can see the Half Moon Estuary, where the Boggy Crone River ends and the Atlantis Ocean begins. All along the path toward the shore, we've planted a variety of trees to help the Spares who now live in these houseboats feel happier." Ambert gestured to the homes.

"Spares live in those?" Thorn asked in awe.

Ambert nodded proudly. "Only as of the past few months, but yes."

"I bet they get crushed by the waves," mumbled Valley.

"Not at all. We've made sure to put enchantments in place to keep the houses safe."

Seven couldn't believe it. That kind of magic was costly and was the sort of thing you only really saw rich witches be able to afford. But not only were these Spare homes kept safe by the town, they were actually nice. They were lined up in a neat row along a dock and all painted different pastel hues. They looked beautiful and cozy and Seven felt a small ache in her heart for the Ravenskill Spares, who didn't have homes nearly this nice, if they had their own places to live in at all. She wondered what it would take to make their homes livable.

"This is froggin' cool," Valley whispered.

"It's wonderful," said Thorn.

They walked back to the museum, which was even bigger than the Hall of Elders. There were massive marble columns on each side, adorned with beavers and foliage. Inside, various tour groups crowded the hallways and exhibits.

"Stay close," said Miss Dewey as they pushed their way through the throngs of witches. Twelve Townians from every town were packed into the museum, making it hard to move. That made it that much worse; everywhere they walked, curious glances followed. Seven's chest constricted, her mind racing with all the possible horrible things people might be thinking about them. She wondered about this so often that she had begun to think maybe some of those awful things must be true. She could hear monstruos, after all. Seven wished she could go inside Edgar's little hideaway, but even if she could find a way to make herself small, she knew Edgar would only say, "Better get your head out of the clouds," or something. The thought of it made her smile, and Seven tapped her rucksack lovingly. It wasn't all bad, she thought. At least she had her mean old toad.

They funneled into one of the museum's emptier wings, and Seven felt like she could breathe again. Ambert was the perfect substitute tour guide. He patiently explained the various paintings and relics, and he told them all about the founder of Crones Cliff Manor, Guillemot Ligero, whose goal had always been to give witches a happier and safer way of life.

"Guillemot fought in the Battle of Oso Mountain over six hundred years ago, and took in Spares who had been abandoned by their families. In fact, he always believed in the rights of Spares and did everything in his power to make sure they were treated fairly. Our system is not perfect, of course—there are still many prejudiced rules concerning Spares in Crones Cliff Manor, and we've only recently begun to see bigger change, but the tallest of trees can sprout from the smallest of acorns," Ambert said.

A modest portrait of Guillemot stared at them from a glass case. He had kind brown eyes and long shining raven hair.

"When walking through Crones Cliff Manor, you'll find his legacy continues today," Ambert said.

"If those houseboats are the norm for Spares, I'm moving," Valley said.

"Same," said Thorn. "Oh my gosh, look."

Thorn gestured subtly toward the entrance of the large

gallery. Three teen witches were walking through the crowd. All three wore dark lipstick that matched their coven pendants of black, green, and purple. The Moth House witch had smudged-on dark eyeliner, clothes adorned with safety pins, and torn fishnets beneath his spring cloak. The witch from Frog House had beautiful, pixie-like features. Her big green eyes were almost the same color as her lush emerald cloak. Her hair fell in shining silver waves down her back. The Hyacinth witch had an elaborate hairstyle, a plait weaved into her long powder-blue tresses, with straight wispy pieces framing her striking heart-shaped face. They looked scary and cool, and as they walked, it was almost as if they moved in slow motion. Seven, Valley, and Thorn watched them, mesmerized, before Valley spoke up and asked, "Who are *they*?"

"Those are the witches I was telling you about," Thorn said. "The shoo-ins for Crones Cliff Manor's costura champions."

"Right," said Seven, remembering Thorn's hours-long rant about how great they were a few weeks back.

They were all seventeen, Seven remembered: Crimson Riddle from Moth House, River Moonfall from Frog House, and Lotus Evenstar from House Hyacinth. They were best friends, according to Thorn, infamous for their talent and cunning and well-known among the Twelve Towns' champion hopefuls. River's family was not particularly well-liked, Thorn had told them. Lotus had been the subject of rumors and ridicule since her once-wealthy family had recently lost their fortune, and Crimson was a wild card known for shunning Witchling world traditions and breaking every rule he could.

The three witches walked right past them, and Crimson turned to wink at the ogling Witchlings.

"Oh hex," Seven said, turning away, her face hot.

Crimson was perhaps the most famous of the trio, since he was not only an amazing costurist but an expert wand dueler *and* an incredible toad racer for Crones Cliff Manor. It was rumored he had his choice of sports to try out for, but since witches could only compete in two, he had chosen dueling and, in the end, his friendship with Lotus and River made him choose costura over toad racing.

"Thorn?" Miss Dewey said, breaking the Witchlings out of their spell.

"Yes?" Thorn asked.

"I thought you might like to see the Hall of Costura History."

"Oh, that would be lovely," Thorn said as they walked to another giant hall, where Thorn clasped her hands in front of her chest and spun, taking everything in.

Ornate fabrics lined with gold or silver hung from the high ceilings, large elaborate ball gowns moved and swayed as if dancing on their dress forms, shoes sparkled from a floor-to-ceiling glass display, and signs detailing the history of costura arts adorned the walls.

"Make sure she doesn't pass out." Miss Dewey nudged Seven gently.

"No promises. This is, like, Thorn heaven," Seven said.

"Ambert and I are going to grab a cup of mudbean juice," Miss Dewey said. "You girls can stay here and look around as long as you like; we'll be right over there at the café when you're ready to go."

"Oh, Valley, what if we get you in a dress like this!" Thorn gestured toward a pink-and-black dress with hundreds of folds.

"Take me with you." Valley opened her eyes wide at Miss Dewey, and Miss Dewey laughed.

But before Valley could escape with the adults, Thorn grabbed her hand and pulled her toward another display. Seven shook her head. "See you in a bit," she said to Miss Dewey and Ambert, and went to join her coven.

Thorn and Valley were standing in front of a wall covered in portraits. From paintings to black-and-white to color pictures, they documented real-life witch fashion throughout the ages. There were pictures of witches in old-timey clothes, sometimes even holding wands, which used to be needed to channel magic long ago and now were only used by Grans and for recreational duels. There were pictures of toad races and weddings and one very old, fading picture of three witches staring straight at the camera, each of them holding a fox.

"They must've been librarians," said Valley, pointing at the foxes.

"Yeah," said Seven, staring. All three witches had haunting looks in their eyes, and the foxes they held were so cute. They wore long dresses, and their hair blew in the wind. Something about it was mesmerizing, and Seven couldn't look away. All around the fox-holding witches were people dressed in some of the most elaborate clothing Seven had ever seen. There were fur-lined cloaks and glittering gloves, silver shoes, and one enormous hat encrusted with jewels, so big you could see the witch's face, but just barely.

"Wow, this picture is old, from 1790!" Thorn inspected the photo closely before walking off with Valley.

Seven stayed to look at the picture, even snapping a sneaky photo with her portaphone, when a young witch came up beside her.

"This is always one of my favorite sections of the museum," said the witch.

Seven looked to her right and nearly gasped. It was a boy, about her age but a bit taller, with casual, expertly cut black clothing. He had a slight tan to his perfect, glowing skin, with dark, deep-set eyes that sort of twinkled when he smiled at her. He pushed his shiny black hair back, and Seven noticed a row of silver earrings on each ear. He was the coolest-looking boy Seven had ever seen.

"I . . . It's my first time here. I mean, not just in the museum, in, um . . . this town," Seven said, immediately cringing.

"Yeah?" The boy opened his eyes wide. "I hope you like it. It's not all great, but what place is? You have to try the Blue Pig Ice Cream Shop if you get a chance. They have a great avocado flavor."

Seven nodded, not sure what to say, but wanting to tell the witch to keep talking.

"Um . . . do you know anything about this picture?" she asked, pointing to a random portrait on the adjacent wall.

"Pfft." The boy smiled, revealing dimples on his cheeks. Seven was done for. "Of course I do! Let's go."

They looked at every single picture, the witch, whose name was Figgs Moonchild, reading each description carefully and adding his own knowledge along the way. Seven didn't want the afternoon to end, but she had to meet her friends.

"I have to go," Seven said. "It was nice hanging out with you. Thanks for showing me around."

"Anytime," said Figgs with a sweet smile and a nod of his head, before taking off farther inside the museum. Seven sighed, then went to find her coven sisters.

Outside, Thorn was so worked up she was bouncing off the walls. It was how Valley got about monstruos and how Seven got about plants. There was no way Thorn wasn't meant to be a costura champion; she was born for this.

"You're gonna get picked, I know it," said Seven.

"I hope so. But . . . I can't help thinking that a Spare's

never been a champion, and I'm too young," Thorn said.

"A Spare's never been an Uncle either, and . . ." Valley pointed at Seven, who just so happened to have a squirrel climb atop her head at that very moment.

"I am not this town's Uncle, but here," Seven said, giving the squirrel a few snacks she carried in her pocket, which had become a habit. A few witches streamed past and studied them.

"Thank you, little Witchling," the squirrel said, and scampered away.

"He messed up my hair," Seven whined. "And Valley has a point. Plus, look at how the Spares are treated here. Not every place is just like Ravenskill."

"And if you don't get picked, we'll hex them," Valley said.

Thorn smiled. "Why is that always your solution?"

"Some witches could use a good hexing." Valley smirked and the three Witchlings giggled as they made their way to the unveiling. It was time for Thorn to learn whether she would be a champion.

CHAPTER FIVE
UNVEILING OF THE CHAMPIONS

THE CRYSTAL THEATER was crackling with anticipation as the Witchlings found their seats for the Unveiling of the Champions. It was fancier than any place Seven had ever seen. Murals depicting Crones Cliff Manor's landscape were painted with rich colors that complemented the glittering crystal walls that had given the theater its name. On either side of the stage were floating seats where the Grans, Uncles, and Oracles of the Twelve Towns all sat above the crowd. If she passed her Uncle trial she would be sitting up there for the next Golden Frog Games. *If,* thought Seven. *A very big if.* Sybell gave Seven a tiny wave as she, Valley, and Thorn sank into the deep velvet seats reserved for them at the very front of the theater. Behind them sat their parents and Pixel.

Seven looked around the theater, which was packed with every witch, fae, and ghost in seemingly the entire Twelve

Towns. Sitting a few rows behind them, Figgs Moonchild caught her eye and grinned, giving her a casual salute. Seven turned around quickly, her face going hot. There was so much going on, Seven could barely hear herself think, let alone hear any creatures. She shifted nervously in her seat, wondering why the Nightbeast had barely spoken to her today. She looked over at Thorn, guilty with thoughts of the creature that had killed her brother, and squeezed her friend's hand. Thorn smiled back, and Seven's heart lurched. She had to find a way to stop this awful connection she had to the beast. If not for her own sake, then at least for Thorn's.

The lights dimmed, the theater quieted, and Enve Lopes stepped out from behind the heavy red curtains of the stage in a shimmering cape. A skinny golden tree sprouted from the stage, stopping right in front of the fae's face. It bloomed with with hundreds of tiny roses in the shape of a microphone.

"Welcome, Twelve Townians, to the one hundred and fifth annual Golden Frog Games!" Enve said, and the theater erupted in applause and celebration.

"I am Enve Lopes, and on behalf of Crones Cliff Manor, I'd like to thank you for attending our humble event: the Unveiling of the Champions!

"The Golden Frog Games are a long-standing tradition of the Twelve Towns, beginning in 1600 by a coalition of House Hyacinth witches. The games are meant to showcase the strengths of our talented residents, inspire friendly competition between the towns, and foster the community and winning spirit our lovely towns are known for!

"As is customary at these games, we will begin with the Unveiling of the Champions for all seventeen of our sports. I will briefly explain the rules . . . I said briefly!" the fae said as the crowd groaned.

"We know the rules—there are no babies here," Valley whispered.

"It's good to be reminded though," Seven said, and Valley rolled her eyes.

"Of course *you* would say that, Salazar."

"Hush, you two," Thorn said, her eyes pinned to the stage.

Thorn was sweating, her cheeks bright red, and she moved her fingers in a weaving motion, like when she was creating one of her clothing pieces. Seven nudged her lightly, and when Thorn looked at her, she quirked an eyebrow, offering one hand palm up for her friend to hold.

Thorn smiled and took Seven's hand on one side and Valley's on the other, her body instantly relaxing. If there was one thing Seven knew, it was that having your friends by your side during hard or scary times helped. She just wished she could find a way to tell them what was happening to her without completely freaking them out.

"Every day we will hold five games across various sports, with each trial advancing the respective team or champion to the next round. Every sport that's won is equal to one point, and every point counts toward each town's individual score. The town with the most wins, wins the tournament. However, as always, there is one individual winner of the games as well, a champion from the winning town, chosen for their exceptional skill, cunning, and sportswitchship. The MVW, or Most Valuable Witch, will touch the coveted . . ." Enve Lopes paused, and an orchestra floated down from the rafters, suspended on either side of the stage as they played a dramatic melody, the music swelling as Enve spoke again. ". . . Golden Frog!"

Enve twirled her cape and, with a bright flash, disappeared. The curtains pulled back, and there in the center of the stage, surrounded by hundreds of twinkling lights, was the famous Golden Frog.

"Ohhhhh," the crowd responded, applause breaking out throughout the theater.

The Golden Frog was, as its name suggested, golden, but it was not simply a trophy, it was a *living* thing. And it was big. Bigger than one Nightbeast paw, a round golden frog with a serene and knowing look in its eyes. Seven wondered if she'd be able to communicate with it.

"And now . . ." Enve Lopes reappeared as the curtains closed once more, hiding the Golden Frog from view. ". . . for the moment we have all been waiting for. The Unveiling of the Champions!"

"I am going to throw up," said Thorn.

"If they don't pick you, they're butt-toads," Valley said.

"Absolute geese," agreed Seven.

The crowd cheered and Seven squeezed Thorn's hand tight. This was it. What her friend had been working day and night to achieve, something no witch their age, and certainly no Spare, had ever done. But now, with a Spare as the next Uncle, who could really say what they were capable of?

The curtains opened again, revealing rows of small, iridescent white cloaks suspended in the air, one for each champion. They were designed by Thorn's very own mother, Thimble Laroux.

"They're beautiful, my love," Thorn's father, Leaf, said behind them, followed by what could only be described as smooching noises.

"They're smooching!" whispered Valley at Thorn.

"I know, they do that all the time." Thorn smiled.

Onstage, the cloaks floated and danced in the air gracefully. They almost looked like jellyfish. A chorus of witches vocalized a haunting melody along with the orchestra, the ethereal music matching the cloaks' movements as it echoed through the theater.

First, the team captains were announced, since not every champion on a team could be called up. It would take too long. The spaceball teams went first.

"Rain Azaleas!" said the announcer, and as the theater cheered, one of the red cloaks onstage floated away, revealing a cylindrical glass globe, the size of Edgar Allan Toad's tank. Someone screamed and the Witchlings turned to see Rain disappear from her seat, then appear moments later inside the glass orb! The crowd clapped at this stunning display of magic.

"They're gonna shrink me?!" Thorn asked.

"It's probably just an illusion spell. I'm pretty sure," Seven said.

But Seven was not pretty sure. Like, at all. She just didn't want to scare Thorn any more than she already was.

Inside, Rain made a batting motion, pretending to watch a ball fly away, and everyone roared with laughter. The town hosting the champion unveiling always made a grand show of the ceremony, trying their best to use never-before-seen magical spectacles during the show. Crones Cliff Manor had really hit the spaceball out of the park.

"Now for the toad racers!" Enve said. Tia Stardust and her toad, Bob, from Thorn's hometown, Boggs Ferry, got the most cheers, followed by Ravenskill's own Holo Vexx. They were the two most famous toad racers in the Twelve Towns.

"I'm cheering for Bob," Edgar said from Seven's cloak lapel.

"He's from Boggs Ferry, you traitor," Seven said, but Edgar just shrugged.

The BMX, or broom motocross, sky-racing champions were announced next, followed by potions trials, bear lifting, and seahorse polo. One by one, the seventeen sports of the Golden Frog Games got their champions, until finally it was the costura champions' turn.

"Oh my goats, I am so nervous," Thorn said.

"We're here for you no matter what," Seven said.

"Same. And if they don't pick you . . ." Valley started.

"We'll hex them," said Seven and Valley in unison.

Before Thorn could answer, Enve began to call the costura champions onstage.

"River Moonfall!" cried Enve. The Crones Cliff Manor section went wild.

River Moonfall, at only seventeen, was already infamous for her magical sewing skills. Her miniature form stood in the glass display with an air of grace and authority, and Seven could feel Thorn shrinking slightly into her chair. River's long silver hair shimmered in the delicate lights of the theater, and she used an enchantment to spin inside the display, making her look like a music box doll. The already raucous crowd got so loud Seven was afraid the roof would collapse. She put small foam earmuffs on Edgar, just in case.

Lotus and Crimson followed for Crones Cliff Manor, as everyone thought they would. This was the team to beat. Finally, it was time for the Ravenskill fashion champions to be unveiled.

"Good luck, Thorn." Her mother squeezed her shoulder and her father kissed the top of her head. Their section of the theater was brimming with excitement, everyone hoping against hope that Thorn would be named champion.

"First up for the Ravenskill fashion champions is . . . Gunnar Grimsbane!"

A tall, handsome witch with umber-brown skin a few seats down from the Witchlings smirked before disappearing into a wisp of smoke and reappearing inside one of the glass displays on the stage.

"He's a House Hyacinth witch, so I bet he's really good," said Seven.

"Two more names, oh please, oh please," Thorn said, squeezing her eyes shut.

"And next, we have . . . Thorn Laroux!"

"OH MY GOATS!" screamed Thorn right before she disappeared in a fluffy cloud of pink and zoomed onto the stage.

"YES!" yelled Valley as she and Seven jumped up and down, hugging. The Witchlings' parents whooped and celebrated even more loudly than the Witchlings. In fact, the entire crowd was thunderous now, with the historic naming of the youngest witch, and only Spare, to be part of Golden Frog Games history. Seven did not dare look up at the fancy balcony seating where Hill witches normally sat, because she knew there would be more than one scowling face. But that didn't matter; Thorn had done it!

From inside her display case, Thorn beamed, her smile so wide and bright, Seven wondered if she was lighting up the whole theater. Now the final champion would be unveiled completing Thorn's team, and marking the end of the unveiling.

"And the final champion of the games . . . is Mayhem Lilitoad!"

Once again, a cloud of colorful smoke shot onto the stage and into the solitary cloaked display case. But this time was different.

A burning purple light flashed across the stage, going straight toward Thorn. The light seemed to move both quickly and slower than dripped honey, and Seven suddenly felt as if she were underwater—she was unable to move or speak, and everything around her was muffled and blurry—as her mind screamed in terror. A whooshing noise, like all the air was being sucked out of the room, rang loudly in her ears. The glass displays rippled in a wave, and cries of confusion and horror erupted from the audience as the purple light clipped Thorn's display and went spinning wildly in the air. The light ricocheted off a column, then hit the case directly beside Thorn, making a sound like a million hissing snakes on impact. The whooshing sound echoed in reverse and the atmosphere returned to normal. Seven could breathe again.

"Thorn!" screamed Seven, getting up to run, but her parents were already up and holding her back.

The cloak fell from the final glass vessel and Mayhem Lilitoad had been turned into stone.

CHAPTER SIX
A PECULIAR HEX

THE GLASS VESSELS onstage spun wildly like cursed tops. Seven broke free of her parents, and she and Valley tried to run to Thorn. The Gran's Guard blocked them as the Town Grans, Uncles, and Oracles descended onto the stage to try and control the wayward magic. Moments later, Graves and their parents were by their side as the rest of the witches in attendance either rushed the stage or rushed out of the theater.

"Please!" said Thimble. "My daughter is up there!"

Cries from the family members of the other champions echoed through the theater, but one voice cried loudest of all.

A sobbing witch who looked a lot like Mayhem came running down the aisle toward the stage.

"Mayhem! My child!" said Mr. Lilitoad. "Mayhem, oh please, no!"

With superhuman strength, Mayhem's father pushed a

row of the Gran's Guard aside and they collided with the floating orbs. Still in their glass displays, the champions careened through the air. The champion displays crashed into one another and smashed. Glass exploded everywhere as the champions fell from their vessels and onto the stage with a horrible crunching sound.

"Oh my Stars, Thorn!" Leaf said.

"Everyone, please, please be calm," a voice said from the speakers. "Take your closest exit and make your way to the Crones Cliff Manor pavilion for medical treatment and calming marbles. Please stay safe and be vigilant!"

The Gran's Guard and town officials began reassuring the crowd and evacuating the theater. Seven and the rest of their group were finally able to run to Thorn, who had tumbled from her glass and was struggling up from the floor, her hands and knees bleeding.

"Thorn, are you all right?" Leaf asked.

"I'm a bit cut up, but I'm fine," said Thorn.

"Here." Seven pulled a calming ointment from her cloak. "This is a ground-up cura-shroom with aloe, it'll take the sting out of the cuts."

"Thanks, Seven," said a teary Thorn. Her mother pulled her into a hug, and the towering Leaf stood over them, a concerned look on his face. All around them, champions who had fallen from their displays were ushered to safety or to the healers waiting in the wings. The glass enclosures that hadn't exploded still danced in unison as though on an ocean wave. The faces of the champions within told another story though. They were scared, or angry, or had passed out from the crash. Worst of all was Mayhem. She had been turned into a miniature stone statue, her hands up, her eyes and mouth wide open in shock—the final moment before the purple magic struck her, frozen in time.

"I will handle them," the Ravenskill Gran, Knox, said to the Crones Cliff Manor Gran, Antares Calarook, and she nodded. Knox raised her wand and the remaining champion glasses floated in unison toward one side of the stage and disappeared into the back.

"You did this!" said a witch, pointing at Thimble.

"What?" Thimble turned to face the man.

"You designed the cloaks, you . . . you probably hexed Mayhem so your Spare would have less competition!" said another witch in an elegant red coat.

"She even has a Spare working in her shop," said someone from the other side of the stage, to many murmurs of agreement.

Pixel, who was beside Thimble, turned a bright red.

"I suggest you watch your tone." Leaf crossed his arms, flexing his enormous muscles as he did.

Thimble held both hands up. "This has been upsetting for us all. But we can get to the bottom of it without throwing around baseless accusations."

"Of course those Spares are involved," said a shrill, familiar voice. Heels click-clacked slowly up the stage steps and the crowd of witches parted to reveal a witch in an eye-assaulting bright yellow dress, with long dark hair peppered with strands of gray, and wearing cow-print heels. Seven shook her head at the sight of her. Rafflesia Dimblewit.

She sauntered to Mr. Lilitoad's side and put one hand on his heaving shoulders. "They should never have been allowed in the games anyway—they've probably hexed the whole thing."

"How is she out?" whispered Seven.

Mrs. Dimblewit whipped around, gleeful malice in her ice-blue eyes. "My kind do not belong in the Tombs. I am a proud Frog House witch, with *means*."

"Don't you dare talk to my daughter like that," Fox said, her voice low and menacing. But Mrs. Dimblewit just sniffed at her dismissively.

Seven was becoming so sick and tired of wealthy witches thinking their gold coins meant they could do whatever they wanted. She balled her hands into fists, the urge to attack Mrs. Dimblewit with magic overtaking her.

"Strike her," said a rumbling voice.

Bright, hot fury built in Seven. Maybe she should listen to the Nightbeast. After all, hadn't the Dimblewits put them through enough last year?

"I have seen them cause destruction firsthand. There can be no other culprit," Mrs. Dimblewit sneered.

"You sound like a warlock," Seven said, rolling her eyes. "That doesn't make any sense!"

"Then why has this never happened before? We're letting Spares in everything and this is the result," Mrs. Dimblewit said, and all around them, witches exchanged concerned looks.

"Enough with these conspiracy theories! A child was just hexed and we need to help her," Fox said.

"Agreed," Talis backed her up.

Mrs. Dimblewit waved them away and turned back to the crowd. "I've even heard that the Spares are recruiting others to disrupt the town! The violence that's been in the papers? All made up by them!" Mrs. Dimblewit's eyes were red, wide, and watery, like she hadn't slept in days. "I'm sure this one is the leader." She pointed at Valley.

Why was Mrs. Dimblewit lying? What would Seven, Valley, and Thorn have to gain from fake horror stories when they had enough real ones to last a lifetime? Many of them thanks to Mrs. Dimblewit herself.

"You leave my daughter alone," Quill said fiercely.

"I won't stand by while these criminals ruin our region," Mrs. Dimblewit said.

"That's funny, didn't you just *bribe* your way out of the Tombs for being a criminal?" Seven scoffed. A few witches laughed and Mrs. Dimblewit turned as red as a devil pepper.

"I will not be spoken to like this by this . . . this . . . rabble!"

"Enough!" Antares said. "I know how Spares are treated

in your town, but you are in Crones Cliff Manor now. I urge you to have a bit more respect for these young witches."

"We should go," Fox said. "Before I do something I regret," she added under her breath.

"Yes, come on." Quill began to usher the Witchlings off the stage, when another witch stood in her path. More witches poured onto the stage, blocking their exit and looking . . . angry.

"We told you that allowing a Spare into the games would be trouble," said one witch with a pointy nose and deep purple cloak.

"Thimble Laroux should be held in our dungeons, at least until the child is unstonified," said another witch.

"*If* they can be," said Mrs. Dimblewit, which made Mayhem's father wail in agony.

"How, exactly, was Mrs. Laroux supposed to have planned a hex on Mayhem when she didn't know she would be chosen?" asked a young witch. It was Lotus, the other fashion champion from Crones Cliff Manor.

"She could've peeked at the results somehow!" said the pointy-nosed witch.

"I heard the Witchlings say they'd hex someone outside the museum!" said another witch.

"We were kidding!" Seven said helplessly.

"I will vouch for the Witchlings and their parent," said River Moonfall. "Thimble was with the committee right before the unveiling and then both she and the Witchlings, with the exception of Thorn, who was in a vessel, were sitting in the audience when the hex was cast. I could see them from my own globe."

"I am a witness to that too," Crimson said.

"As was I," said a witch with dark hair who stepped beside River and nodded. It was Figgs, the witch from the museum.

"My assistant, Figgs," said River, as she smiled warmly at him.

"The word of another *Spare* means nothing," Mrs. Dimblewitt hissed.

Figgs was a Spare? Nobody had assistants his age, unless that were the case. But he was dressed in the finest of clothing and treated like an equal by River, like a friend.

"There's something else the genius Mrs. Dimblewit failed to notice," said the Oracle, holding what was left of Thorn's scorched glass vessel. "The hex came from the right side of the stage. It went straight for Thorn and missed, hitting Mayhem instead. Whoever cast it meant to stonify *Miss Laroux*, not Miss Lilitoad. Besides, there is only one witch on this stage with a record of using forbidden magic, and it's not Thimble." The Oracle winked at Seven as Mrs. Dimblewit began to screech and the adult witches began to argue.

"That's not just any forbidden magic, it's an arenisca hex," whispered Graves. "I didn't think it was possible."

Seven, Valley, and Thorn exchanged looks. They had heard *that* before—but witches would find a way when it came to forbidden magic. They knew that all too well.

"We can not trust the suppositions of this child Oracle and a Spare crew of rats!" Mrs. Dimblewit wailed.

River and Lotus narrowed their eyes at the hysterical witch, but when Crimson curled his lip at her, Mrs. Dimblewit took a frightened step back.

"I am one hundred years your senior, and I've seen your future." The Oracle whispered the last part. "It's not pretty."

"Why, you—you—" Mrs. Dimblewit stammered. "I still demand an investigation!"

"And an investigation you shall have," said Antares, to which Knox nodded.

"But it remains that Mayhem has been turned into *stone*. Stone!" said the pointy-nosed witch. "The kind of magic that can turn a witch into an unliving thing—into an object—is not normal and hasn't been seen for . . ."

"Many, many years," said Knox. "It is not the kind of magic any of us should take lightly."

Knox looked at Seven and she knew, in an instant, what the Gran meant: archaic magic. The Cursed Toads, who were the only known witches to use archaic magic in the past century, were literal toads right now, sitting in their tanks in a highly guarded prison cell. But if wasn't the Cursed Toads, then who could've done this?

CHAPTER SEVEN
A VISIT TO MOTH HOUSE

EVER SINCE THE BLACK MOON CEREMONY last fall, Seven did everything she could to avoid walking past the coven houses. It wasn't that she was still devastated about being a Spare. She had accepted it . . . mostly. But if Seven was being completely, diary-worthy-only-Edgar-Allan-Toad-knew-because-she-forgot-he-could-speak honest? Sometimes it still made her sad. Being in House Hyacinth had been her dream for years, and no matter how much she loved Valley and Thorn, or how much she believed in her coven, a little piece of her would always long for the bright purple light to have shown up in her necklace that night instead of the red. It was just one more secret to add to her stash. Her secrets were getting harder to keep every day, but Seven knew she could not break. Delphinium had, and look where it had gotten her.

But on this particular afternoon, as she left school,

followed by ten raccoons, the coven houses just couldn't be avoided. If anyone knew about hexes, it was the Moth House witches, and one witch in particular: Graves. Not only had Graves known the name of the stone hex but Moth House had the famed Library of Hexes, which might hold some much needed information about the hex too. Seven really hoped Graves could help them before something truly awful happened to Thorn.

The night before, the Witchlings had made plans to meet at Evanora's Tea Room and then walk over to Moth House together. But even with so much on the line, her coven hadn't shown up. Seven had waited for Valley and Thorn for ages before giving up and leaving on her own. She had of course messaged them on her portaphone—Valley hadn't answered and Thorn had said she was busy getting ready for the first trial with Gunnar. Traitors.

"'Scuse me, young Seven," said a woman carrying an enormous log toward the center of the games.

"Sorry," Seven said, stepping aside.

"They should step aside for you, Uncle Seven," said Cheese, the leader of the ten raccoons who followed Seven everywhere. The rest of the half-monstruo creatures clapped in agreement.

"It's okay, I'm a regular witch just like they are," Seven said.

"An Uncle witch!" exclaimed Sopa, another raccoon, to more polite applause.

Seven looked over her shoulder and smiled. They were walking behind her in single file as if she were a line leader at school. Sometimes Uncles gave animals their names, but usually they were named by their parents, and those names were almost always humdrum names or their favorite foods. The members of her raccoon fan club were all in the latter camp. There was Sweet Potato, Chicken Finger, and Tostone, to name a few. As weird as they were, she'd begun to find comfort in the raccoons who had become like her shadow.

A stream of builders carrying materials walked past them. All of Ravenskill was being decorated for the games, which were set to begin in just two days. Not to mention, every champion and Twelve Townian who wanted to watch the games would be staying in Ravenskill for the next few weeks. That meant younger witches would also be taking classes at Seven's school, and the coven houses would be filled to capacity. There was much to prepare. The gazebo was covered in intricate undulating streamers enchanted to look like mermaid hair and imported from troll country especially for the tournament. There were banners and flags for each coven lining the streets: purple for House Hyacinth, aquamarine and silver for House of Stars, orange and pearly white for Goose House, black and gray for Moth House, and pink and green for Frog House. But no red for the Spares. Seven sighed.

Festival carts were being set up with everything from

fireworks to organic batjelly to sugar-feathered cloud cakies and golden frog plushies, all for tournament goers to buy. Rides were being erected along the Boggy Crone River, cheerful music played from every corner and shop, and there were supplies and construction everywhere you looked. At the center of town, a large structure was being erected where the public sentiment points that would count toward the Most Valuable Witch prize would be tallied.

Seven yawned and rubbed her eyes. She had trained at four in the morning, like she normally did, then had a full day of school, including volunteering to help with toad-handling club since she could talk to all of them now. As she walked on, a young witch, cloaked by the shadow of a tree, stared at her, and Seven shook her head. This was normal for her now, to be stared at all the time, but she still wasn't used to it. Seven smiled, but the shadowy figure was gone. Weird. She was so tired now she was seeing things. It was a wonder she was still upright, but she had to make it to Moth House.

"And to help me," said a familiar voice.

"Not now," Seven whispered.

"If you do not come, I will find a way out. And I will be very angry and also cross," said the Nightbeast.

"Those are the same thing."

"When will you come?"

"I'm not coming."

The Nightbeast growled low, and long, and menacingly.

Seven shivered. "I'm . . . I'm sorry."

"What for?" asked another voice, and a startled Seven whipped around quicker than a racing toad.

"Valley, what the hex—you scared me!"

"Sorry. I've been behind you for, like, ten minutes though. Who were you talking to?"

"Uh, just some birds," said Seven. A lie, but she couldn't exactly tell Valley that she was hearing the Nightbeast's voice in her head day and night.

"Are they gonna follow you everywhere?" Valley gestured at the raccoons.

"Yeah, they're my friends," Seven said a little snippily.

"Friends!" the raccoons said in awed voices. Maybe she shouldn't have said that.

"Where were you? I waited for you for ages." Seven asked, still annoyed.

"Oh, sorry, I was in the library looking some stuff up," Valley said, her eyes pinned straight ahead.

Seven quirked an eyebrow. Valley wasn't the library type.

"I know, I know." Valley rubbed the back of her neck.

Seven shook her head. "No, you've been going through this mega thing with your parents and I don't blame you for being distracted. I'm just tired and cranky."

Valley put her arm around Seven's shoulders and smirked. "Crankier, you mean." The two Witchlings laughed as they walked together down the coven house road.

Goose and Frog House were both by the river, a great source of stress for the diligent Frog House witches, who were disturbed at all hours by Goose House antics. A few Frog House witches sat on the lawn of their emerald-colored house, pink-and-green philodendrons draping the slated sides like one of Thorn's elaborate crochet projects. They wore their pink spring robes and had their noses in heavy-looking textbooks. A few sat in rocking chairs knitting or drinking tea with little delicious-looking cakes. They were kind of like old people. Next door, the blood-orange Goose House sat happily on a grassy knoll. Witches did cartwheels on the lawn or practiced dance routines for imaginary concerts. A few of them waved enthusiastically at Seven and Valley, and Seven gave a little wave back while Valley just raised her chin up slightly in acknowledgment. Valley was *so* froggin' cool. Seven had spent so much time being annoyed with her former bully that she had never noticed it, but now she couldn't help but admire Valley. Sometimes she even found herself copying her mannerisms so she could maybe be a little less of a giant nerd, but she would never tell Valley that. Seven would take that one to the grave.

Seven and Valley entered an archway of willow trees lining the road. They swayed and bowed like a line of ballet dancers, and the smell of vanilla and lavender swirled in the air around them. When they emerged from the shade of the dancing trees, a grand house twinkling blue and silver in the afternoon sun greeted them—House of Stars.

Large windows were open to the warm afternoon breeze, and inside Seven could see witches fluttering about like colorful butterflies, rolls of fabric in their arms, enchanted makeup-enhancing mirrors in their hands, and magic rollers curling into witches' hair as they sat staring at their porta-phones. The witches outside lounged under parasols drinking lemon lily water and chatting, their elaborately decorated spring robes glimmering with pearls and crystals. Most of them ignored Seven and Valley, but a few smiled in their direction kindly and with curiosity. They were beautiful and almost hard to look at in a group like that, but Seven was used to it—both her parents were from House of Stars, after all.

"Did you ever find out where the Nightbeast was being kept?" Valley asked.

"No, why?"

"Just curious."

They walked on for a few hundred toadstools until finally they got to the cemetery surrounding Moth House. A large, corroded black fence separated the cemetery from the road, and Seven swore the temperature dropped several degrees the moment they walked through the gate.

"Reminds me of my old house," Valley said with a sad smile.

Last year, Valley and her mother, Quill, pen name *the* V. V. Avenmora, aka Seven's favorite author, had moved out of Blood Rose Manor, a creepy mansion on the Hill, and into a small, cozy apartment in the center of town. Sometimes, when she saw how much the divorce of Valley's parents was affecting her, Seven felt guilty for telling her mother about Valley's dad hurting her, but she knew she'd done the right thing. Valley was safe now. And happier.

"Come on, I don't wanna still be here when it's dark out," Seven said.

"What. A. Chicken," Valley said, laughing as they climbed the tombstone-dotted hill toward Moth House. The higher they climbed, the foggier it became, and when they finally reached the top of the hill, it was like entering the eye of a hurricane—quiet, eerily so, all the sounds of Ravenskill disappearing with a *zwipe*-like noise, as if it were being swallowed by the sky.

The weather had changed altogether, and Seven and Valley huddled close as they knocked on the ancient-looking door. Gray clouds hung low around the house, and a light mist frizzed Seven's curls up immediately, much to her annoyance. She had *just* washed her hair. Flashes of lightning illuminated the clouds, and a howling wind that sounded a little too much like a wolf echoed far away. Seven didn't dare mention it, in case it was really the Nightbeast.

"Why do they have to be such weirdos?" Valley asked.

"I think it's cool. The weather is a level-seventeen enchantment," said Seven.

"Only a level-seventeen nerd would know that," said Valley.

Seven narrowed her eyes as she held back a smirk, and Valley's laugh echoed in the gloomy air.

Of all the covens, Goose and Moth had been the nicest to them. Frog House witches were mostly indifferent, too busy to be bothered. Hyacinth witches had been downright mean sometimes and overly friendly at others, and with a few exceptions, House of Stars had pretended they didn't even exist. But Seven had been open to friendship with anyone who was decent to her and found that in each coven, there were at least a handful of witches who showed them kindness.

The door opened and a tall boy with hair over both his eyes appeared. He wore all black, with sleeves that were pulled down to his knuckles, and when he pushed his hair to one side, they saw his eyes were lined heavily in coal pencil.

"Yeah?"

"We're here for Graves," Seven said.

"Finally. She, like, literally won't shut up about you." The witch walked away, leaving the door open for Seven and Valley to walk through. They exchanged looks, holding in their laughter. Teenagers were absolute geese sometimes.

The tall Moth House witch walked up the stairs as Seven

and Valley waited in the foyer. It was big and dark but not uninviting, with elaborate red-and-gray tilework, white chrysanthemums hanging from the ceiling, and rounded wooden doors leading to what Seven assumed were rooms. *Or maybe the kitchen,* she thought as her stomach reminded her, not for the first time, that she had slept through her lunch hour. The black chandelier overhead was made of what looked like iron branches, and it cast a faint glow over them as they waited.

From one of the rooms upstairs, Graves emerged. She slid down the curved banister and landed gracefully in front of them. Outside of the formal cloaks Seven was used to seeing her in, Graves looked froggin' cool. Her deep brown skin was dusted with iridescent glitter at the cheekbones, like one of the House of Stars witches, and she wore her blue-green hair in choppy waves that hit her shoulders, with one side pushed behind her ear to show her collection of earrings. But besides that, Graves was all Moth House—from her dark eyeliner to her all-black clothes to the skeleton rings she wore stacked on each finger. Thorn had said once that of all the Moth House witches their age, Graves was the most stylish, and Seven couldn't help but agree.

"You're here, hi, been waiting," Graves said in her gravelly voice, with a sideways smirk to rival Valley's.

"Sorry, got caught up in toad club," Seven said.

"Oh, is Edgar here?" Graves's eyes went wide.

Seven tapped her pocket gently. "Say hi."

Edgar popped his little head out, looked up at Seven with a scowl, said, "I am not a circus toad," then went right back into her cloak pocket to nap. Her pocket was enchanted to mimic a pond, a spell the Gran had taught her after Seven found out she'd be the next Uncle. She found having Edgar around soothed her anxiety, and lately she was having a lot of that.

"He said hello," Seven said brightly.

"Looked like he hexed you," Graves laughed. "Hey, Pepperhorn."

"Sup." Valley smiled and Seven quirked an eyebrow at how red Valley's pale cheeks suddenly were. *Interesting.*

"Shall we?" Graves gestured toward an archway to their right, and the three witches wound their way through the dark corridors of Moth House.

"Farolito," Graves whispered, and a bright orange flame appeared in the palm of her hand right as they got to a steep, spiral staircase.

Ivy crept up the stone walls of the passageway, and a draft made Seven wrap her arms around her body. It was dark and quiet here, and Seven struggled to keep her eyes open, her body upright. As she walked, she held on to the cold stone at her side and couldn't help but think of her warm, comfortable bed right now. She would give anything for just a few hours of sleep and to shut out the world, but how could she rest when Thorn was in danger?

"So, about the Nightbeast?" Valley asked in a whisper as they walked.

Seven bristled. "You and the Nightbeast questions. Why are you obsessed with it?"

"I just think it's cool that they can keep it somewhere that no one can get to. And creepy. If they can do that to the Nightbeast, they can do it to anyone," Valley said.

Graves discreetly looked back, a curious expression on her face. She was very clearly listening to their conversation. Not that she could help it.

"The Nightbeast is dangerous." Seven felt hot breath on her neck, as if the monstruo were with her right now.

"Why didn't they set it free somewhere far away, like the Enchanted Grim, instead of keeping it captive and near everyone?"

Seven couldn't understand what Valley's preoccupation with the Nightbeast was. She was famously obsessed with *hunting* monstruos. So why, now, did she suddenly want to free the most gruesome of them all?

"You should be more worried about Thorn right now than the Nightbeast," Seven snapped. *And me.* She knew it wasn't their fault. Her friends had no idea about the monstruos still speaking to her, but it didn't stop her from feeling alone. And afraid.

"I *am* worried about Thorn but . . . I just . . . something tells me the Nightbeast needs help too," Valley said softly.

"The Nightbeast is perfectly fine and has everything it needs," Seven said a bit too loudly.

In the distance, a low, ominous growl rumbled, and Seven jumped back and right into Valley, who screamed at the same time.

"What?!" Graves asked.

"Nothing . . . it's just creepy here." Seven lied. It wasn't creepy here; in fact, the dark house was pretty cozy.

Valley composed herself, then cleared her throat. "Maybe we should think things over. The Nightbeast is being punished, when it wasn't really in control."

"If Thorn heard you talking like that, she'd frog out. I don't wanna talk about it anymore, Valley, really. Don't you remember the nightmares Thorn used to have about the Nightbeast? How much seeing it kill Petal traumatized her?"

"I remember the dreams where she was rocking it like a baby . . ." Valley said.

"Valley, stop!" Seven pleaded.

"Okay, but—"

"Here we are," said Graves.

They were standing in front of a massive black-and-gray thicket. It must've been at least twenty toadstools high, and it pulsed slowly, almost like it was breathing. Seven knew that the door led to a place she'd only ever read about but had never actually been to. The Library of Hexes.

CHAPTER EIGHT
THE LIBRARY OF HEXES

"I CAN'T BELIEVE I'm actually going in," said Seven.

"She belongs in Frog House," Valley said to Graves, who giggled.

But Seven didn't mind being called a nerd. She was about to see, firsthand, a rare collection of hex-related books and artifacts that were only held here.

Every house had a special room with magic specific to their coven. House Hyacinth had the most extensive collection of combat magic; House of Stars had appearance-related enchantments for everything from changing the color of clothing to changing individual facial features, if only temporarily; Frog House had an arsenal of uncloaking magic—spells that would uncover truths, reveal buried treasure, or unravel illusions; and Goose House had all the magic that had to do with cunning and charms. (Goose House also had a stash of explosives-related magic, of course.) And Moth House had the Library of Hexes.

Dark purple berries hung from the vines weaving through the thorns, and Graves took one and looked at Seven and Valley.

"You have to eat one to go in. It's a deathberry," Graves said sheepishly.

I ate the deathberry and knew that my fate would not be a pleasant one. That I would die at the hands of the witches I called friend. Seven remembered the passage from Delphinium's diary, one of her very last entries. She had broken into Moth House as a last resort, to try and get whatever information she could from this very library. It hadn't helped, so far as Seven could tell, but she had yet to read Delphinium's final entries either . . . she couldn't bring herself to. Seven could only hope that she would have better luck.

"Um, are you sure they're safe?" Seven asked.

"Yep," Graves said. "Most times you just lose an eyelash or something."

"And what happens other times?" Valley asked.

"Shouldn't be anything *too* bad?" Graves chuckled.

Valley and Seven exchanged looks.

"But! You either eat one or the door won't let us in. Every coven room has a price."

"Fine," Seven said. "Count of three."

"One," said Graves.

"Two," said Valley.

"Three," said Seven, and all three witches popped the dark berries into their mouths.

They tasted sweet and bitter all at once, peaceful and filled with every anxiety Seven had ever felt. Like the answer to a question she'd been wondering about her whole life was on the verge of being revealed, but remained just out of reach. Her heart thumped hard, and behind her closed eyes flashed a vision of her as an old witch, wrinkled and surrounded by people smiling at her. An old toad on her shoulder. The vision shifted and Seven was a teenager surrounded by dark clouds, and a dagger was coming toward her fast, but someone was running to her side. Before the dagger made contact, Seven opened her eyes and took in a big gulp of air, like she had been underwater.

"What was that?" she asked.

"Did you see something?" Graves asked.

Seven nodded slowly, holding a hand to her chest.

"Sometimes the berry tells you different ways you might die. Nothing is set in stone though, no need to worry," Graves said. "I've seen loads of stuff that never came true."

"Did you see anything, Valley?" Seven asked.

"Something weird." Valley shrugged. "I saw Thorn in the moonlight hurling a hex at me."

"Ha." Seven threw her head back. *As if that would ever happen.*

The thicket shook awake, creaking and groaning as it opened to the Library of Hexes. The three witches entered. Inside was a dim hall made of stone and lined with bookcases. Tables were scattered throughout, covered with papers and various plants. There were jars filled with eyeballs and skulls, normal things like that, and then some not-so-normal things—pots with dirt and what looked like fingers sticking out of them and tiny leaves sprouting from their skin, a chalice with a protruding nose that sniffed at the air, chairs with human hands where the clawed feet should be.

"Is that—are those—what are those?" Seven asked.

"They used to be witches," sighed Graves.

Seven covered her mouth, and Valley looked like she was going to be sick.

"They were hexed at one time or another with undoable kinds of magic. It's inhumane to just throw them away, and we can't save them because the magic prevents it. Trust me, we've tried. So they live out their lives here. I come and talk to them sometimes so they're not lonely."

"What happens when they do die?" asked Valley as she sat in one of the normal-looking chairs.

"They turn into regular furniture," said Graves, which sent Valley almost flying out of the chair and right into Seven, who held in a laugh.

"Don't wanna be embarrassing in front of your *crush*," whispered Seven as Valley straightened herself up.

Valley's eyes went wide, and then she narrowed them at Seven. "Don't say anything weird."

Seven zipped her mouth shut and locked it, but she refused to wipe the annoying grin off her face. It was payback for Valley telling the whole school that Seven had a crush on a boy witch named Hurricane in fourth year.

But Graves hadn't seemed to notice anyway. She walked across the room, scanning the shelves, and climbed a small staircase. She pulled a slim white book from the top shelf and signaled Valley and Seven over

"Here it is." Graves threw the book to a waiting Seven and then climbed down. "There's info on rare hexes in that book, and I know I read something about the arenisca hex in it once."

"The Book of Unliving." Seven read the title, which was written in metallic green letters. A whistling wind rustled around them as the words left her lips, and Seven and Valley exchanged a look. Seven quickly gave the book back to Graves.

"Don't worry," Graves said. "It's just enchanted to be creepy here."

Graves led them to a comfy spot in front of a fireplace. Rugs were strewn everywhere, along with big furry pillows that Seven was afraid to go near in case they were made of *someone* instead of some*thing*, but they gathered close around the book as Graves read.

"Okay, the arenisca hex was created by some old witch of unknown origins blah-blah, but it was outlawed, along with a whole list of magic, around the same time the Black Moon Ceremony was created."

"So, hundreds of years ago," Valley said.

"Right. Witches were becoming too powerful, combining covens and having no limit to their magic, which is how spells like this were even possible. It takes a level of magic none of us are capable of because our covens are limited."

Seven nodded. This was the entire point of the Black Moon Ceremony—only a certain number of witches were admitted to the covens each year, and the rest became Spares. It was the price they paid to keep the Twelve Towns safe from magic like the stone hex, or the archaic magic the Cursed Toads had used to control the Nightbeast. Only witches who had multi-coven capabilities could use that kind of powerful magic, so multi-covens were banned.

"Many of these spells were heavily guarded and kept within covens or sometimes even families, either for security reasons or for financial reasons, as other witches paid handsomely to have these spells performed. It says here that a . . . witch from an unknown house found a way to expand a witch's bones and calcify their entire body using magic. Gross," said Graves.

"Do you think that's how the stone hex works?" Seven asked.

Graves nodded. "It says the hex causes the victim's bones to turn into stone that takes over their entire body, even absorbing the *skin*, and spreads until . . ." Graves looked up at them. "Until it reaches their heart. If that happens, they can never be un-hexed. They stay that way forever. It's supposed to be incredibly painful, and the hex itself is almost impossible to stop once it's begun. The hex is so powerful, it changes the atmosphere, makes it heavier and harder to move in. So everything around it feels slowed down, except for the hex itself. Only a very powerful witch could do this, I bet," Graves said.

Seven remembered feeling weird, like she couldn't move, when the hex had been cast. Her stomach lurched as she thought of the hex reaching a witch's heart and killing them: Mayhem. If the healers weren't able to help her, she would be a statue forever.

Seven looked over at one of the human-hand chairs and shivered. "Is that how that furniture hex worked?"

"That magic is even *older* than the stone hex, even more powerful. I don't know if the older witches know where it comes from but I definitely don't. I'm a little freaked out to even find out, if I'm being honest." Graves's cheeks went red and she looked at Valley, who shifted closer to Graves and put one hand on hers in support.

"Is there any way to stop the arenisca hex?" Valley asked.

"I dunno. The book talks about the origins of the spell but not the cure."

"Rats. Couldn't be that easy, I guess," Seven said.

"Well, if we can't find info about how to stop or cure it, we need to figure out who's doing this. Think: What *kinds* of witches could wield this magic? Who is the most likely to hold on to superpowerful old magic like that?" Valley asked.

"There's really no way to know for sure . . ." Graves said. "Maybe a very old witch?"

"Or a witch with a long family history . . . Someone from one of the influential families might be a good place to begin," Seven offered, remembering that almost every witch they'd come up against last year was from the Hill, where the wealthiest, oldest families of Ravenskill lived. The Dimblewits, Valley's dad, and all the Hill Society witches who supported them fit the bill.

"That barely narrows it down," Graves said. "And literally everyone from the Twelve Towns was there the night of the unveiling."

"Oh goose, you're right," said Seven, discouraged. "At least we know a bit more about how the magic works. Thanks a lot, Graves."

Even if they hadn't gotten anything that would help protect Thorn, knowing a bit more about how it worked was a start.

"Sure, happy to help. But if anyone asks, you never saw this or were in here," said Graves.

"Secret's safe with us. I'm gonna go, I have a goose-load of homework to get done and I have to be up at three in the morning again," Seven said as a small yawn escaped her mouth.

"We should probably get out of here anyway. If anyone catches me, I'm toast," Graves said.

They made their way out of the library and to the foyer of Moth House, where a few witches were chatting or passing through. None of them looked at Seven or Valley weirdly. They smiled softly or nodded, and Seven thought, not for the first time, that Moth House witches might not have much in common with her, but they always made her feel welcome. Or at least not judged.

"See you later, Seven," Graves said, but her eyes were on Valley, who gave her a small nod as if they were cementing an unspoken agreement.

Valley and Seven walked down the hill, the sun already setting behind the trees.

"We didn't learn much, but I'll write everything down the moment I get home. Never know what could come in handy. Plus, now we know we have to act fast if, Stars forbid, someone else is stonified," Seven said.

Valley cleared her throat. "So . . . do you think that we'd be able to at least *try* and find the Nightbeast soon?"

Seven stopped in her tracks. "Valley, were you even listening to me?"

"I was! You're gonna write everything down, I heard you, I'm just . . ."

"Okay, I've had it. What's your obsession with the Nightbeast? Why this sudden interest all day? Spill, or I'm gonna go back to the library and find a hex for giant pimples."

"Fine, okay, I'm . . . figuring out a way to set the Nightbeast free."

"You're *what*?"

"Hmmmm," said the familiar voice of the Nightbeast, both in Seven's mind and far away.

"I know what it's like, okay? To be misunderstood. You told us yourself that the Nightbeast was being controlled by the Cursed Toads. That it didn't even want to kill Petal . . ."

"It could've been lying to me, Valley."

"And what if it wasn't? We're keeping an innocent animal imprisoned, while the witch that taught the Cursed Toads magic is running around somewhere."

"They're probably already dead, whoever they are—"

"What are the chances of that, Seven? The Cursed Toads weren't the brightest stars in the sky; they had help. You know it, I know it, the Gran knows it. I wouldn't ask you to help if I didn't have a really good reason," Valley said softly, her voice haunted with the ghost of something she wasn't saying.

Seven felt like she might collapse. On top of everything else she had to deal with, now Valley was adding more pressure to her load. She wanted to forget the Nightbeast ever existed, to stop hearing its voice night and day, not start a crusade to free it.

"What about Thorn? We should be worried about her right now. She could be in danger, and if she finds out you're trying to free the Nightbeast . . ."

"Then we won't tell her. Not for now." Valley's voice was pleading, and Seven rubbed one hand over her face.

"I think you're being a butt-toad right now."

"And maybe I am, but I really think it's the right thing to do."

Seven sighed. "This is a bad idea. Horrible, but if you won't let it go, then the smartest way is to take it step-by-step. We should start by finding out how the investigation behind who was controlling the Nightbeast is going. Since we think the person who controlled the Nightbeast could be connected to the stone hex, it will help on both fronts." Seven couldn't just jump in and help her free a monstruo, especially not one that had hurt Thorn and her family so badly that they were still grieving, but she would look into it if it helped them figure out who was behind the hexing.

"So you'll help?"

"When have I ever said no to you?" Seven said. *Or to any- one.* "I have training with the Gran in a few days. I'll ask her then."

"Thanks." Valley smiled, and then, looking at Seven, who was not smiling at all, Valley's face fell in concern. "You're not mad?"

Seven wanted to yell that of course she was mad! But she

could see the eagerness behind Valley's eyes. And the hurt. She was going through a hard time with her parents' divorce, and Seven didn't know, maybe this was her way of feeling better or something. Seven knew what it was like trying to take control of something, of anything, when you felt like your world was upside down. She wanted Valley to be okay, even if it meant she'd have even less time for herself.

"I'm not. Come on, let's get off this hill before it gets any darker."

"Actually . . ." Valley's cheeks went red. "I'm staying for a bit. I've been meaning to tell you but . . . Graves and I are sort of girlfriends now."

Valley looked up toward Moth House, and Seven followed her gaze: Graves was waiting at the door.

"Oh," said Seven, trying not to let the annoyance creep into her voice. So she'd agreed to help Valley and now she was getting ditched to walk home through the cemetery alone.

"See you tomorrow?" Valley said, already racing up the hill, but Seven didn't bother to respond.

She knew Valley wouldn't be able to hear her anyway.

CHAPTER NINE
CREEPING PHLOX HILL

AS GOLDEN HOUR approached on the day before the games, all the witches in Ravenskill gathered on Creeping Phlox Hill. Each of the Twelve Towns had its own version of the flowery hill, and it was tradition in every Golden Frog Games for champions to have their pictures taken there. It was also an opportunity for Twelve Townians to get pictures taken with their favorite champions. It was an enormous deal, made all the more enormous this year by Thorn, the legendary Spare champion. At least, that was what the *Squawking Crow* had begun calling her.

"Come on, Seven, we're almost there!" Fox called out as they climbed the flower-festooned hill. There were rows of flowers in the colors of the covens, reaching all the way up the hill, and a few grassy lanes for witches to walk through. It was beautiful and the perfect place for pictures.

Seven was out of breath as she tried to climb, yet somehow her mother was going twice as fast while carrying Seven's big baby brother, Beefy.

"Does she secretly do bear lifting or something?" said Talis, who was pushing Beefy's empty stroller and wiping sweat from his brow. The hill was quite steep.

Seven laughed. "I think she must."

Beefy was looking back at them from over Fox's shoulder, his brow knitted in concern.

"Down, please, Mama!" Beefy said assuredly.

The moment Fox put him on the ground, he toddled back down the hill and took Talis's hand.

"Papa, sit," Beefy said, guiding Talis lovingly into the stroller.

"I'm fine, Beefy baby," Talis tried, but Beefy was having none of it. He made Talis sit in his oversized stroller and pushed him effortlessly up the hill.

"Papa tired, Beefy help," Beefy said, and Seven and Fox exploded in laughter as Talis looked back at them helplessly.

"I guess he noticed Dad was exhausted." Seven shook her head. Beefy was growing up way too fast, and it made something tug at her heart. She wished her baby brother could . . . well, stay a baby forever.

"Let's run," Fox said, and she grabbed Seven's hand as they ran up the hill together. The warm breeze smelled like honey and freshly cut grass as Seven and her mother ran, laughing and out of breath, the sun warming their brown skin.

They reached the picture area, where a few small tents for champions to rest and have their hair and makeup fixed by House of Stars witches had been erected. Thorn still hadn't emerged from her tent, so her parents walked away to mingle with some other adults, and Seven settled on the grass next to Valley to wait.

"Did you—" Valley started, but Seven held a hand up.

"If you're gonna ask about the . . ." Seven looked around and lowered her voice. ". . . Nightbeast, don't. I haven't had a moment to even think about it."

"I wasn't gonna bring it up," Valley said, but her bright red cheeks said otherwise.

Seven immediately felt bad and scooted closer to her friend. "Are you holding up okay?"

Valley, who was hugging her knees to her chest, looked away and shrugged. "I'm used to people talking about me."

"Not in the newspaper though. It's okay if things are hard. You don't have to be strong with me."

Valley turned, giving Seven a curious look.

"I just mean . . . I know when people are being terrible to you, you put your guard up, but I'm not going to make fun of you if you need to complain or be mad. You can be yourself with me."

Valley's eyes watered and she wiped them quickly with her sleeve, her face red and blotchy.

"You can cry too," Seven said softly. "That's okay too."

Her eyes still wet with tears, Valley smirked and nudged Seven gently with her shoulder. "You're not bad, Salazar."

"Yeah, yeah." Seven smiled.

"To tell you the truth, I'm kinda goosing out about the whole stone hex thing more than anything else right now," Valley said. Okay, she wanted to change the subject. Seven could do that.

"Me too. We *need* to figure out who the hexer is," Seven said.

"But where do we start?"

Seven held her head in her hands in despair. "I have no idea."

Her mind felt foggy and sluggish, and she was having a hard time doing her normal strategizing. Seven felt a presence on either side of her, and when she looked up, River, Lotus, and Crimson had sat down next to her and Valley on the grass.

Valley was trying hard to look cool and unfazed, but Seven's jaw was pretty much on the floor.

"We've been wanting to say hi." Crimson smiled. "I'm Crimson Riddle."

"We know who you are!" Seven said much too loudly. On instinct she held one hand out, and Crimson slowly extended his, looking side to side in confusion as Seven took his hand

and shook it forcefully. River smirked, her button nose twitching as she did, and Lotus threw her head back and laughed loudly, her powder-blue hair shimmering in the sun.

"It's great to meet you," Seven said.

"Sorry, she's weird." Valley smiled.

"I am," Seven said.

The older witches all laughed. Seven had made them laugh twice!

Just then two witches, arms interlocked, blue spring robes sparkling in the setting sun, walked up to them.

"Aren't you that Valley Pepperhorn Spare?" said the taller of the two girls. She almost sneered as she said it, her long, hooklike nose scrunched in disgust.

"Yeah, so?" Valley said.

"You're pretty brave to show your face in public after what your dad did," said the other witch, who had a short brown bob and looked . . . strangely familiar.

"That's . . . interesting coming from you, Aphra," Lotus said slowly.

"It's all over the papers," continued Aphra, ignoring Lotus. "It's a shame that they let just anyone take advantage of living in the Twelve Towns. If you ask me, Spares who aren't working for a respectable family should be exiled."

The tall witch by her side nodded emphatically.

"It's a good thing nobody asked you, then," Crimson said.

"Ugh, the Dimblewits are the worst," River grumbled.

"Dimblewit?!" Seven blurted.

Aphra *Dimblewit* sniffed. "No doubt you've heard of my aunt and uncle, then?"

"Heard of them—we helped get them sent to the Tombs," Valley said giving Seven a high five.

Aphra blanched, and the older teens laughed.

"Run along now, Aphra," River said sweetly. "Before Seven calls the Nightbeast."

Aphra grabbed her friend's arm in fright and Seven froze, but as River laughed, Seven knew she had only meant to scare the mean witches. Nobody *really* knew about the Nightbeast.

"Come on, Ember. We don't want to be seen with their kind. A thief"—Aphra pointed at Lotus, and then whirled on Valley—"and a Spare that even her own father doesn't want."

"Hey!" yelled Seven fiercely. She got up and stood face-to-face with Aphra. Well, almost, since she was a good toadstool shorter, but she was ready to fight right here if she had to.

A few witches around them had noticed the commotion and begun to stare. Valley's face went red, and Lotus's eyes filled with tears.

"Haven't you been cruel enough for one day?" River shot the awful witches a withering look.

Aphra smiled at Seven. "I am just getting started."

"Do your worst," Seven shot back.

Just as Aphra looked like she was about to shoot a spell at

Seven, Crimson casually flourished his hand, sending sparks of fire at Aphra's and Ember's feet.

"What do you think you're doing!" yelled Aphra.

"Go away." Crimson waved them off. "Before *I* do my worst."

The two witches scowled, and Aphra gave Seven one final dirty look, leaned in, and whispered, "Don't you worry, Seven Salazar. We'll win the fight when it counts." Then she and Ember walked away. *What were they talking about? What fight?*

The rest of the witches around them went back to their conversations, the argument defused. "I didn't know there were more Dimblewits." Seven shook her head.

Lotus nodded. "Unfortunately they live in our town. Aphra's always been a bit of a bully, but she's been even worse since her aunt Rafflesia moved in with them. She came to our town after getting out of the Tombs, and they've been causing trouble ever since."

"Aphra swore she'd be named a champion, but wasn't. And she's been even meaner ever since," Crimson said.

"They've been absolutely awful to the Spares," said River. "Figgs won't even go near them."

Seven turned to Valley. "You okay?"

Valley shrugged, but her face was ruddy, her eyes still watery. "She's not the first person to say something like that."

Lotus looked at Valley, seeming to consider her. Then she

cleared her throat and clicked her long, sparkly nails together. "Last year my dad convinced a bunch of other witches to put coin behind a lost-dragon-scale excursion. It was supposed to return triple their gold—indeed, my father put almost all our own coin into it—but . . . the excursion party didn't make it back."

"Eaten by sirenas," said River, shaking her head.

Seven shivered. Sirenas might look like beautiful water-dwelling witches from a distance, but up close they were hideous, scaly monstruos. She hoped to never find out for herself.

"The other witches thought the whole excursion was a scheme, and my family paid what little we had left in our coffers back to them to try to make amends. It wasn't enough—we still owe them thousands of coins, and I and the rest of my family have been labeled thieves."

River and Crimson nodded, dark looks in their eyes.

"They've been talking about my family in the newspapers and gossip programs for months. They've called my father and mother every cursed word under the Stars, they've taken everything we had away to pay for a tragedy that was not of our making, but do you know what they can't do?" Lotus said, looking straight at Valley.

"They can't break us. Because we have one another. And they can't take away our wins. No matter how many dirty looks Aphra throws at us, it doesn't change the fact that we are champions and she is not. There are those who can be happy for others' successes, but Aphra is not one of them. Instead of working harder to make it next time, she let her bitterness take hold. She blames everyone else for what she could not do, including us. She doesn't think we deserve to be champions, that only witches like her should win anything. But you win by keeping your head high and proving them wrong."

Crimson and River both put their hands on Lotus's shoulder and squeezed.

"'The best way to make them eat their words is to win no matter what,' that's what my grandmother and my great-great-grandmother Fortuna before her always used to say, and she was the smartest witch I've ever known."

Valley's face brightened.

"It's our turn," said River, pointing at the waving photographer.

"We'll see you later?" Crimson said, standing and wiping the grass from his ripped black pants.

"Sure," Seven said.

"Keep your head up, Witchlings," Lotus said as the three teen witches made their way to their very long line of waiting fans, and Seven and Valley made their way to Thorn's tent.

At the photo area, Seven's parents were chatting happily with Thorn's parents and Valley's mom. When Thorn emerged from her tent to raucous cheers, she looked more beautiful than Seven had ever seen her. Her makeup was soft and pretty, and her black hair shone in the sun. Perhaps the best part though, was her dark red tiered jacket dress. Thorn had made it specially for this occasion, an ode to their Spare colors. Seven swelled with pride. A photographer helped Thorn pose. They put a flower in her hand, customary for Witchlings' portraits, though Thorn was no longer a Witchling.

"Why are they making her pose like a kid?" Valley complained.

"I don't think they'll ever stop seeing us as Witchlings." Seven rolled her eyes.

A row of photographers were standing at the ready, and a long line of witches were waiting their turn to take a picture with the youngest champion in the history of the games. She was the most popular champion of the day, it seemed.

"Thorn!" yelled Seven, and they cheered and waved at her as Thorn beamed.

Seven was so proud of Thorn. And she just knew that none of the champions had any idea who they were up against. Seven would bet her plant collection that Thorn came out in the top five, at least.

As they all took pictures with Thorn, Valley and Seven could barely contain their laughter and joy. Thimble and Leaf, Thorn's parents, both wiped their eyes as they watched her. Seven wondered if, even in happy times like these, they thought of Petal too.

"Okay, just need to go sign the ledger of champions and we can go have ice cream," Thorn said breathlessly.

She went over to a giant golden book, which was being supervised by Alaric the ghost and Jonafren from the Hall of Elders, out of his Enve Lopes costume and in a sensible sweater-vest. Alaric waved happily at Seven and Jonafren sighed, admonishing Alaric for not paying attention. Thorn signed her name and wrote a message, and everyone clapped loudly for her as she ran back over to her friends. But before they could get away, Alaric, with Jonafren in tow, stood in their way, tutting at Seven.

"Seven! Oh, I have a *bone* to pick with you! You haven't come to see me in weeks! I thought you forgot about me altogether. You know, I even baked you cookies a few days back because I was sure you'd come for my thirty-year office anniversary. And you know how I feel about using ovens, me dying by fire and all, and then you just didn't show? Heartbreak!" Alaric screeched dramatically.

Seven held back a laugh, but not for unkind reasons. Alaric was just like this. Dramatic, and fun, and over-the-top.

"I'm so, so, so sorry. I've been real busy with training and all," Seven said.

"I know, I know. You're a special gold star now. All three

of you are, my Stars! And now you don't have time for old friends," Alaric said with a smile. "So, what schemes have you been up to lately?"

Thorn blushed. "No schemes, promise!"

"Doubtful," Jonafren said.

"You really should come by the office soon," Alaric said, and Jonafren shot him a dirty look.

"You've been doing a great job as Enve," Seven said, trying to defuse the situation.

"Hasn't he just?! Ugh, I tell him all the time, he should take that show on the road, forget about this office stuff, but," Alaric sighed, "he just loves it there, don't you?"

Jonafren grumbled.

"He loves the office supplies, and truthfully"—he pitched his voice to a whisper—"I do too."

The Witchlings giggled.

"We have more champions to attend to, Alaric," Jonafren said with a tight smile.

"I'll be waiting for you at the office! Toodle-oo!" Alaric said as Jonafren pulled him away.

"Ice cream time!" Thorn said.

Seven thought about what Lotus had said, and a glimmer of hope bloomed in her heart. Despite all odds being stacked against them, Seven, Valley, and Thorn had continued to prove everyone wrong. They had beaten the Nightbeast—at least sort of—they had stopped the Cursed Toads, and Thorn was a champion. Valley was fighting through scrutiny from every witch in the Twelve Towns and had still managed to find someone she cared about in Graves. No matter how much people knocked them down, they kept getting back up. Maybe that meant there was a chance for Seven to become a real Uncle—to stop the Nightbeast's voice, to break free of the curse of being a Spare, and be *someone*. Seven smiled, knowing she could do it all with Valley and Thorn by her side. They walked with their arms linked with one another, their parents trailing them. As the sun dipped farther behind the hill, lighting the world up in brilliant hues, Seven thought of how grateful she was to finally have a group of friends that nothing and nobody could tear apart.

CHAPTER TEN
THE FIRST COSTURA TRIAL

RAVENSKILL'S SPORT STADIUM, which was shaped like an egg and affectionately called the Spegg, was filled to capacity. It had also been enchanted a sparkling gold color for the games, making it glimmer in the sun. Seven had waited for Valley out front for a whole hour before she gave up and went inside, and now she was so far from the stage, all the witches looked like ants. During normal events, Spares would be up in the nosebleed seats anyway, but the Golden Frog Games were different. *Supposedly.* It was supposed to be first come, first served, but families that employed Spares almost never let them sit alongside them. So Seven was surrounded by other Spares. And they were staring at her.

Seven put her rucksack in the seat to her right, saving it for Valley, as a pair of teen witches walked past her whispering.

"Hi," she tried, but they just turned away and walked faster.

"Sheesh, you'd think I'm cursed or something."

"Give 'em a break. They're understandably nervous around you," said Figgs as he slid into the other empty seat next to Seven with a wide smile. He smelled like a strawberry sundae. Seven resisted the urge to scream.

"What for? I'm just a Spare loser like the rest of them," Seven snapped, and immediately regretted it. Lately, whenever she was nervous or uncomfortable, she acted like an absolute goose. Although she had talked about it with her witch doctor, Dr. Blackwood, she was still having a hard time controlling her emotions. She had started to see him at the Gran's request, to make sure she was okay after everything that happened last year. Seven felt like a broken cauldron that had exploded after a faulty potion, and she was trying to put herself back together piece by piece. But whenever she thought she'd fixed one part, another would get messed up again. Getting better was hard work. It didn't help having the entire Twelve Towns talking about her when she was just a kid. She might've had her full powers, but deep down, she did still feel like a Witchling.

"You can't be serious," Figgs said, not unkindly. "Of course everyone is nervous. I am too." Figgs looked at Seven pointedly.

Seven took a deep breath and tried again. "Sorry, that was a warlock thing to say."

Figgs held his hands up, as if to say "No worries." But Seven really didn't want him to think she was awful.

"I just mean I'm no different than anyone else here," she said quickly.

Figgs cocked his head to the side. "Would it really be all that awful if you were?"

Seven didn't know what to say, but the words echoed in her mind as she looked around the Spegg.

Covens, who were mostly sitting together, made a sea of green and pink, purple, aqua and silver, blood orange, and black as they gathered in different sections. Seven and Figgs settled in to watch the trial, grabbing some snacks as a vendor flew by on a broom. Seven looked toward the entrance every few seconds so she would see when Valley arrived.

The maintenance crew was spraying the stage with anticheating magic, and the lucky witches who'd gotten there first were settling in the front row. Including Valley! Seven spotted her sitting next to Graves, and they were chatting happily while sharing fairy floss. Seven narrowed her eyes.

"This is so froggin' cool," Figgs said.

"Yeah," Seven grumbled, "the coolest."

She wanted to run down there and yell at Valley. Why hadn't she remembered they were supposed to meet up? Why hadn't she at least messaged Seven? Now that she'd found Graves, it was like Seven didn't even exist. Annoyed, Seven flourished her fingers and whispered, "Pastel."

A round cake materialized in her other hand, and she took a big, angry bite.

"Um . . ." Figgs said.

"Sorry, do you want some?" Seven said, her mouth full of the creamy, sugary sponge cake as she held out what was left of it to Figgs, who surprisingly took the rest and ate it.

"You're not supposed to be able to use magic at that level yet, right? Unless it's an Uncle thing?" Figgs asked as he chewed.

"Nope, it's just a Seven thing. I think I studied so much, my magic broke." Seven wiped her mouth.

"Witches of the Twelve Towns!" Enve Lopes was suddenly onstage, and the crowd cheered wildly. Figgs was clapping excitedly, and he elbowed Seven softly, smiling as if to say "Come on! This is fun!"

Seven smiled back reluctantly, if only because Figgs's happiness was contagious, and she joined in with the cheering. She was here for Thorn, she reminded herself; everything else could wait.

"Welcome to the first costura trials of the Golden Frog Games! I present to you your costura champions!"

More cheering and screaming ensued as each Town's champions emerged. Twelve teams, and thirty-five champions in total, were introduced. When they announced Thorn and Gunnar, the stadium erupted.

Thorn waved at the crowd shyly while Gunnar glided

around like royalty, his large cape floating gracefully behind him. Thorn looked around and the Crones Cliff Manor champions smiled at her, River even giving her a thumbs-up.

Seven stood up, a guttural scream coming from her throat. "THORN, YEAH!!!!"

She knew how nervous Thorn must be and she hoped she could hear her somehow, or at least feel how much Seven was pulling for her. Suddenly Seven felt the Spegg spin around her, and she staggered backward into her seat.

"You okay?" Figgs asked. "Water, please!" he called out to a flying vendor, who brought a lily pad cup filled with icy cold water. Figgs gave it to Seven, who gulped it down greedily.

She wiped her mouth, still out of breath. "Thanks. Sorry, I screamed too hard."

Figgs threw his head back and laughed.

Seven *had* screamed too hard, but she was also so tired, deep down in her bones tired, that any bit of exertion made her light-headed. She'd have to try and take it easy for the rest of the match, in case she really did pass out.

"Now, for today's challenge," Enve Lopes said, "each team will have exactly one hour to complete the trial using the pool of materials available to them here." She gestured at an enormous closet, its doors flung open to reveal reams of fabric and thread and all sorts of fashion thingamajigs. It looked like the inside of Thorn's room.

"Each team will work together to complete the given task

and then demonstrate it for our crowd. Once the clock stops, all magic will be halted immediately. Each team will be scored on innovation, styling, and utility. The lowest mark you can receive in each category is a one, the highest, a ten." The announcer gestured toward a table of judges just off the center of the arena. "The final criterion is crowd sentiment, which goes toward the team's overall score and each champion's overall score as well. Crowd sentiment accounts for five points, so it is very important. Choose wisely, witches."

Crowd sentiment was a controversial but crucial part of the games. The game officials used emotion enchantments, a highly volatile branch of magic that House of Stars witches specialized in, to gauge the feelings toward each champion and team. Currently, River Moonfall was the favorite to win the games, should Crones Cliff Manor take the cup. But in the end, it would be the witch with the most crowd sentiment points *from* the winning town who would be the Most Valuable Witch.

The crowd cheered loudly and the announcer cleared her throat.

"Now, for the challenge. Each team will be tasked with constructing an item of clothing that will transport them across a body of water safely."

Seven thought of the freezing-cold river last year during their battle with the Cursed Toads and the Nightbeast, and how Thorn's cape had saved them. She hoped having that experience would help Thorn now, but by the worried look on her friend's face, she wasn't so sure. Gunnar looked smug, but that seemed to be his face all the time. There were always officials at the games to make sure witches were safe, Seven reminded herself as she located two witches in Spegg staff uniforms on either side of the platform stage. The champions were granted a few moments of discussion before the announcer spoke again.

"Good luck to our champions, and begin!"

The champions ran to the open closet and began pulling materials. Thorn was focused, her brow furrowed, her arms already filled with supplies. She was trying to communicate with Gunnar as she worked, but he didn't seem to be listening. Her teammate grabbed a swatch of leather, then put it back down, then grabbed a shoelace and discarded it on the ground. The other teams were already busy at work at their respective workstations, with mannequins and scissors and supplies strewn about.

Lotus, River, and Crimson were making a dress of some sort. Another team seemed to be working on pants, another on a cloak. Meanwhile, Thorn was still gathering supplies, and Gunnar was at their workstation measuring his . . . feet?

"What is he doing?" Figgs asked.

Thorn dumped all her supplies on the table and quickly wrapped Gunnar's feet in a thick-looking material. It was suddenly apparent to Seven that Thorn and Gunnar were making shoes . . . well, Thorn was. Gunnar sat, feet up, as Thorn pieced together the shoes around his feet, her needle weaving in and out at her instruction, sparks of light and wind dancing around her as she masterfully put the shoes together. Seven had no idea if the shoes would work, or if what she was doing was considered difficult, but Thorn was holding her own, to say the least. She didn't look out of place or overwhelmed or out of her league: She looked like a champion.

Gunnar said something to Thorn and they stopped working. Thorn shook her head no and Gunnar seemed to insist.

"There seems to be some discontent between the Ravenskill champions," said Enve in a faux whisper.

The crowd visibly shifted to stare at their team, and Thorn looked around, her face red. She turned back to Gunnar, said one more thing, and he nodded. Thorn sighed, switching out one piece of hide for another. Gunnar smiled smugly; he had gotten his way.

"I hope he didn't just mess everything up," Figgs said.

"He *was* chosen as a champion. No matter how much of a butt-toad he seems to be," Seven said. "He's gotta be a little good at this."

Thorn pointed to the floor, where she put a piece of material under his feet and traced frantically with a mouthed spell Seven could not hear, followed by a flash of light from her fingers.

"Cortar, probably," Seven said to Figgs. "She always uses that one to cut."

Figgs nodded. "Impressive precision."

It was true. The material cut perfectly around Gunnar's feet. Thorn raced back over to the table and began to work. She yelled something at Gunnar, who got up and began helping her sew pieces of the shoe together. After every stitch, Thorn closed her eyes and uttered a spell, infusing magic into every single bit of thread. The process took longer, but maybe it would make the shoes work better. Thorn wiped at her forehead and kept her head down as she sewed and hammered and used spells to cut and pull and pieces together while Gunnar assisted her.

Seven's heart was pounding so hard, she had to take several deep breaths and remind herself it was only a game. *A game where someone has already been turned to stone*, she remembered, but dismissed the thought just as quickly. Thorn would be okay—Seven wouldn't let anyone come near her, even if she really did have to summon the Nightbeast.

"Five-minute warning!" said Enve. Lotus, River, and Crimson were already finished and tidying their workstation, but all the other witches began to work at an even more frantic pace. Everyone in the crowd seemed on edge, the air sticky with anxiety and excitement. The covens made waves in their house colors, chanting their coven cheers and yelling the names of their respective town champions. It was nice to have a fellow coven member compete, thought Seven, because even if your town didn't win, you could always find a champion from your house to cheer for. And this time, Seven had Thorn. Not just Seven, but all the Spares, she realized as she saw the bright smile on Figgs's face. The thought warmed her heart, and she stood up, clapping and screaming wildly. Figgs copied her and together they yelled Thorn's name so loudly that soon the other Spares were joining in. A rush of adrenaline took over as the Spares united over their champion.

Then Enve Lopes stepped up to her mic, and Seven knew it was over.

"Time!" All at once the needles, sewing machines, and flicking wrists stopped and the crowd cheered. This was the moment of truth.

Everything shook around them and, from the wooden floor of the Spegg, a roaring river materialized. Seven's breath caught with the memory of the river that had almost drowned the three Witchlings last year. She held one hand to her chest and took deep breaths to steady her heart. The fear felt so real, but it was just an enchantment, she reminded herself. She was safe right now and so was Thorn.

"First up, we have Boggs Ferry!"

The champions stepped forward. One witch with royal-blue hair was wearing their creation: a sharply cut black blazer. The blue-haired witch walked toward the edge of the water, then pressed one of the buttons on the blazer. The crowd gasped as a stunning golden cape unfolded from the back of the garment. All at once the water rushed toward her and she jumped forward, gliding down gracefully and landing with one foot on the water, the cape keeping her suspended like a hummingbird. The crowd clapped and cheered as she skipped over the choppy water—but then a particularly high wave shot at her and she lost her balance. One foot slipped under the water and the witch cried out. She stumbled, got tangled in the cape, and sunk straight down into the water with a piercing scream.

Seven stood, raising her hands up instinctively. Beside her, Figgs was doing the same.

"It's cold!" the witch screamed right as she was about to be fully submerged. Two of the officials on either side of the river flicked their hands, and she was pulled up and out of the water. As the crowd applauded, Seven let out a breath and sat back down, glancing at Figgs. He had a sheepish look on his face to match her own.

"How many points do you think they lost for that?" Figgs asked.

"No clue, but it's gotta be a lot. She could've drowned."

The number ten flashed overhead in giant red letters, with a crowd sentiment score of just one that was pulled from emotion magic.

The next teams went, using everything from gloves, which did not work very well at all, to pants, which were surprisingly effective. The Crones Cliff Manor team presented their dress—a beautiful water gem–encrusted gown with a built-in cape, worn by Lotus. She glided effortlessly across the water and only had one small mishap when the water got very choppy and wind blew around her, temporarily tangling the cape of her dress and stalling her mid-glide. But after just a second or two the cape was straightened out, and she made it to the other side of the river in record time. They had gotten the highest score, and most cheers, yet, with thirty points overall, including the highest crowd score of four.

Thorn and Gunnar went last. They stepped up to the river, and Seven could see the sweat on Thorn's forehead, her flushed cheeks, the way she pumped her hands into little fists every few seconds. Seven bit her lip, nervous for her friend and hopeful that this would all go okay.

"Fingers crossed," Figgs whispered.

"Thorn's got this," Seven said, hoping her friend could feel Seven's confidence radiating from the bleachers.

"Thorn Laroux and Gunnar Grimsbane for Ravenskill!" Enve said as the crowd erupted in cheers, but nowhere were they louder than the Spare section. Seven swelled with pride as Thorn looked up, right at her, and gave her the biggest smile.

"The Ravenskill team is one champion down, so let us see how they fare. Begin!"

Thorn grabbed Gunnar's hand and led him to the edge of

the river. She seemed to be giving him instructions, as Gunnar smiled at the crowd. Thorn did what looked like a little dance and some witches in the audience laughed.

Gunnar jumped up and landed, legs apart, knees bent, right on the surface of the water. And then he began to . . .

"They're tap shoes!" Seven said.

Gunnar danced and spun on the water. Every wave that came his way he was able to use as a literal step. A few icy rocks materialized and Gunnar slid expertly across them, making the entire sequence look like a dance routine from an old black-and-white movie. It was brilliant. With the other items of clothing, the weather or the water had gotten in the way of a completely uneventful crossing of the river. But Thorn had thought to make the first point of contact with the water the magical item. So no matter what, Gunnar was upright, and tap-dancing across. The faster the river churned, the faster his legs went. It was likely, Seven thought, that the dancing magic was built right into the shoes. Quicker than a world-class racing toad, Gunnar danced, his arms moving in a windmill motion as he smiled and danced his way to the other side of the river. The cheers from the crowd were so loud this time, it made Seven's ears ring. She was too busy cheering and screaming herself to mind though.

Figgs was jumping up and down and cheering right alongside her, which surprised Seven just a bit.

"Won't River be upset you're cheering for the competition?" she asked, out of breath and giddy with excitement.

"No, she's not like that. Don't worry. She's actually nice to me."

Finally, it was time for the judges to post their scores.

"A thirty-five! The first perfect score of the games!" said the announcer, and the Spare section got so loud, Seven was afraid they'd blow the roof clean off the Spegg.

The overall games crowd sentiment changed as well, and as the names flipped, Seven had a secret hope it would change to Thorn.

"We have a new crowd favorite!" the announcer said. "Gunnar Grimsbane!"

Seven scowled, but she had to give it to Gunnar: His presentation had really made the shoes shine. The Ravenskill team hugged happily and waved at the crowd. The champions lined up to do the customary handshake at the end of each trial to demonstrate good sportswitchship. River and Lotus both hugged Thorn with big smiles on their faces as Crimson gave her a low five. A few other witches stopped to talk to Thorn and Gunnar, but the vast majority just . . . ignored her. Some of them shook Gunnar's hand, and he smiled nervously, eyeing Thorn, but most walked past her. One witch even shoulder checked her, to which Gunnar did step in, a pleasant smile on his face as he said something that made the witch's face go a ghostly pale color. Thorn smiled, Gunnar squeezed her shoulder, and they exited the stage with the rest of the champions. Seven felt a wave of relief that no hexes had been cast this time. Security had been amped up to the absolute highest level, and maybe that had worked.

The Spegg began to empty out, and Seven and Figgs ran to wait at the side entrance for Thorn.

"Salazar," a familiar voice said, and Seven narrowed her eyes.

"Oh, you remember I exist?" Seven said as Valley and Graves walked up to them.

"Don't be weird, I just got here first and we got seats."

"Thanks for saving me one!"

"I got excited and forgot, sheesh."

"Whatever." Seven turned back toward Figgs. If Valley was gonna be a butt-toad and forget her because of her new friend, then she could do the same.

Valley hooked her arm through Seven's and nudged her toward the Spegg and away from Figgs and Graves, who smiled at each other uneasily.

"Hey, did you look into what we talked about?" Valley whispered.

"Huh?"

"The Nightbeast, remember?"

"Oh my gosh, you are *obsessed* with the Nightbeast."

"Seven, we have to help it. I heard that they might try to . . . kill it."

"What?" Seven's eyes opened wide. Something clenched

at her heart, something very painful. The thought of the Nightbeast being hurt made her feel sick and awful and all clammy. It made her feel like destroying something.

"Wait, how do you even know that?" Seven asked.

"I've been looking into it, trust me. We can't let them hurt it. The Nightbeast is innocent."

"We don't actually know—"

"The Nightbeast is what?"

Seven and Valley turned in unison, and there, standing with their gym bags, were Thorn and Gunnar.

"Thorn, great job in there!" Seven tried.

"What did you say about the Nightbeast, Valley?" Thorn didn't even look at Seven. She had never ever seen Thorn look so mad.

"Erm, that's my cue to be off!" said Gunnar in a lilting accent as he spun and walked quickly away from the impending fight.

"Thorn, listen. Please. Seven said the Nightbeast actually felt bad and the Cursed Toads were controlling it . . ."

"And it killed my brother. Don't you care about that at all?"

"It's just misunderstood. It's not a bad animal . . ." said Valley.

"It's not an animal at all. It's a monstruo!" Thorn yelled, and a few people did turn to stare now.

"Hey, goats, maybe we should talk about this somewhere else," Seven tried.

"And you were gonna help her?" Thorn asked Seven.

"Me?! I was just trying to find out who was behind the archaic magic." Seven pitched her voice low. "I didn't technically agree to anything."

"You *did* say you would help me." Valley crossed her arms in front of her, and now both she and Thorn were staring at Seven.

"I . . . don't know what to do, okay? I want to be there for both of you but I can't do everything!"

"Oh, poor Uncle Seven. It's so hard being famous and having all that magic, huh?" Valley said.

Seven narrowed her eyes. "Don't be a butt-toad, Valley. I didn't ask to be Uncle, and I've got my own froggin' problems."

"Yeah, big deal. You're a champion." She pointed at Thorn. "And you're destined to be the second-most-powerful witch in town. And what am I, huh?"

Seven flinched. As mad as she was at Valley, she hadn't thought about her feeling left out.

"Valley—" Seven started, but Thorn interrupted her.

"According to the conversation I just overheard you having, you're a selfish witch who wants to free the thing that killed my brother, Valley," said Thorn.

"Is that really what you think?" Valley asked. "That I don't care if the Nightbeast killed Petal on purpose?"

"On purpose or not, he's dead because of it. You weren't there when it happened. You didn't have to watch—" Thorn choked up, her eyes pooling with tears, and then suddenly her mother, Thimble, and her father, Leaf, were rushing toward her with flowers. Thorn straightened up and wiped her eyes immediately, trying not to let the pain on her face show.

"Thorn, we're so proud!" her dad said as he scooped her up and kissed her forehead.

Thimble wiped her face with a fancy pink handkerchief that matched her designer suit and threw her arms around her family. Just then River, Lotus, and Crimson emerged from the Spegg and congratulated Thorn good-naturedly.

"Do you all want to come to our house for the celebration?" Thimble asked.

"Sure," River said, but when Seven opened her mouth to say yes, Thorn put her hand up.

"No," Thorn interjected. "I don't think Valley or Seven will be able to hang out or talk for a while, in fact. They're so busy with their plans. Come on," she said to River, Lotus, and Crimson, who looked at one another and cringed.

With that, Thorn took each of her parents by the hand, walked away from her coven mates with her new friends in tow, and didn't look back.

CHAPTER ELEVEN
UNCLE LESSONS

SEVEN STOOD AT THE ENTRANCE to Starlight Cottage and practiced what she would say. The sun had just begun to rise, but she was used to being up at this time. She was training at the Gran's house today instead of the forest.

"I'm just curious about the Nightbeast investigation," she said softly.

"No, make it more confident," said Cheese the raccoon. The rest of the raccoons sat along the flower-strewn stone ledges leading to the Gran's home.

"Yeah, how about"—Breadstick the raccoon stood on her hind legs and put her chin up—"any updates on the Nightbeast investigation?"

The other raccoons gave her a round of applause and Seven shook her head.

"You know you don't have to follow me everywhere, right?"

"We like you." Tostone the raccoon nodded and the rest mimicked him.

"We brought you treasures." They held their little paws out, and in them was an assortment of trash—old apples, portaphone cords, coins, and discarded spell bottles.

"I . . . appreciate it?" Seven smiled awkwardly. If she brought any more raccoon gifts into her house, her parents would kill her.

"You are nice. Not like the old Uncle, ew," said Cheese.

"Ew," mimicked the others, some spitting on the ground in disgust.

"I will never be mean to you. I promise," Seven said, and the raccoons gave her a round of applause.

"Wish me luck?"

"Good luck," they said in unison, then sat down to wait for her.

"You seriously don't have to wait for me," Seven said.

"We love you, Seven Salazar," said Cheese, and the rest clapped again. "We will be here when you finish training."

Seven gave them a tight smile and a wave and then knocked on the Gran's door. She knew it was useless to argue with the raccoons, but she still felt bad. They waited for her every morning after training, even if it was raining or snowing. Maybe she could get Thorn to fashion them little raincoats or sweaters . . . if Thorn ever spoke to her again, that was.

The door flew open and the Oracle stood there with a smirk on their face.

"You're late."

"Only by a minute," Seven said.

"The Gran is going to be extra tough on you today. Hope you're ready to get your butt kicked." The Oracle's smile spread.

"Boooo!" the raccoons chorused, and Seven held in a laugh.

"Nice try, Sybell, but I'm *always* ready." Seven smirked, giving the Oracle a high five as she walked past them and into the house.

"Good luck, Sev—!" The raccoons' voices were cut off as Sybell closed the door.

"She's in the backyard; better hurry," the Oracle said.

It was funny; when she'd come to Starlight Cottage after their first run-in with the Nightbeast's minions, the cucos, she'd been in awe of this place. Now she was here every week and it felt more like an after-school club than the legendary Gran's house. Well, an after-school club that was first thing in the morning and where she was almost mauled to death once during a training session. She had gotten used to Sybell's sense of humor and they had become sort of friends. The Oracle was a mystery to most Ravenskill residents, but Seven knew now that Sybell was actually about one hundred and twelve years old, which for Oracles was more like seventeen. They had become their town's Oracle after their grandfather Mancio had passed away and become a Star, as all Oracles did when they left this life.

"He was seven hundred and five, a family record," Sybell had told Seven proudly.

It was nice having someone closer to her age, at least sort of. Seven had been spending so much of her time with other Town Uncles, or Grans, or her parents, and she'd heard more than enough about back pain and insurance.

Seven walked through the cottage and out onto the stone patio.

The backyard meant combat training. Turns out you have to know all sorts of things when you're the second-most-important witch in a town. She had wanted to be a reporter, to be witching world–famous for her words, sure, but to be in charge of one of the Twelve Towns? To be responsible for the safety and happiness of all the animals within it? To be able to protect and fight for them if another monstruo should appear? It wasn't what she'd pictured for her own future, and she wasn't sure, if she was being completely honest, that it was what she wanted.

"Hello, Seven," the Gran said. "You can take your shoes and socks off today." The Gran was sitting on a wooden platform in the middle of her backyard, her purple spring robes gathered around her like frosting on a fancy cake—a reminder that the Gran, like many a great witch, belonged to

House Hyacinth. *The best coven,* Seven's brain said instinctively.

"All the covens are great and have merit," she heard Dr. Blackwood's voice counter. He was always reminding her to try to reroute her thinking whenever she had thoughts that made her feel bad, but it was easier said than done. Plus, what if the thoughts were true? She'd be lying to herself if she denied that, statistically, House Hyacinth had the most successful witches in the Twelve Towns.

All around her, there were willow trees and dogwood trees nestled so close together they looked like long green hair dotted with pink flowers. They created a canopy that let just enough sunshine in to make the grass warm beneath Seven's feet, while also making the backyard feel a world apart from anywhere else in Ravenskill. Lanterns hung from moss-covered branches on rough ropes, and rare plants lined the perimeter of the cozy yard. A fresh breeze wafted through the air as the Gran smiled at Seven and gestured for her to join her.

"Sorry, Gran," Seven said. "I know I'm a *little* late, but just a little. Are we doing combat training today? I was thinking, maybe we could look at some of those old Uncle training videos you mentioned last time? I was super curious about the monstruo invasion of 1983 . . ."

"Perhaps next time. Today I thought we'd focus on offensive combat."

Rats. It would be difficult for Seven to talk to the Gran

about the Nightbeast if she was busy blocking spells. But she knew better than to push back on what their lessons were. Every time she had, she'd ended up getting bitten or hexed by some cursed creature when training with another Town Uncle and wishing she'd just listened to the Gran or Sybell. Besides, with someone going around stonifying witches, it couldn't hurt to work on her offensive magic skills.

"Okay," Seven said, rolling the sleeves of her long black shirt up.

The Gran stood with a grunt before Seven could run over to help her. "My back is not what it used to be," said the Gran, and Seven nodded knowingly.

"I actually made you something! It's in my rucksack, but it's an ointment I made from devil's claw plants I grew myself. It's supposed to really help with old—I mean, with aches," Seven said with a chuckle, her face going hot.

The Gran laughed and waved Seven off. "Old is not an insult, it is proof of survival. It is a blessing. May we all reach the age of achiness." The Gran winked.

Seven gave a small, relieved laugh, and nodded at the Gran. She was ready.

They stood fifteen toadstools apart, and Seven tried not to be nervous.

"I want you to feel the grass beneath your feet, Seven. To try and connect with it so that it may help you in battle," said the Gran.

"The grass?" Seven asked skeptically.

"All magic is taken from nature, but nature does not just mean 'animals'—you know this well. While a Town Uncle has a special connection with the critters all around us, they can also form strong bonds with the trees, the flowers, the dirt beneath our feet, and, yes, the grass. All these things can help you not only in your daily tasks, but in battle."

"How?" Seven asked. She felt like a toddler witch sometimes. *How, why, what?* Over and over again. She was surprised the Gran wasn't sick of her.

"You, as an Uncle, are granted additional blessings from nature. But when any witch uses a spell or enchantment, it comes from the nature that surrounds them."

Seven began to understand slowly.

"So it helps in combat . . . because I can control their magic, sort of?" she asked.

"Not control, but sense with signals, communication with nature, *intuition*," said the Gran. "Let's say I am about to hit you with a freezing spell. Before the spell emits from my wand, I must pull from nature to create that magic. It must begin as a thought in my mind and then as the action. Perhaps I will pull from a cold stream of water deep beneath the earth . . ." The Gran eyed Seven expectantly.

"Oh," said Seven. "By communicating with their surroundings uncles can anticipate what magic you might use. So if you pull the magic from the stream, I can use my power to find out your move from the stream before it happens? Kind of?"

"Precisely. Let's put the theory to the test. Just as you open your heart and mind to the animals, be open to the blades of grass beneath your feet. To the leaves of the willow trees above. Use their wisdom to help you best me. If you can." The Gran smiled wide.

Though she had struggled to get up just moments before, the Gran looked like a warrior witch now, one open hand up to block her face while the other wielded her wand.

Seven's heart thumped wildly. She had no idea what she was doing.

"Ready?" the Gran asked.

"Ready," said Seven.

She tried to feel what the grass was telling her, or the willow trees, or anything, but all she could hear was the very faint chant of "Seven, Seven, Seven" from the raccoons on the other side of the brick wall separating the backyard from the alley behind it.

"Viento!" The Gran thrust her wand forward, and a strong gust of wind shot at Seven.

"Bloquear," Seven tried, throwing her arms up in an X motion as she stepped forward with one foot. She was pushed back, her feet scrambling for purchase against the grass and dirt. Finally she stopped, just short of the brick wall on the far end of the yard.

"Sorry," Seven said, dejected.

"It was only your first try," the Gran said as Seven jogged back into place. "You will get it. Trust in yourself."

Seven nodded and put her hands up in a defensive stance, one foot behind the other.

"Take your time. Close your eyes and really try to connect with the ground beneath you. I won't strike until you're ready," the Gran said.

Seven nodded again and closed her eyes. She took deep breaths in, the same way she did the first time she had trained with the Gran and opened herself to the animals of Blue Mountain Forest on that chilly January morning. Their voices had flooded her mind almost immediately. *It had been easy,* she thought. But then, slowly, other voices leaked into her mind like the drip, drip, drip of a faucet. The voices of monstruos. Before long, they had taken over. And Seven knew it had been too good to be true. Nothing ever came easy for Seven Salazar. She had to fight for the things she wanted, and even the things she wasn't sure she wanted. She had to fight for her friends, for her grades, for her magic. Fighting was nothing new.

She breathed in and out, taking in the smells around her, the light breeze, the sticky-soft feel of spring grass newly uncovered from layers of snow. She felt the dew that would come in the early morning, the soft tap of rain against the ground. She felt the worms wiggling many toadstools beneath the soil, the ants marching in line, the bones of animals long gone.

When she opened her eyes, there was a fire in them she had never felt before, an intensity and focus that would've really come in handy during her math test the other morning. The Gran nodded, a proud smile on her face, before she hurled another spell at Seven, but this time Seven was ready.

A voice whispered an unintelligible word and Seven strained to hear, but it was so low and so faint. She focused all her energy on the feeling of the ground beneath her feet like the Gran had told her to. The word unfolded like a piece of paper; layer by layer it came apart until finally she heard, ever so faintly, the whisper of the spell paliza in the air around her. At the same time the words left the Gran's lips, Seven countered with her own paliza spell, nearly stopping the Gran's magic midair.

"Well done, Seven!" the Gran exclaimed.

Soft claps came from inside the house, and Seven looked to find Sybell giving her a thumbs-up. Little raccoon cheers erupted from the alley. She hadn't stopped the Gran, or even really heard the spell before she cast it, but she had felt something. Now she just had to work on her timing.

"That was cool," Seven said.

"Look." The Gran made a circle with her wand and a mirror appeared before Seven's face. Her eyes were a weird swirling green-and-blue color; they were glowing as if there was a fire inside them, and they lit everything in front of her a soft hue of green.

"Oh my goats," Seven said, holding her hand up to her face. "I look . . . incredible."

The Gran threw her head back and laughed. "This is what it looks like when you are in tune with your true power, when you give in to it and don't fight your nature."

Seven winced. Her nature was something far worse. A Monstruo Uncle. If only she could tell the Gran, but she was afraid of what it might mean about her. No, she'd be able to stop it, if she just worked hard enough.

"Okay, back to work," the Gran said.

Seven nodded, throwing her hands up with a renewed sense of confidence. They practiced like that for another few hours, Seven getting closer and closer each time. Soon she was completely exhausted and the Gran was satisfied with her progress.

They practiced the entire day, taking a break to eat some cheesy hot sandwiches Sybell had made and which Seven had just been in the mood for. Of course, Sybell knew that. The sun was just beginning to set behind the trees around them as the Gran dismissed her for the night, and Seven finally saw her opportunity.

"Gran, can I ask you something?"

The Gran raised an eyebrow.

"Have you found out who was behind the archaic magic?

Is someone still out there who can control the Nightbeast and make it attack again?"

The Gran sat down on a mushroom-covered tree stump and let out a breath as Sybell came out with a tray of colorful healing tea, handing one cup to the Gran and one to Seven.

"Thank you, Sybell." The Gran took a big sip. "We haven't found anything substantial yet, but things have been complicated by the—"

"Stonification spell?"

The Gran nodded gravely. "That is archaic magic as well," she said.

I knew it, thought Seven.

"It doesn't seem likely to us that it's a coincidence that archaic magic was used to control the Nightbeast, and is now being used to stonify a champion. It's possible that the Cursed Toads were being led by someone, and that that person is still out there . . . But, Seven, I do not want you—"

"Gran, they went after Thorn. Isn't it my job to protect my coven?"

"Seven, you do not know that for sure—"

"If something happens to Thorn, it will be my fault. I'm the Uncle, and Thorn and Valley are Spares. I have to make sure nothing happens. Otherwise, what's the point of this magic, if I can't even use it to keep my friends safe?"

"Seven—" the Gran tried again, but Seven was not listening. Her face was hot, and she held her cool hands to her cheeks in an effort to calm down. "I don't want you to tell me not to get involved. That's impossible! I can't just sit around trying to talk to squirrels when something bad might happen! I have to stop them! I have to—"

She was feverish with the desperation of all the things she felt and didn't know how to say out loud. She was afraid, and worried, and so very tired, but she felt that now, being a future Uncle, she was not allowed to complain about things the way she used to. Now she had to keep things in like the adults around her did, like her parents, like the Gran. She had to be strong, and calm, and hold it all together and figure it out, and make everyone happy. She just didn't know how.

"Seven!" The Gran almost never raised her voice, and she had never raised it at Seven before. Not like this.

Seven felt faint then, and she only didn't collapse because there was a chair to hold on to just inches from her hand. But she did stumble a bit, and the Gran's face softened instantly as she rushed over to her.

"Seven, oh, Seven," the Gran said as she helped her sit.

"I'm fine. I just got light-headed."

The Gran kneeled down as Seven sat, holding her hands and looking up at her.

"You're burning up," the Gran said, and there was a heavy worry in her eyes. "Sybell!" she cried out, but the Oracle was already beside her, holding a cold glass of some pink, icy drink that made Seven's mouth water.

The Oracle handed the cup to Seven, she took a sip, and almost instantly Seven felt her face cool and the sharp pain in her chest dull.

"Seven, have you been sleeping? Have the animal voices been too much?" the Gran asked carefully.

Seven hesitated. This was the moment. She could tell the Gran she'd been hearing the Nightbeast's voice, and that she could hear monstruos more than she could hear animals. She could tell her that she was afraid. This was her chance.

"I'm just tired because of the training," she said instead.

"And that's all it is?" the Oracle asked in the same careful, quiet voice the Gran was using.

"Yes. That's all."

The Gran and Sybell exchanged glances. Knowing glances. It worried Seven even more.

"I want to put your mind at ease. Listen closely: The Twelve Town Grans and I are investigating the Cursed Toads' magic as thoroughly as we can and making sure the Nightbeast is safe and secure. The Committee on Magical Misdeeds is investigating the stone hex with help from the Council and the Gran's Guard. We're all working together and we're all working hard to make sure we find out who is behind this so that it doesn't happen again and none of the other champions get hurt. So I am asking you not to put this on your shoulders, because they are already carrying enough."

It did calm Seven a bit to know all those witches were working on the archaic magic case, but there had to be *something* she could do . . .

"I see the gears in your mind turning already, Seven, and again, I am asking you, do not try to take this on. I will not allow it and have already alerted your parents and every other adult who might have information not to get you involved. You are so capable that it is easy to forget you are only a child. It is *our* job to take care of *you*, not the other way around. Understood?"

Seven nodded and handed the empty glass back to the waiting Oracle. It didn't sit right with Seven that, last year, the three Witchlings had essentially been on their own, and now adults wanted them to take a back seat to everything going on. But she knew deep down, the Gran was right. She knew she should listen, and rest as much as she could.

"I understand," Seven said.

The Gran nodded and patted her hand. "That's all for today, and you deserve a few days off for rest." The Gran pointed as she said it. *"Rest."*

"Yes, Gran," said Seven. "I promise I won't get involved."

Because what was one more lie when Seven was already drowning?

CHAPTER TWELVE
ALONE

SEVEN SAT IN HER ROOM and brooded. For the hundredth time that day, she picked up her portaphone, but there were still no messages. She had been trying to get in touch with Thorn and Valley all morning, but neither of them was answering. Just as she was about to walk over to their houses and bang on their doors, Thorn sent a message back.

"I'm with Gunnar, getting ready for the next trial."

That was it. Thorn never messaged so . . . coldly. Seven's heart lurched, her chest aching with the familiar heaviness that always seemed present these days, but at least she also felt relief. Thorn was safe; that was all that really mattered.

Seven put her phone down. There were so many things she wanted to talk to her friends about. She wanted to know if they were okay, talk about the hexer and the growing unrest around Spares. Rumors of an increased push to strip

Spare rights had begun surfacing, spearheaded by none other than Mrs. Dimblewit. It was all too much to handle, especially on her own. She needed someone to lean on.

Just then her phone rang. It was Valley. Seven's heart soared as she picked up and Valley greeted her.

"Hey, Salazar. Sorry I didn't answer earlier."

"It's okay. Listen, I talked to the Gran about the thing. Wanna get together and I'll catch you up?"

"Uh," Valley said, sounding distracted, and Seven heard another voice in the background. The voice said something else and Valley laughed before coming back to the phone. "I wish you had told me earlier! I'm kinda busy helping Graves with something today. What about early tomorrow morning or . . . ?" Valley trailed off, and someone else said something to her. "Right," Valley said to someone who Seven guessed was Graves. "Can I get back to you? I'll call you really soon, okay?"

"Oh, okay," Seven said softly, the pressure in her chest getting more intense. "Do you maybe think—"

But before she could finish, Valley let out a loud laugh on the other end at something Graves had said. "Talk to you later, Seven!"

And then she hung up. Seven stared at her phone, her eyes watering. When had everything changed between them? She shoved her phone under her pillow before burying her face in her bed and screaming. They were supposed to be a coven, they were supposed to be there for one another, but lately none of that seemed to matter. Seven turned over and stared up at the ceiling, remembering the last time she'd felt this terrible, right here in her room, looking up at the same star-covered ceiling: the night of her Black Moon Ceremony. Seven thought about going downstairs to talk to her parents or cuddling Beefy for a while, before remembering they weren't even home. Between their jobs, Beefy getting bigger and needing all sorts of attention, and Seven's training, she barely even saw them anymore.

It felt . . . really lonely.

Seven felt left out.

She grabbed her portaphone from under her pillow and bit her lip. She scrolled through the names on her contact list and her finger hovered over one name that used to be her go-to, her ace, her only friend. Before she could talk herself out of it, she pressed call, and her old friend picked up almost immediately.

"Seven!" said Poppy Mayweather. "I'd been meaning to call you."

CHAPTER THIRTEEN
POWERFUL IN ALL THINGS

SEVEN HAD ONLY EVER wanted to be a Hyacinth witch. And so, in her first year, while every other Witchling in her class diligently visited each coven, Seven had only bothered with House Hyacinth. It was the one time when she hadn't done her homework, because she was so sure that *this* was always supposed to be her home. Except . . . it wasn't. And now she was standing in front of a shining purple door that had to be at least twenty toadstools high, about to go in while knowing she would never be one of them.

"Seven!" Poppy opened the door and pulled her inside before Seven could protest.

"Hi, oh gosh, you're strong," Seven said.

Poppy smiled and flexed her muscles under her flowery purple dress. She hadn't always been this strong, but House Hyacinth took great pride in their athleticism. They were not just powerful at magic, which was what many people interpreted the "powerful in all things" part of their motto to mean, but masters of sport, agility, and combat.

"Wow." Seven spun around in the entrance hall, which was decorated with celebratory banners of House Hyacinth's many championships. They hung from the ceilings and sparkled in the light of the gold chandelier overhead.

Enchanted wallpaper dotted with purple flowers swayed as if they were in a meadow, sturdy-looking armchairs were also accented in Hyacinth's signature purple, and an enormous glass cabinet held what must have been hundreds of trophies from every sport imaginable.

"This place is even more incredible than I remembered," Seven said.

"It is pretty neat." Poppy blushed.

Unlike the much quieter Moth House, there were many witches walking through the adjacent halls, yelling excitedly or arguing about test answers.

"My otter is dehydrated, I'm pretty sure," lamented one witch in an ottersleigh uniform as a friend consoled him.

Poppy led Seven through a long hallway with portraits of past Hyacinth witches, and into a room. It wasn't until they were inside with the door shut that Seven realized where they were: Poppy's room.

The room looked just as Seven imagined: regal yet cozy, with heavy-looking wooden bunk beds, a large oak desk strewn with spell books and papers, and velvet curtains adorning each floor-to-ceiling window, pinned aside to let in a stream of warm sunlight. It smelled fresh and flowery and inviting. Seven's heart lurched as she suddenly remembered how they'd always talked about rooming together once they got into House Hyacinth. Well, at least it had happened for Poppy. She smiled warmly at her old friend.

"You doing okay? Valley and Thorn being weirdos?" Poppy plopped into one of the wooden chairs.

"They are being kind of different. Not any weirder than usual, just . . . not around as much," Seven said.

Seven told her old best friend all about the hard time she'd been having with her coven as Poppy plopped down next to her on the floor. "It must be hard not being able to be there for Valley when you know she's sad."

Seven nodded. "I really miss her. Is that weird?"

Poppy cringed. "It is a *little*, but only because it's Valley. And you used to be so afraid of her."

"I was not afraid of her!"

Seven and Poppy stared at each other for a moment, then started laughing. "Okay, okay, I did hide from her a few times. She was scary, but it was all a misunderstanding. Valley is cool." Seven looked down and smiled to herself.

"Maybe she just needs some time," Poppy tried. "Remember how hard it was for me when my moms got divorced?"

"I remember," said Seven, who had spent many a night comforting a crying Poppy about her fighting moms.

"And I know when we got in our big fight, it took time for me to figure things out. And I sort of needed to be on my own to really think about it, you know?"

Seven nodded. She wanted to be a good friend to Valley, and maybe sometimes that meant giving someone space. It would be hard, but she would do it.

"Are you okay aside from the coven stuff? You look kinda like the time you stayed up all night writing your spider silk essay," Poppy said, and Seven nearly burst into tears.

Seven felt a pang in her heart, because nobody knew her as well as Poppy did. Poppy had been there when Seven had remembered on the very last night of winter break that she had an entire five-page essay due on the benefits of spider silk in combat. Poppy had convinced one of her moms to let her sleep over that night, and as Seven fervently researched and wrote her paper, Poppy had brought her snacks and told her jokes. She'd stayed with her the whole time, just like they had been there for each other their whole lives. When they'd been sorted into different covens, everything had changed. But Seven wished that, somehow, they could've remained best friends instead of becoming kind of awkward, new, getting-to-know-each-other-again friends.

"I'm all right besides being sleepy all the froggin' time," Seven said, smiling widely. *And the Nightbeast, and all the other monstruos who won't stop talking to me*, she wished she could say and nearly did.

"Okay to come in?" a familiar voice said outside Poppy's room.

"Come in!" Poppy said and Tia Stardust entered, followed by her girlfriend and fellow toad-racer, October.

"Hey, Seven," Tia said, and Seven had to remind herself to be cool. Tia was literally famous, and though they'd hung out with her and October briefly last year, it was still strange to talk to her like it was no big deal.

"Hi," Seven said, her face going hot.

"How's Thorn doing?" Tia asked. The two witches sat on the floor next to her and Poppy.

Seven shrugged. *She hates me now.*

"Are you gonna ask her or should I?" October said.

"Ask who?" Seven asked. "Me?"

"Yes." Tia smiled. "I hope you don't mind us butting in like this but . . . we were worried about Thorn and the rest of the champions."

"But especially Thorn," Poppy said. "Since the Spares don't have a larger coven system and all."

"Oh." Seven looked down at her feet. She didn't know why she was ashamed. She loved Thorn and Valley and she was glad to be in their coven even if they were just Spares, but . . . she didn't want anyone feeling sorry for them either. Seven was, she reminded herself, training to become the second-most-powerful witch in Ravenskill. That was some-thing to honk at, wasn't it?

"Don't get us wrong, we know you're all capable and we wouldn't have been able to do the stuff you witches did last year," Tia said.

"No way. The Nightbeast gives me the creeps," Poppy said.

"I do not like that," the Nightbeast's voice whispered, and Seven shuddered. *Please, please not now.*

"But covens have a pact with one another—danger for one, danger for all. It means if one of us is in trouble, we all help," Poppy said. "It's not fair the Spare coven doesn't get that level of protection."

"We had learned about the impossible task in class of course, but it all felt so long ago, we had no idea how terrible it was until you had to fell the Nightbeast. Twelve-year-olds shouldn't have to be on death's door just because of some magical contract. You shouldn't have been left on your own," Tia said.

Seven looked around at the Hyacinth witches. They all had some form of purple on, their house color, and they were the embodiment of their motto: valiant, virtuous, powerful in all things. Were they really saying they were going to help Seven? Help her coven?

"After Mayhem was stonified, we decided we need to help you. If the adults won't step up, we will," October said.

"I will personally make sure nothing happens to Thorn.

'Today for you, tomorrow for me,'" Tia recited the famous Twelve Townian saying. "We have to look out for one another."

"I . . . don't know what to say," Seven said. "Thank you. I am so worried about Thorn and we're kind of in a fight right now—I know she wouldn't ignore you if you offered to help."

Tia and October lived in Boggs Ferry, where Thorn was from. Tia used to be Thorn's potions tutor back when she lived there, and Thorn was a huge fan of hers. Seven knew if Tia offered to help protect Thorn, she'd readily accept.

"So that's a yes?" Tia asked.

"I would be a butt-toad to turn down your help," Seven said. She was . . . relieved. She didn't have to tell them everything that was going on, but with them helping, Seven could focus at least some of her energy on the other two thousand problems she had.

"Good, because we also have theories," Tia said, taking out her portaphone.

"Theories about the stone hex?" Seven asked.

"And who could be behind it," October said. "Look."

Tia held up her portaphone and on it was a picture of a page from an old book. It had gray flourishes on every corner, and it looked very familiar to Seven.

The Book of Unliving. The same book Graves had gotten them access to.

"We're friends with Crimson from toad racing and he

snapped a few pictures for us since we didn't want to go into the Library of Hexes ourselves," Tia said.

"Did you know you have to eat a deathberry to go in? No way." October shook her head.

Seven chuckled nervously. "Ha ha, yeah, who would do that?"

Poppy gave Seven a curious look.

"A . . . friend of ours looked into that book too. Thanks for trying, but there was nothing really helpful there. Sorry." Seven shrugged.

October scratched her head. "I thought at least knowing a Moth House witch created the arenisca hex would've been helpful. You don't think it would help narrow down suspects?"

"Wait . . . what did you say?" Seven asked.

Seven tried to think back to her visit to Moth House. She hadn't remembered Graves mentioning a Moth House witch had created the spell.

"It says here that a Moth House witch found a way to use magic to fuse and calcify bones, in other words, the perfect ingredient for a spell that turns you into stone," Tia said, pointing at her portaphone.

Seven put her hands on her temples, trying to remember through the fog of her brain. Graves had said . . . she had said the book specifically *didn't* say what kind of witch had created the hex. Yes, Seven remembered clearly now. But why would Graves lie?

"Can I see?" Seven asked, and Tia handed her portaphone over.

The infamous arenisca hex is sometimes known as the stone hex. Its first known use was on the eve of the first-ever Black Moon Ceremony, although it is contested by some historians that its origins long precede the Witchling World sorting tradition. Although the name and family name of the creator of the arenisca hex is unknown, its origins can be traced to Moth House.

Oh my goats.

Seven looked up at the Hyacinth witches. Her heart was racing with panic, her eyes wide. "Are there other books of the unliving? Or is the one in Moth House the only one?" Maybe the book Graves had read from was different from the Crones Cliff Manor book; that would explain it.

"No, this is the only copy of that book. There are maybe other Moth Houses with something similar, but Crimson got this one from Ravenskill since he's here for the games. Why?" October asked.

Maybe Seven had misremembered or something, but if she hadn't . . . maybe Graves was covering up for someone. Or maybe she was involved herself and it was why she was getting so close to Valley. Seven had a sinking feeling then that Valley might be in danger.

CHAPTER FOURTEEN
A GRAVE SITUATION

SEVEN SAT ON THE STEPS of her house and compiled a list of suspects. It was a beautiful spring day, pink dogwood tree flowers dancing in the wind as her neighbors tended to their gardens or nodded kindly to her as they walked by. Some also gave her curious looks, which she didn't blame them for, since ten raccoons and Beefy sat all around her on the stoop. They were nibbling on grapes Fox had brought them, the raccoons talking to Beefy as he cooed unintelligibly back at them. The raccoons didn't seem to understand that he couldn't talk to them the way Seven did, but Beefy didn't seem to mind and they were keeping one another entertained as Seven worked.

It was the day of Thorn's second match and it was a double—she'd be competing in back-to-back events. Seven had just a few hours before it started, and she wanted to make the most of her time and focus on her investigation. The two motives Seven could think of were that someone had a grudge against Spares, or that someone wanted to sabotage champions in order to win the games. Mrs. Dimblewit was on her list of witches who would've happily tried to use the stone hex on a Spare, along with her awful niece Aphra. The other fashion champions would benefit the most in the games from taking Thorn out, making them all fairly suspicious. Next Seven wrote down *Moth House witches*. The hex was created by a Moth House witch and Graves could've lied to protect someone from her coven. And at number one, Seven reluctantly wrote the name *Graves Shadowmend*.

Seven tapped her pen to her chin. "But why would Graves do that? What's her motive?"

"Graves, Graves, Graves," the raccoons began chanting, and Beefy screamed happily at what Seven imagined were just chittering noises to him.

"He okay?" Talis stuck his head out of the first-floor window and looked at Seven.

"Yeah, Dad, he's just raging with the raccoons," Seven said.

Talis shook his head and laughed. "She says he's raging with the raccoons, amor!" he yelled back into the house.

"Okay, then." Seven heard her mom's voice in the distance, and she turned back to her notebook.

Seven couldn't think of any reason why Graves would

want to hurt Thorn—or anyone for that matter. But unless she *was* protecting someone, why else would Graves lie? She had no grudge against Spares. She was *dating* a Spare . . . but that didn't mean it was genuine. Seven really hoped that wasn't the case. She tried to remember anything that connected Graves to the games, anything she'd said or done in the few times Seven had met her that might explain her lying.

As she racked her brain, she watched Beefy holding one of the raccoons and rocking it like a baby. It had fully fallen asleep and the other raccoons had lined up for their own turn. Seven shook her head.

Seven looked through her notes, but found nothing helpful. By the time she'd finished, eight out of the ten raccoons had been rocked to sleep by Beefy and placed gingerly on a tuft of grass in their small front lawn.

Could Graves want to sabotage the games? If Graves was a champion herself and wanted to win, that would make sense, except she wasn't, but—

"Maybe someone she knows is!" Seven shot up from her seat.

"Think, think, Seven, think," she whispered to herself. Graves had mentioned someone before the costura trials . . . her sister! If she was in the Golden Frog Games, maybe she had something to do with the hex, and that would explain why Graves lied about the origins of it.

Seven did a bit of digging on the witchernet and found

her name . . . Wren Shadowmend. She searched the current champion database and under the magic dueling team she found her. Aside from her short purple, pixie haircut and nose ring, Wren looked just like Graves. Seven covered her mouth with her hand. This was horrible.

The last thing she wanted to do was cause any more fights within her coven, but she had to warn Valley about Graves. She brought Beefy inside, left the sleeping raccoons on her lawn, and ran to warn her friend.

Seven reached Valley's building on Division Street and looked up. Usually, her mother, Quill, kept the windows open if they were home—and they were open now. Before Seven ran up to the second story, something in the window display of Vikram's Telecaster Shop caught her eye.

"Thorn Laroux, Golden Frog Games youngest champion, is making history," said a familiar witch from the wall of tele-casters in the window display. It was Tiordan Whisperbrew, Seven's idol and the star reporter of the *Squawking Crow* newspaper. They were in a grand-looking room with all-purple furnishings and a roaring fire behind them. Must be a Hyacinth common room in one of the Towns. They were sitting opposite a line of witches seated in fancy-looking chairs. Some were champions and some were spectators, including Aphra Dimblewit, who had a smug look on her face, and the head of the Toad Racing League, Orion Hook. And one witch who Seven knew well. Her jaw dropped when she realized who it was.

"Thorn?!"

She was sitting with *the* Tiordan Whisperbrew! Being interviewed on some sort of special report by the looks of it. She hadn't even told Seven! Seven had seen Thorn at school. She'd waited for her after her advanced wand theory class and Thorn just . . . walked past her like she didn't even exist, and now she was sitting with the one person Seven admired more than anyone in the world. Seven's heart swelled with a mix of pride for her friend and hurt.

She stood there watching the rest of the short interview, Thorn looking shy but holding her own as Tiordan asked her how she felt about being a Spare champion, what her parents thought about it, and how she was balancing her schoolwork.

"And your friends?" asked Tiordan, tucking a strand of wavy brown hair behind their ear. "Famously, you are in a coven with future Uncle Seven Salazar and heir to the Blood Rose fortune, Valley Pepperhorn."

"Heir . . ." Seven said out loud. It's what the newspaper had said as well, but Valley had never mentioned anything about being an heir.

Thorn was silent for a moment, her cheeks going red, and Seven's eyes watered. She was hurt that Thorn was ignoring her, but if she was in her shoes, if the Nightbeast had killed

Beefy, would Seven be willing to help it? Thorn wasn't wrong when she told them off, but Valley wasn't wrong either: The Nightbeast had done things against its will. So was it fair to blame it for Petal's death if it had not been responsible? Maybe it wasn't Seven's decision to make, she realized. Maybe Thorn was the only one who could decide that.

"I'm sure Seven will make a great Uncle, and Valley will . . ."

"*Everyone* knows she is a troubled girl," said Aphra, cutting Thorn off. "It is unfortunate for both Thorn and Seven to be placed with her. They are a legendary Spare coven, if such a thing even exists, I suppose, and Valley, well, it is no surprise that she is unexceptional. Considering her family." A chilling smile crossed Aphra's face as she looked directly into the camera.

Seven's heart froze up just as something loud crashed upstairs, and in moments the front door to Valley's building flew open and she walked out.

"Valley!" Seven said, coming after her.

"What?" Valley said. Her hands were in her pockets, and she looked mad enough to spit fire.

"You okay?"

"Did you see what she said?" Valley looked at Seven. There were tears in her eyes.

Seven nodded. "They don't know you. They're just basing everything on gossip."

"And it's all true!" Valley spun on Seven and threw her hands up. "My dad *is* terrible and everyone knows what he did and . . . I'm embarrassed!"

"He should be embarrassed, not you. You didn't do anything wrong," Seven said.

"That's not what it feels like. Everyone's always judging me and my mom." Valley choked up. "She . . . It's complicated. It's not like she let things happen to me. My dad was sneaky, he made me keep quiet." Valley rubbed her arms as if she were cold, and tears spilled down her cheeks.

"Don't cry, Valley." Seven went for her hand but Valley pulled away.

"Seven, don't. I wanna be alone right now."

"Okay, but remember, I'm your friend. You can talk to me about stuff. Thorn is your friend too; you're just going through a rough patch."

Valley looked up at Seven, her mascara-rimmed eyes reminding Seven of her raccoon friends. "I don't know if Thorn *is* my friend, honestly."

"Valley, please . . ."

"She didn't even defend me! She kept quiet." Valley pointed at the telecast display. "She knew I was watching or that someone would watch and tell me, and she just sat there!"

Seven bit her lip. It was kinda hard to defend Thorn right now, except that Seven understood *why* she was upset. She couldn't say that though.

"Are you on my side, or hers?" Valley said suddenly.

". . . What?"

"It's simple, are you on *my* side, or *Thorn's*?" Valley crossed her arms.

"You can't ask me to choose between my best friends."

Valley scoffed. "Some friendship."

"I wanted to help you, that's why Thorn is mad at me in the first place."

"Sure, blame me. But if it weren't for your stupid Uncle powers, we wouldn't even be in this mess. This was your fault, Seven."

Seven took a step back. Was Valley right?

"I . . ."

"Save it. Don't follow me," Valley said, before turning around and stalking away, probably to go to Graves. Seven suddenly remembered why she'd come here in the first place. She had to tell her about Graves, just in case she really was in danger. Even if it made Valley hate her.

"I have to tell you something, about Graves!"

Valley stopped, turned around, and quirked an eyebrow. "What?"

Seven got closer to her, and they were standing in the middle of the brick road, face-to-face. "Graves kept something from us when we were at the library. She lied about *The Book of Unliving*, not saying what kind of witch created the arenisca spell," Seven said quickly.

Valley shook her head. "Yeah right, Graves wouldn't lie about that."

"Except she did." Seven took out her portaphone, showing Valley the picture of the page she'd had Tia send her.

Valley read it and her face went even paler than usual, but when she looked up, her eyes were full of anger. "So what? There could be more than one of these books, maybe Graves—"

"No, Valley, Crimson got this from the same book. Only the Ravenskill Library of Hexes has it."

"So are you blaming Graves for the stone hex now?"

"Of course I'm not! But it's weird that she lied, Valley, and we should ask her why. For Thorn's sake."

"Why are you trying to hurt me? Graves is the only person who understands what I'm going through, and you're trying to take that away," Valley said.

"I'm not, I promise. I just—I'm trying to be a good friend to you!"

"Well, you're not. You're making everything worse, and this time I'm gonna walk away and if you follow me," Valley said, her voice trembling, "I *will* hex you, Seven Salazar. So don't test me."

Seven stood there, her mouth open and her heart shattered as Valley walked away from her.

She wanted to run after Valley, but her boots were firmly planted in the ground. Seven closed her eyes, and she felt the dirt beneath the brick, the roots of the trees lining the street speaking to her and keeping her grounded. *You're okay,* they seemed to say, even as Seven bit back tears.

She opened her eyes and began making her way to the Spegg. It was almost time for Thorn's next match. Today's event was super intense and Seven wanted to be there to cheer Thorn on and keep an eye out for Wren and Graves now too. If she hurried, maybe she could catch Thorn before her match and tell her how hurt Valley was. There had to be a way to fix this, Seven thought, a wave of nausea overtaking her as she left Division Street and walked to where the Ravenskill Mudbean House was. She would talk to Thorn, then talk to Valley again somehow, and she'd figure out why her powers were failing, and she'd ace her Uncle trials, and she'd find a way to make the Nightbeast stop talking to her . . .

The world around her spun, and Seven's head felt like a balloon that was floating away in the sky.

She took a ginger jelly from her pocket and popped it in her mouth. The candy, which she had made with her mom at home using her very own ginger plants, gave her a shot of energy.

"I'm gonna be late," Seven murmured, running through the bustling streets of downtown Ravenskill toward the Cursed Forest. The MVW point counter floated over the gazebo, and now River had pulled ahead with crowd sentiment points, with Lotus in second and Thorn in third! Maybe Thorn could snatch it from her today. Seven stepped into the woods to take the shortcut toward the stadium, the fear she used to feel here all but gone. She could hear the monstruos after all, and they were not interested in eating her today.

The ground was thick with roots and fallen branches as Seven scuttled through the Cursed Forest. She was pushing brambles aside when her eyes found two glowing red ones staring back at her from the ground.

"Whoa." Seven jumped back, her heart pounding, her hands up in defensive mode. But then the thing on the ground chirped sadly, a soft, terrified sound, and Seven heard a gentle voice say from somewhere in the trees, "Please, help us."

She looked closer and realized the thing on the ground was a skeleton bird, a baby one. And it was hurt. Seven dropped to her knees beside the wounded monstruo and gently ran her fingers over one of its skeletal wings.

"He is unwell," said a spindly voice from above.

At least one hundred skeleton birds were perched on the branches above her. A chill ran over her. Skeleton birds were, like . . . the mascots of the Cursed Forest. The monstruos you could see most often, flying overhead in the middle of the night, their red eyes glowing in the dark. But this time, there was something different in their demeanor. Their shiny bone-white heads were cocked to the side, their eyes . . . soft. They were worried about this baby bird, and were looking to Seven to help it.

Seven looked down at the bird, and it shivered, soft cries

of pain coming from its tiny beak. Seven carefully placed one hand under its head and furrowed her brow. She tried to see where the bird was hurt, but it was hard to tell.

What do I do?

Seven racked her brain, thinking of what plant, or spell, or lesson from her Uncle training she could utilize to help this baby bird. She tried to connect to the dirt beneath her legs, but was met with a piercing scream that seemed to come from every corner of the Cursed Forest, and she abandoned that idea swiftly.

"Will you help, or will you not help?" asked the same bird from the branch above. She began to sweat.

"I'm trying," she responded, and the skeleton birds leaned forward as one, the trees creaking beneath their weight. "Do you know where the baby's hurt?" asked Seven.

The skeleton birds shook their heads no in unison, and Seven sighed.

"How can I help you?" she whispered to the baby bird. "Tell me what to do."

Just because she could speak to these monstruos did not mean they could talk back. A baby was still a baby, even if it was a cursed creature. And this creature had not yet learned to speak. If only she could look into its mind, maybe she could figure out where it was hurt exactly and . . .

That's it.

Seven tried to communicate the way she did with the

Nightbeast, through her mind. Almost instantly, she heard a low growl.

"Now now," said Seven, and the Nightbeast fell silent. Seven ran her hands over the baby bird's tiny legs, its wings, and finally its heart. A wave of heat overtook her, a pain piercing her own chest. *There*, she thought. The bird's breathing began to slow, a rattling noise accompanying it, and Seven wasn't sure how she knew, but it was . . . dying. Her own heart began to race; Seven had to help, she was their Uncle. They had nowhere else to turn and she could not fail them.

"Please, help our baby," said the birds desperately, and a fevered determination took over Seven. It was as if she was not herself. Something around her, the trees, the wind, the touch of sunlight that reached the glade where she sat, all spoke to her at once, giving her strength, and something even more important than that . . . understanding. Seven put her hand over the bird and closed her eyes. She could feel them rolling back inside her head, a squishy, disgusting feeling, but with it came a bright gold power Seven could see in her mind's eye. Her eyes flew open, and it was as if she were floating above herself, watching the scene. Seven's hands were over the bird, her head back, only the whites of her eyes visible as a warm golden glow came from her hands.

The baby bird cried out, and Seven heard a pop; whatever disease had grabbed hold of its heart was stopped. But she knew that was not enough; she had to pull it out. Seven gathered every ounce of power she had and swirled her fingers in a circle over the baby bird's heart. The sickness gathered around her fingers like fairy floss—except gray, and gooey, and smelling of death. Once she was sure she'd gotten it all out, she cast it away and the baby bird fluttered back from the brink of death.

The bird flew to his family in the trees.

"Thank you, Uncle," said the birds, and Seven tried to get up but found she couldn't.

She was faint, taking deep breaths in and out, rubbing her eyes with one hand as the other kept her upright on the ground. Everything around her looked blurry. Where was she? Why had she come to the forest in the first place?

Seven looked around; every direction looked the same to her. How deep in the woods was she? When had she gotten lost? Why couldn't she remember where she was going?

The woods around her began to spin faster than the whirly ride at a fair. The voices of animals spiking then dropping, the notes off-key and clashing to make a nightmarish song of voices that pushed in on Seven until she was forced onto her back, shaking. Red eyes peered down at her, glowing and big, growing with every passing moment. It was the very last thing she saw, before the whole world went dark.

20th December 1789

Tonight, the monstruos do not speak to me, but scream.
I fear they've tired of waiting and if the witches of my
town do not burn me, the monstruos will consume me
instead.

—From the diary of Delphinium Larkspur, the
Monstruo Uncle

CHAPTER FIFTEEN
THE RULE OF MIRRORS

"YOU DO NOT LOOK GOOD, Uncle," said a voice hovering over Seven. She opened her eyes and found ten pairs of tiny beady eyes staring back at her. The raccoons all nodded in agreement with Cheese, and Seven tried to sit up, only to be met with tiny hands pushing her gently back down.

"You are hurt," said Sopa.

"I'm missing Thorn's event . . ." Seven tried again.

"It is missed," said Tostone. The ten little animals looked up at the sky and Seven noticed for the first time that it was dark. How long had she been out here? She reached for her portaphone and saw that it was nearly six p.m. and that she had about a billion missed calls. She'd been out here for over three hours! Still, Thorn's event today was a double. She could still make the second half if she hurried.

She sat up now, shooing the tutting raccoons away and

pushing past what remained of her dizziness. She had to go support Thorn and make sure nothing happened to her and . . . to Valley. Seven didn't have definitive proof Graves and Wren were behind the hex yet. But she was still super froggin' suspicious of them, and if they were going today, Seven could keep an eye out for any warlock behavior.

"Uncle Seven is sick," said Breadstick the raccoon.

"Rest, rest is good," said Puddin.

"I have to go, so you can either help me or fight me," Seven said, knowing full well there was no way she would ever fight them. *One* raccoon would be a formidable opponent, let alone ten of them. Besides that, they'd sort of become her friends. Maybe even, weirdly, the only beings she could count on right now. She wouldn't even be capable of using a freeze spell on them. Seven struggled, trying to stand but finding she couldn't. She closed her eyes. Her whole body felt weak, her brain felt foggy, and she was, Seven had to admit, afraid. She was alive, which was a bonus, but what if next time she wasn't so lucky? Uncle or not, this was still the Cursed Forest.

"I'm too sick to use a strong healing spell," Seven said, and the raccoons nodded sagely. "I'll have to use something weaker."

Seven thought of the spell her mother used to heal her scraped knees or Beefy's runny nose. It would be enough to help her body recover temporarily, she hoped.

She held her hands up and pulled as much magic as she

could from the forest around her. "Sana, sana, colita de rana."

At once, a warmth spread through her body and Seven felt well enough to stand with some help.

"Can you goats help me stay upright while I get used to walking, please?"

The raccoons were . . . overcome. Their eyes watered as they nodded in unison, holding their little paws together in glee. Seven had never asked them for anything, they were just always there, and now that she finally had, they seemed overjoyed.

Seven got up with their help. The raccoons used their hands and bodies to prop her up and spotted her as she walked in case she fell over. It was kinda comforting, and Seven smiled to herself. She might not have Valley and Thorn right now, but she had these creatures to lean on, and she was grateful for them.

At the Spegg's entrance, Seven hugged each raccoon quickly, then made her way inside. People were still getting snacks and taking bathroom breaks before the next match. Seven walked in and looked around, warily taking in her surroundings. From a nearby row of seats, Poppy waved her down. She gestured for Seven to come sit with her. There was an empty seat next to her. Had Poppy saved her a seat? Seven's heart swelled.

"Hey," Seven said.

"Where've you been? I called your portaphone, like, two hundred times. I was worried," Poppy said.

"I was training, sorry," Seven replied.

"Hey," someone said behind her. Figgs. "Is anyone sitting here?" He pointed to another empty seat next to Seven's.

"Nope, go for it," Poppy said. Seven introduced them as they took their seats, but she was screaming internally. She was suddenly aware of the grass in her hair and the dirt on her clothes, but something even more peculiar was happening. Seven's body felt different. Moments earlier, she could barely walk without the raccoons' help, but now she felt strangely . . . strong. Seven felt more awake, more energetic, than she had in months. She felt like herself.

Giving in to the monstruos is terrifying . . . but wonderful. She recalled a passage from Delphinium's diary and wondered, once again, if the very same things were happening to her. Had her strength returned because she spoke to the skeleton birds? Because she had used her magic to heal a monstruo?

"Witches! The second match is about to begin!" Enve Lopes was suddenly center stage, with a tiered dress made of holographic material and a shiny silver glitter wig to match.

The audience clapped and yelled, and Seven's stomach did somersaults with anticipation.

"How did Thorn do in the last round?" she asked Poppy.

"She did well! They had to make gloves with an enchantment of their choosing. Thorn's turned bitter things sweet, but the other top teams scored way higher, and Thorn and Gunnar dropped to third. Lotus, Crimson, and River are in first now."

Seven bit her lip. She wanted Thorn to win so badly, no matter how much they were fighting right now.

"Our next challenge is to design clothing using the Rule of Mirrors," said Enve, and the crowd murmured excitedly. This would be particularly challenging.

"Using the Rule of Mirrors," Enve said, "each team shall create one ensemble for one of its members and another for a particularly challenging population of our community . . . GHOSTS!"

A stream of specters floated down from the dome above them and landed on the platform at the center of the arena.

Everyone cheered wildly as the champions were each assigned a ghost to design evening wear for. Thorn looked determined if a bit nervous, but Gunnar patted her back encouragingly. He had seemed like an absolute goose at first, but Seven was glad he was actually supportive. Seven could see Thorn jumping up and down clapping when they were paired with their friend from the Hall of Elders, Alaric. He sashayed toward Thorn, twirling dramatically to thunderous applause. Enve Lopes rolled her eyes, but a small smirk escaped her lips.

"Each team of champions has one hour to complete a head-to-see-through-toe look for their respective ghost and a matching ensemble for one champion on their team. As some of you may know, ghosts always wear the clothing from their death day, and any other clothing they wear *must* be ghost clothing and *must* fit over their death day ensemble. The outfit must also consist of fabric that has crossed over to the other side. Our contestants not only have to design these looks but figure out a way to make the normal fabric, ghost fabric."

The audience buzzed with anticipation and chatter, and Seven could see Thorn trying to work out how to transform the fabric, her face one of deep concentration. Gunnar looked quite lost.

"Ready? Begin!" the announcer said, and like the last match Seven had gone to, the witches ran to grab fabrics.

River put the fabric on a mannequin as Crimson lobbed spells at it and Lotus cut and sewed things on their table. The Sleepy Hollow champions were using invisibility spells, which worked somewhat, but Seven knew invisible didn't equal dead. And Thorn and Gunnar were coming back from the fabric closet with . . .

"A burlap sack?" asked Poppy.

Instantly Seven knew what Thorn was doing. A smile spread across her face. They had used a spell to practice on a burlap sack before, when they were training to fight the Nightbeast. The Ravenskill champions began filling the burlap sack with thousands of colorful beads, and when they finished, Thorn pointed her hands at the bag.

"Viviente!" she said, and the sack began to morph and move like it was made of putty.

It shifted until it became a burlap version of Alaric. It walked around Thorn's area exactly like Alaric, and the ghost looked at it in amazement.

"I know I'm not exactly the smartest witch here, but this doesn't make a whole lot of sense to me," Figgs said.

"It's risky, but it's brilliant actually," Seven said, pretty sure she understood Thorn's plan. "She's going to put the fabric on the fake Alaric and, um . . . kill it."

"Whoa," Poppy said.

Using a killing spell wasn't normally allowed for anyone, but during the games the rules were different. It would be incredibly dangerous in a stadium filled with witches, but Seven was almost positive this was what Thorn intended.

The minutes passed as Thorn worked on the burlap sack, and Gunnar worked beside her on a costume made from shining iridescent fabric. After every stitch, cut, and mend, they whispered a spell, eyes closed, as was Thorn's method. It took longer than all the other champions, but Thorn put extra care into every stitch, just as her mother, and grandmother before her, had taught her. Soon there were mere minutes left on the clock. Some of the champions were struggling, their enchanted fabric turning visible or falling apart.

Lotus and River were guarding their creation closely, not revealing their hand and keeping their exact plan out of sight. But when Thorn seemed stuck on one stubborn stitch, River had come over and helped, patting a grateful Thorn on the back and returning to her team with a smile. It wasn't against the rules, exactly, to help another team, but it was rarely done. River and Thorn had become close though, so Seven wasn't surprised. Her coven sister could charm just about anyone.

Finally Thorn put the clothes on the burlap sack, scrambling as the seconds ticked by.

"Five minutes!" Enve said.

"Cúpula!" Gunnar threw his hands up and a glassy liquid dome formed around him, Thorn, Alaric, and the burlap Alaric.

A protective dome in case the spell backfired, Seven thought. Killing spells were all high-level and if Seven was right and it was Thorn's plan, a million things could go wrong. Thorn or Gunnar could get killed. Alaric was safe, since he was already dead.

As Gunnar held his hands up, maintaining the protective dome, Thorn turned to Alaric and gestured at him to close his eyes. Alaric gulped, stepped back, and did what Thorn said, covering his eyes and turning away. Thorn whispered a spell, holding her hand to her heart, her own eyes closed, then they shot open and she threw her hands out, fire streaming from her to the sack. The dome around them shook with the force of the magic, and the crowd gasped, but Gunnar held strong, his chiseled face red and sweating. In just moments, fake Alaric had crumpled to the floor and Seven winced. Real Alaric had died in a fire caused by the Cursed Toads' faulty magic, so it was no wonder Thorn had not only told him to look away but had whispered the spell.

It was the moment of truth, and the entire stadium seemed to be waiting to see if Thorn's gamble had worked. Thorn ran over to the sack and picked up . . .

A beautiful ghost fabric ensemble. Gunnar disengaged the dome and beamed at Thorn. She clapped in delight, then pointed at the other garment they'd created that was on the table. Gunnar grabbed it, then together with Alaric disappeared behind a closet wall to get changed just as Enve called time and the creation period was over. They had completed the task; now it was time to see if they had created something worthy of a win.

The ghosts appeared one by one: some in regular fabric, their champions unable to ghostify their designs, with normal see-through fabric in a sort of work-around that got low scores from the judges, and two teams—Faeton and the Crones Cliff Manor team—that had actually managed to create ghost fabric and designed a sharp suit and elegant gown, respectively. But all the clothing felt a bit off somehow. Sleeves slipped off shoulders, or pants were hiked up a bit too high, or gave the ghosts unfortunate wedgies. Every actual ghost ensemble didn't quite fit the ghost models, and Seven marveled at how difficult it must be to get this right if Lotus, Crimson, and River couldn't nail it completely.

Lastly, it was Ravenskill's turn. Alaric and Gunnar each revealed one sparkly boot at a time, their toes pointed, and the audience cheered wildly. Seven whistled and screamed alongside Poppy and Figgs. Alaric and Gunnar emerged with a final, flourishing twirl, and the crowd gasped at the sight of them.

Their twin capes glittered in holographic rainbow colors. The look was reminiscent, Seven thought, of the Oracle. Thorn had managed to infuse some color into Alaric's clothing by using light magic, an ingenious move, and although it was clearly made of ghost clothing, it matched Gunnar's outfit perfectly. And maybe her method of killing the fake Alaric had done something special to the fabric because it was snug and fit well on his body, unlike the other contestants, who had managed to complete the challenge by creating loose and flowy designs. Beneath the cape was a sheer shirt with three stripes across the front, each a different color and each glittering like the cape. Their pants looked shiny and laced up on either side, the lace shimmering to match the cape and high, sparkling boots. Finally, a large brimmed hat sat perfectly on each of their heads, slightly tilted over one eye for dramatic effect, a giant multicolored, shimmering feather sticking out from the top. Alaric and Gunnar acted like reflections of each other, one living, one dead, and their movements were completely in sync. It was by far the most stunning design of the night, and the audience applause proved that.

"Excellent!" Enve said, and the crowd settled in for the score.

The teams got anywhere from three points to an impressive twenty-five, but it was clear that the two top performers were once again Ravenskill and Crones Cliff Manor. When it was finally time to announce how Lotus, Crimson, and River had done, the stadium went quiet.

"With eight innovation points, six utility points, a perfect ten for styling, and a crowd sentiment score of four, the Crones Cliff Manor team receives twenty-eight points!"

People cheered loudly and Seven held her breath for the announcement of Ravenskill's points.

"With ten innovation points . . ."

"Yes, yes, yes!" said Seven, leaning forward in her seat.

". . . a ten for styling, a perfect ten for utility, and five crowd sentiment points, the great Gunnar and Thorn Laroux, our youngest champion, have done it again! A perfect score for the Ravenskill champions!"

The Spare section absolutely *exploded* now, and Seven got up and screamed her head off, hugging Poppy and then . . . Figgs. Both of their cheeks turned bright pink.

They all watched the giant scoreboard overhead, and

even with Ravenskill's high score, the previous match's score meant Thorn and Gunnar were only in second place. Crones Cliff Manor had *just* managed to squeak by, but Ravenskill was catching up.

"Watch out!"

A burst of light zigzagged toward the stage, and all the champions took cover as it tore through the closet with deadly precision heading toward Thorn.

Seven jumped up. This was what she had been afraid of. Just like the last time, she suddenly felt as if she were underwater, unable to move quick enough to help her friend.

With what looked like tremendous effort Gunnar grabbed Thorn's shoulders and spun her out of the way, blocking her with his own body. At the same time, someone in a black hooded cloak jumped in front of them both. The spell clipped Gunnar and the mysterious witch, sending all three of them tumbling before the hex hit someone square in the chest.

"Alaric, no!" Seven screamed.

The ghost froze, suspended in place like someone had stopped time. The crowd was surging away from the stage, and Seven tried to run toward it but was being swept up in the stampede. She fought her way through the crowd, but when she finally made it to Thorn's section of the stage, she and Gunnar had already been carried out by the Gran's Guard.

"Thorn! Thorn!" Seven cried out as she ran after her

friend, but she was too late. The witch in the black cloak bumped into Seven as she ran out and nearly knocked her over. There was blood on her clothes and Seven couldn't see her face, but just as she slipped from view, a wisp of pink hair escaped from her hood—Valley. Seven stopped where she was, her heart pumping. Poppy and Figgs caught up to her and they watched somberly as a member of the Gran's Guard covered Alaric's frozen form with a blanket. Seven looked around at the remaining champions, at the remaining witches in the crowd . . . it could've been anyone in here. Any one of them could've just tried to stonify Thorn. A cascade of teal-green hair caught Seven's eye, and her gaze locked with Graves, who was staring at her from across the Spegg. Her sister was by her side, arms crossed. They were in perfect line of sight to cast the hex, and Seven had failed to stop them. A fiery rage grew in Seven's heart, and the Nightbeast's growl was a comfort in her mind.

CHAPTER SIXTEEN
A BEAST IN RAVENSKILL

DAWN, ON THE NINETEENTH OF JANUARY.

It was cold and Seven had been sick.

"Seven, in order to gain an animal's trust you must communicate your intent with not just your voice, but body language," the Gran had said.

Seven had tried again and again to convince a hummingbird to eat from her hand, but it had flown away unhappy and she had gone home dejected. It had taken her another four weeks to pass this Uncle lesson.

Sunset, on the twenty-fourth of February.

Snow blanketed the ground, and Seven hadn't slept more than ten hours in the past week.

"It is not . . . normal for monstruos to talk to Uncles, no, but so long as it was just the first time your powers manifested, you will be fine. I promise," the Sleepy Hollow Uncle had told her.

Seven had looked down, still ashamed of what she could do, still too afraid to tell the truth.

Dawn, on the first of March.

"If you're going to talk to them, you have to learn the rules. When an aggressive animal approaches you, always concede the right of way and let them lead the conversation. Never try to dominate a dangerous creature. Always be calm," the Oracle had said.

Morning, on the ninth of March.

Seven had fainted after using her Uncle powers, not for the first time. She had a hard time breaking free of the darkness that had taken her, of the voices of beasts that would not let her rest and were drowning out the voices of the animals she was meant to help. She did not tell anyone. She did not know what to do. And she was afraid.

The lessons Seven had been learning for the past four months ran in a loop in her mind as she waited to emerge into the center of the outdoor space that had been prepared for the Uncle exhibition.

A few days had passed since the last costura event, since

Alaric had been turned to, not stone exactly, but a sort of ghost statue. The monstruo voices had become stronger since then, and so had Seven. Thankfully, both Thorn and Valley were okay after the last hex attack, not that she heard it from them. Gunnar had been injured but was recovering, but poor Alaric had joined Mayhem in the Bluewing Infirmary for the healers to work on. And now it was time for her Uncle presentation, where each Uncle had to complete a different task to show off their powers. Seven had been assigned birds, which was one of her weak points, but she didn't have a choice. She would only need to summon them, and though she was nervous, she was hopeful she could pull this off.

The crowd was cheering loudly on the other side of the concrete wall. The Castle Point Uncle, Forrest Thornheart, was completing a dance routine with puppies, and Seven had to follow *that*. *Just great*. With a final round of applause, Forrest ran into the locker room area where Seven was waiting. He was covered in sweat, and twelve adorable corgi puppies followed him, their ears flopping.

"Good luck out there, it's a good crowd," Forrest said as he wiped the sweat from his forehead and gave the puppies treats.

"Thanks," Seven said.

"Uncle, we want to dance some more!"

"We want to play!"

"Where is the ball?" the puppies were saying all at once,

and Seven couldn't help but smile. She walked toward the exit, too nervous to speak as an attendant with a clipboard and a headset microphone gave her instructions. Seven wasn't even sure what the witch was saying.

"Got that?" asked the attendant.

"Um, could you repeat it?"

The attendant sighed. "Just summon your birds, then send them back home. Make sure you tell them not to fly too close to the audience; it's packed out there. Oh, and try not to summon anything big . . . like birds of prey, you know? There are lots of baby Witchlings in the audience and we don't want to scare them. You have five minutes, okay?"

Seven gulped, and before she had a chance to tell her she wasn't okay and she wanted to do anything but go out there, please, she was thrust out into the open air and met with a roaring crowd.

They were cheering so loudly, they almost drowned out the incessant voices of animals and monstruos. It was the most well-attended Uncle exhibition in Ravenskill history, she'd been told, everyone hungry for a glimpse of the Spare Uncle. She looked out into the crowd and found her parents and Beefy. They were cheering wildly and it gave her a boost to see them. She spotted Miss Dewey with Ambert, Poppy sitting with Figgs—which only made Seven nervous all over again. She searched for Valley and Thorn as she spun around looking at the cheering witches, but she couldn't see them.

When she reached the center of the large stadium, a voice came over the loudspeakers. "Our next Uncle, Seven Salazar!" People cheered and applauded politely, but Seven could see more than a few disapproving looks.

The announcer continued her introduction. "Seven Salazar is the historic *Spare* Uncle, the first of her kind. Her Uncle-ship is creating much controversy in the Twelve Towns, but let's see what she can really do."

Seven's heart sank as the atmosphere around her became thick with tension.

"And now, the Ravenskill Uncle-in-training! With the power of summoning BIRDS!" the announcer said.

The audience erupted in applause again and Seven knew this was it. This was her moment. She closed her eyes, pushing everything else out of her mind and focusing on her many lessons. They looped in her brain again as the crowd fell completely silent.

Body language.

Calm . . .

She was not normal.

She was just like Delphinium, and if any of them knew . . .

No, no, no. Don't think about that part. Just summon the birds. Call them to you, then send them home.

Seven tapped deep into the place where her magic lived, nestled in her heart, and she called to the birds.

"Come," she said. "Please, I need your help."

Moments passed, then minutes. The crowd began to get restless; Seven could hear them talking and moving around, but she did not open her eyes. She called and called and called them, but they did not come.

Until one bird, a blue one, flitted into the stadium from above. There were scattered, unenthusiastic claps, except for the section where her parents, Miss Dewey, and some old ladies were sitting, which was as loud as a handful of witches could be. A few more birds began to trickle in and Seven was relieved that she would not be a complete failure. Not puppies dancing, but not zero birds either.

Suddenly a healthy flock of birds swept into the stadium, making graceful loops and displaying a rainbow of wings. The crowd cheered loudly. And relief washed over Seven. She had done it. She let her Uncle magic rush through her veins, throwing her hands up in victory.

That's when everything went very, very wrong.

Screams erupted from the locker room area and her raccoons emerged, tugging on her long black hoodie.

"Uncle, pick us up," they said.

"We're scared," Pasta said.

"What's happening?" Seven said, but before they could answer, complete and total mayhem erupted around her. The arena was flooded with hundreds of animals of every kind, from birds, to horses, to dogs and cats, to . . .

"WILD BEARS!" someone screamed, and the crowd,

which had already been streaming out, began to run wildly. "Mom! Dad!" Seven yelled as her parents tried to run toward her. Miss Dewey was holding Beefy as Ambert helped her get away.

"This way, away from the arena!" The Gran's Guard used their magic to herd witches away from Seven, her parents swept up and taken to safety. *At least they're safe*, thought Seven. Anywhere Seven went, the animals might follow; she had to stay where she was and try to send them back.

"Go." She threw her hands up. "Go home!"

Power rippled through her body, stronger magic than she'd ever felt before. Seven felt a shift in the air and, for a moment, she thought she had done it.

But then an enormous roar echoed through the amphitheater. The ground rumbled beneath her, a sinking feeling in her stomach making her ill.

"Goodbye!" the animals all said, except the raccoons, who had climbed onto her back or were holding on to her legs.

"Seven," a voice said, and panic, pure, overwhelming panic, took over just as the Nightbeast tore through the stands.

Piercing screams came from every direction as the remaining witches ran for their lives.

"Go, you have to go," Seven told the raccoons as she wrestled them off her.

"No," they said. "We stay with Uncle Seven."

"Stay behind me, then," Seven said as she ran toward the Nightbeast.

A group of Uncles appeared, hands up, walking in unison toward the creature but clearly afraid. They wouldn't be able to talk to it, of course, not like Seven could, but still they were trying to calm it with their Uncle powers. Seven could feel their magic coursing through the ground just as well as she knew this would do nothing.

The Nightbeast was threatened, and it was going to lash out.

"Get back!" Seven yelled just as the Nightbeast ran toward the wall of Uncles and they scattered, some running straight toward the exit while others bounded into the locker room area. All but Cymric, who stood his ground, and Seven was grateful not to be alone. She was so scared, she didn't know how she hadn't already passed out, but adrenaline kept her going. She had to stop the Nightbeast.

"Seven," the Nightbeast said. "Why have you brought me here?"

Seven blanched. She had summoned it?

"The Gran is coming!" one of the Guardsmen said, running to her side.

"Stay back. It's just afraid and you're making it worse," Seven said.

Cymric made his way toward Seven, trying in vain to calm the Nightbeast with a corralling spell, but with an effortless swipe of its paw, the beast sent Cymric flying into the stands.

"Cymric!" Seven screamed.

The Gran's Guard rushed forward then, and the Nightbeast snapped in their direction, then pushed at them with its head. The Guards were knocked out, leveled, and it had been no effort at all.

The Nightbeast roared, and Seven could feel its fear, its pain. She wanted to reach out and . . . comfort it.

The pull she felt to it was not normal; this beast could eat her and half the witches still in the stadium. She should've been running scared, but instead, all she wanted to do was stroke its fur. To help it feel safe. She extended her arm, the Nightbeast taking a tentative step toward her, when suddenly two elderly witches were by her side, their hands up.

"What are you doing? Please, go! You'll get hurt!" Seven said.

"We won't leave you," said a voice that sounded just like Thorn.

Seven looked to her right and left, and realized who the little old witches were: Her coven had come after all.

"Does this mean you two aren't mad anymore?" Seven asked.

"No," Valley said. "Still mad."

"Same," Thorn said. "But that doesn't mean we're gonna abandon you."

Valley nodded, and Seven bit back her tears.

"Seven, step away!" The Gran swooped down on her broom and landed right in between the Nightbeast and the Witchlings. She held a wand up to block the Nightbeast, and the monstruo growled, low and menacing.

"Gran, don't hurt it!" Seven said, feeling a horrible pang of sympathy for it.

"Seven, you have to cast a spell. I cannot do this without an Uncle's help," the Gran said.

"What do I do?"

"Sereno," the Gran whispered. "You must repeat it three times."

"Okay, I'll try," Seven said.

The Gran still had her wand up on the Nightbeast, trying to keep it back with magic, but even she was struggling against the legendary beast.

"Go, Seven, GO!"

"Sereno," Seven said, closing her eyes and pointing her open hands at the Nightbeast. "Sereno, Sereno!" she said, and with a gust of wind and a stream of bright purple light, the Nightbeast lay down slowly, enormous paws tucked under its body as it closed its eyes.

"Transport it to the habitat, quickly!" the Gran instructed her Guard. "The spell will only last so long."

The Gran was sweating and shaking. She turned to Seven. "Seven, how did you just do that?"

"I . . ." Seven looked to Valley and Thorn. "I don't know."

"I assume this is your coven in disguise, but I won't ask why you're using magic above your skill level . . . again. Instead, I'll tell you this. It took three Grans and three Uncles to lock up that Nightbeast, and you just set it free on your own. There is something going on with your magic, Seven Salazar. And it is becoming too dangerous to ignore."

CHAPTER SEVENTEEN
ROTTEN RUMORS

SEVEN WANTED TO HIDE under her bed forever, but she had to go to school instead. The worst alternative to hiding, actually. It was bad enough everyone thought she had summoned the Nightbeast, but to have to endure the cardboard-adjacent pizza they got for lunch on Wednesdays was too much to ask.

"I can drive you," Talis said as Seven ate breakfast the morning after her disastrous performance at the outdoor arena.

"It'll just look like I'm scared if you do that. I'll walk like I always do. Thanks, though."

Fox put her hands on her hips. "What about Valley or Thorn? I haven't seen them around here in ages. Are you girls fighting?"

Seven cringed. Did her mom have mind-reading powers or something?!

"They're just busy. Thorn's a champion, and Valley is always with Graves nowadays . . ."

Graves. The name only made Seven's stomach flip. She had to find out if she or Wren were the hexers if it was the last thing she did.

Talis and Fox looked at each other.

"Are you upset because you'd rather be spending time with Valley like Graves is, or . . . ?"

Seven was pulled out of her train of thought. "What? No, Mami, oh my goats." Seven covered her face. "I don't like Valley that way!"

Seven really didn't, even though if she did, her mom and dad were the last people she'd tell. And it wasn't because Valley was a girl. Seven didn't care much about that. In the past six months alone, she'd had short-lived crushes on ten people in her class. Her brain was becoming a menace. Besides, there was . . . maybe someone else she might like that way, she thought, thinking of ink-black hair and soft brown eyes.

"You're going to be thirteen this autumn. It's normal to have feelings for people and for those feelings to get confusing," Talis tried.

"Mom, Dad? I know you're trying to help, but you're *killing* me right now. It was just nice having Thorn and Valley around all the time, and now I'm on my own more, that's all!"

"You have me," said Edgar from his tank.

"I know, Edgar, and I love you," Seven said.

Her parents' eyes widened for just a moment, and then they seemed to remember, *Ah yes, our daughter can literally speak to animals*. It couldn't have been easy to get used to, but they were doing their best. She couldn't imagine what they would say if they knew about her monstruo powers. The Gran had tested her for any irregularities in her magic and had so far found nothing, but they were all still worried about her after the Nightbeast incident, and had decided Seven needed a break from her Uncle training while the Gran continued her testing. Ironically, she had never felt better, but she agreed, since it would give her more time to find the hexer. So long as nobody found out, she wouldn't end up like Delphinium.

"A protest broke out overnight in Boggs Ferry as unrest surrounding Spares and their place in the Twelve Towns grows," said Tiordan Whisperbrew from the small telecaster in their kitchen. Seven turned her attention to the screen.

"Accusations of cheating and sabotage have taken center stage in this year's Golden Frog Games as the youngest champion, Thorn Laroux, advances in the games, and a deadly stonifying hex terrorizes the Twelve Townians."

A picture of Thorn and Gunnar during the last costura trial flashed on to the screen.

"In Boggs Ferry, a small group of Spares clashed with anti-Spare residents, as a protest demanding expansion of Spare rights was quickly extinguished. The Boggs Ferry Gran assured residents only four Spares were involved and there was nothing to be alarmed about." Tiordan cut their eyes in a way that Seven thought meant dissension, but she hoped they weren't against Spare rights. That would crush her.

"A protest?" said Seven, in awe. It might've only been four Spares, but . . . she could never remember this happening before. Was . . . was it because of her coven? she wondered.

"In light of the recent violence against Spares, and the threat to champions' safety, security has been increased and a new champion security detail has been put in place to ensure the safety of every competitor. A similar petition to increase security for Spares was struck down by the Gran's Circle, citing fear of increased tensions."

Seven shook her head in anger. Of course Spares didn't get any protection.

Seven was taking the last sip of fresh guava juice when the doorbell rang. Beefy ran toward the front door, a new thing he was doing now, and Seven went to stop him.

"Careful!" Fox cried out as Seven and Beefy thundered through the house.

"No, Beefy, no, *ugh*, door," Seven said, struggling to pick up her giant baby brother. She walked with him hanging from her arms, his legs so long they nearly touched the floor anyway, and went to open the door.

Beefy grabbed the doorknob before Seven could put him down and flung the door open to find Figgs standing there.

Seven wished she knew a spell to make herself disappear,

or at the very least, fix her hair. Or put pants on Beefy.

"Um, good morning!" Figgs gave a little wave. "Your trusty school escort is here, at your service."

"School escort?" Seven asked.

"Poppy mentioned she'd be coming to walk you to school in case anyone tried messing with you, so I asked to tag along. Also I still don't know the way to your school." Figgs laughed.

Seven was about to hex Poppy's name when she noticed her running down the road toward her house.

"Seven! Hi!" Poppy reached her door, out of breath. "Want to walk to school together? Figgs, hi!"

Figgs gave Poppy a small wave.

"Okay. I still need to get ready though."

"I know we're early. Was hoping Mr. Salazar made his famous pancakes?" Poppy wiggled her eyebrows.

Figgs's stomach grumbled, and he gave Seven a wide smile.

Seven laughed. "Come in, sorry. Figgs, this is Beefy, my baby brother. Be careful with him, he's strong. Mom! Dad! My friends are here. Can they have pancakes?!"

Seven put Beefy down and ran upstairs to change while her parents chatted with Figgs and Poppy and made them some breakfast. Seven hoped her mom and dad didn't say anything embarrassing, but she didn't have time to worry about that. Plus, her dad's pancakes were delicious enough to cancel out anything they might say. After a quick shower, Seven refreshed her curls, threw on her nicest black jeans and her Kill Le Goose band T-shirt, and ran downstairs.

Figgs and Poppy were finishing up their pancakes while her parents asked them about school. During the Golden Frog Games, school-age witches from out of town took classes at the hosting town's school, which meant Figgs would be at the Goody Garlick Academy for the next few weeks. No big deal. It was all fine! Seven had put on a tiny bit of her mom's under-eye eraser potion to cover up the dark circles being a busy Uncle-in-training had gifted her. Just in case.

"We should get going." Seven grabbed her rucksack from the hook in the kitchen and threw it on.

"Yeah, I have a cat care quiz today first thing," Poppy said, wiping her mouth. "Thanks for breakfast! I've missed your pancakes."

Fox smiled. "You're always welcome here, Poppy. It was nice to meet you, Figgs."

Seven's friends said goodbye and thanked her parents again before walking to the front room to leave.

Seven's mom grabbed her arm. "Are you wearing my makeup?" she whispered.

"Just a little." Seven's eyes opened wide.

Fox shook her head and patted the area under Seven's eyes a bit, then nodded. "Better. I will show you how to wear it if you want. Have a good day, baby. Be good." Seven looked back nervously to make sure Poppy and Figgs hadn't heard their conversation.

"Bye, Mom, bye, Dad, see ya, Beefy," Seven said quickly, pulling her friends with her as she walked out. When the door closed behind them, Seven let out a sigh of relief.

"Everyone's been talking about Thorn. They think she's cheating," Poppy said as they walked to school.

"How can she cheat?! She's twelve and a Spare!" Seven threw her hands up. It was a warm spring day, the birds sang to Seven about how the worms were tasty, and in the trees on either side of the road, Seven saw ten little tails trailing them. She could hear the Nightbeast's soft snores, and though she tried to block that out, she was relieved it was okay after the summoning incident.

"Uh, I seem to remember that the three of you beat the Cursed Toads?" Figgs said.

"And you're kinda the next Uncle," said Poppy.

"Fine, but still, why would she take out her own teammate? That doesn't make sense," Seven said, but even as the words left her mouth, she knew the people talking badly about Thorn had an excuse there too. "But I guess . . . she hasn't needed Mayhem much anyway, has she? The witches who hate us think we're arrogant, that we think we can do anything we want."

Figgs and Poppy nodded.

"That's enough for them to convince themselves Thorn is responsible, even if she's not. And if the real culprit isn't caught, Thorn will get the blame even though we know the hexer is targeting her," Figgs said.

"Then let's hope Gunnar doesn't get stonified, because then Thorn will just get thrown in the Tombs," said Poppy.

"I don't think we can just leave it up to hope," said Seven. "I have a plan."

Seven had been practicing her tracking magic on Edgar, and she was pretty sure she had gotten it down. It was time to put it to actual use. They had a school assembly that day, where every witch would be in close proximity. There, Poppy and Figgs would help Seven place trackers on Graves, Wren, Aphra, any school-age fashion champions, including Gunnar. It would break Valley's heart if she knew they were tracking Graves and Wren, but something suspicious *was* going on with them, and she needed to follow the lead and see what she found. If Seven pulled the spell off correctly—and that was a big *if*—she'd be able to engage the trackers while they were all together in the Goody Garlick auditorium. Then they'd know the locations of their suspects and intermittently get sound recordings from them too. Seven hoped they'd be able to overhear some clues, or maybe even catch the hexer at the scene of the next crime. It wasn't a perfect plan, but it was the only one Seven had.

"Hmmm." Figgs tapped his chin. "I like this plan, but all the costura champions have been onstage with Thorn, so they wouldn't be able to actually pull off the hex, right?"

Seven nodded. "I thought of that too, but there's always a possibility they're working with someone else. The Cursed

Toads hadn't been working alone. Maybe whoever the hexer is, is working with them too."

Morning classes went by in a whir of poisonous plants, healing rituals, and spell casting. During the safety assembly before lunch, Seven attached trackers to the rucksacks of Graves and Wren and their Moth House friends. Poppy and Figgs were busy doing the same to the school-age fashion champions on her list—all older. They had managed to attach the trackers on most of their target's rucksacks or cloaks, but had missed a few of them. Seven would attempt to get the remaining five during lunch.

Finally, lunchtime came. Poppy had saved Seven a seat in the Hyacinth section, just like they'd planned. Not surprisingly, many of the champions in their school were House Hyacinth. There were a few Frog House witches at Poppy's table as well. As Seven picked up her lunch tray, she planned her route to Poppy's table. It would be a bit of a zigzag to get to the few champions on her list, but she'd have to risk looking like a butt-toad.

"Vigilar," she whispered under her breath as she lightly brushed her hand over one of the Moth House witches' bags on her way to her table. She would wait to check the crystal later, but the warm buzz in her pocket made her feel as though it had worked. She managed to get to three more before people started giving her funny looks, and she resigned herself to sit and have her lunch.

With the witches at her table distracted by food and gossip, Seven chanced looking at her twenty-sided crystal. It was lit up on almost every side. Seven smiled, looking back up and patting her pocket, when a witch on the other side of the lunch hall caught her eye: Valley. She was sitting with Graves and staring at Seven. Seven nodded at her, but Valley looked away and Seven's stomach sank. Valley could hate her all she wanted, and if she knew what Seven was up to, she'd probably never forgive her, but Seven couldn't risk Thorn, or anyone else, getting hurt because of them. If Graves was up to no good, Seven Salazar would be the first to know.

CHAPTER EIGHTEEN
THE CURSED NEEDLES

A PINK-AND-ORANGE SKY shimmered behind the champion tents in the Goody Garlick Academy spaceball field. Seven and Figgs walked through the rows of open tents where champions practiced or mingled.

"Gunnar should be around here somewhere," Seven said. "He does his daily workouts here around this time according to my spies."

"You mean your raccoons?" Figgs cracked a sideways grin.

"Yeah, those goats," Seven giggled. Figgs nodded.

"All right. I have to go check in with River, then I'll find Gunnar and do my tracking sneakiness." Figgs winked. "Good luck!" Figgs did a little backward run and smiled at her before taking off. The moths that lived in Seven's belly whenever she talked to Figgs swirled and she had to admit, at least to herself, that she might actually have her first-ever big crush. What a distressing thought.

She kept walking in the direction of the Ravenskill champion tents, going over her plan. She had to tell Thorn about Graves and Wren, and how she was planning to track them. If Thorn was going to keep safe, she had to know who her potential foes were.

As if she'd summoned her with her mind, Wren Shadowmend came walking swiftly from the direction of Thorn's tent, clutching her cloak and looking behind her. Seven took a step back instinctually, about to put her hands up as Wren got closer, when the older witch turned between another row of tents, disappearing from Seven's sight.

Seven shook her head, and pulled out her notebook, quickly scribbling the moment down. Just in case. Finally, she reached Thorn and Gunnar's tent—an iridescent yellow-and-aqua color that shimmered in the setting sun. Tia Stardust was standing watch outside.

"Hey, Tia," Seven said.

"Hi." Tia smiled. "You visiting Thorn?"

Seven nodded.

"Great, I need to grab some dinner. Be right back!" Tia jogged away, leaving Seven alone. She was grateful that Tia had followed through with her promise to keep an eye on Thorn. It made her a little less worried about her friend.

Seven lightly slapped her cheeks and tried to focus:

She had other fish to fry. She grabbed her portaphone and sent the message she'd drafted earlier to Valley, hoping it worked and that this visit would serve two purposes. Seven took a deep breath, then stepped into the entrance of the tent. It was cozy and strewn with carpets and sewing supplies. Thorn was sitting on a fluffy-looking chair, her legs crossed beneath her, needle in hand and deep in concentration.

"Hi, can I come in?"

Thorn started, then looked up from the needlework she was doing. "All right, but just for a few minutes. I'm busy."

Seven's chest tightened. Thorn had never, ever been cold to her and it hurt more than she wanted to admit.

"Are you doing all right?" Seven asked, taking a seat on a chair beside Thorn.

Thorn shrugged. "I guess. My parents don't want me to go on in the games. The Circle of Grans is thinking about outlawing Spares from participating in future games because of all the trouble I've caused."

"What?! That's bogus. And you haven't caused any trouble," Seven said hotly. "Whoever the hexer is, *that's* who's to blame."

"This . . . might be my only shot at ever being a champion. I won't give it up." Thorn looked down, wiping her eyes quickly. Seven cleared her throat.

"Speaking of the hexer," Seven said. "I have some new info."

"Oh?" Thorn quirked an eyebrow, and Seven told her

about Graves and the information she'd withheld from *The Book of Unliving.*

"Does . . . Valley know?" Thorn asked.

"Do I know what?" Valley said, stepping inside the tent.

Seven felt sick, but also pleased. Her plan had worked.

"I got your message. What's the emergency?" Valley narrowed her eyes at Seven. She had a fading pink welt on her face.

Seven stood up. "Our coven breaking."

Valley rolled her eyes. "It's not *breaking.*"

"I dunno, maybe it is," Thorn said, looking away.

"Are you two going to keep fighting forever, or grow up and talk this out?" Seven said.

"Maybe I don't want to talk to her," Valley said.

"Same," Thorn said.

"Then why did you go to her last trial and jump in front of the literal stone hex for her?" Seven leveled at Valley.

"What? No, I didn't," Valley scoffed.

Thorn looked at Valley curiously.

"Then how'd you get the injury?" Seven smiled triumphantly as Valley's hand flew to her face.

"You did?" Thorn asked.

"Of course she did—she tried to hide under a black cloak but I know it was her. Then the both of you used the little old lady spell I cast on you goats last year during my Uncle trial. If you didn't care about each other, or me, you wouldn't go through all that trouble," Seven said.

Valley and Thorn were silent then, staring at each other. Seven smiled.

"You don't hate me?" Valley asked sheepishly.

Thorn sighed. "No, I don't hate you and I . . . do miss both of you but . . . I'm really hurt. You want to help the creature that killed my brother. How would you all feel?"

"I hear what you're saying, but that's not *one hundred percent* true," Seven said, and Thorn shot her an annoyed look. Seven held her hands up in a gesture that meant "Wait, let me explain."

"Valley wanted to find out *for sure* if the Nightbeast was actually responsible or if someone used it and it killed Petal against its will. She wanted to find out if it was still dangerous because it's being kept in captivity right now. And we think it might be suffering."

For a moment, Thorn's eyes opened wide, but she shook her head and painted a scowl on her face again.

"The night we fought it, it told me that the Cursed Toads had been controlling it and making it do things it didn't want to do. That Nightbeasts don't hunt witches anymore," Seven said.

Thorn's face went red and she turned back to her sewing. "I know all that, but it still killed Petal."

"I know, I didn't want you to *live* with the thing, just find out the truth. We saw how they used magic to manipulate witches, even the Gran! You didn't blame the Gran for the things she did while she was hexed," Valley said.

"Of course not, she did them against her . . . will." Thorn sighed. "I know what you're saying, but I *saw* the Nightbeast hurt my brother. You can't expect me to just forgive it."

"You don't have to forgive it, ever. I never expected that. All I wanted was to find out if it was actually innocent because they might kill it," Valley said.

"Kill it?" Thorn asked.

Valley nodded, and Seven looked at her curiously. She still hadn't explained why she thought the Nightbeast might be killed. Valley cleared her throat. "It's in the Twelve Town laws. I looked into it. If something as powerful and as volatile as the Nightbeast is putting Ravenskillians in danger, then the bylaws state it should be put to death."

All the blood rushed from Seven's face. Powerful, volatile . . . couldn't her own magic be described the same way?

"If the Nightbeast really was being controlled by three Uncles using archaic magic, it wouldn't have had a chance," Seven said.

Thorn let out a heavy breath. "Okay, maybe I shouldn't have gotten so mad at you so quickly."

"You had every right to be mad. I should've talked to you about it first." Valley rubbed her neck, her face red as a tomato.

"Thanks," Thorn said in a small voice.

"And is anyone mad at me still for any reason?" Seven asked, on the verge of tears.

Thorn looked up at her, with her own tear-filled eyes. "No, Seven, and I'm so sorry!"

Thorn burst into sobs, and Seven and Valley both ran to hug her.

Seven's heart had felt like it had broken, not in a million pieces, but into three, and now it felt like it was back together again. Things still felt a bit awkward between them, but Seven hoped that would change with time.

Valley let go first, and wiped her nose with her sleeve. "Enough mushy stuff, we've got a butt-toad hexer after Thorn. What are we gonna do?"

Seven and Valley both sat beside Thorn, who picked up a long strand of gray hair from her sewing kit and scrunched her nose. "Weird," she said, then turned back to needlework.

"Any clues?" asked Valley.

"Figgs and Poppy helped me put trackers on a few of the fashion champions and other possible suspects," Seven said. "Like Aphra Dimblewit."

"That's a start," Valley said.

"What about Graves?" Thorn asked softly.

"What about her?" Valley snapped.

"Didn't Graves lie about a Moth House witch creating the stonifying hex?" Thorn asked.

Seven nodded.

"Graves has nothing to do with the hex. There's no way she'd ever do anything like this," Valley said.

"If it was anyone else, we'd follow this lead and you know it," Seven said.

Valley looked away angrily.

"It doesn't mean she's guilty, but maybe she knows something," Seven said.

"What if we just talk to Graves? I bet there's a simple explanation," said Thorn. "But—ow!"

Thorn dropped the needle she was using and grabbed her hand. There was blood dripping from her finger. The needles in Thorn's kit began to shake wildly.

"What in the . . . ?" Thorn said, seemingly mesmerized. There was a blank, glassy stare in her eyes that Seven didn't recognize.

"Thorn, get away from there!" Seven yelled, but before she could get up, the needles shot up from their case and turned on Thorn, plunging right at her face.

Thorn quickly shielded her face with a pillow, the first wave of needles plunging deep into the cushion. Meanwhile, others zoomed away and looped back, coming right for Thorn again.

Seven scrambled to her feet and threw her hands up. "Detener!" But once again, the needles swerved and came at Thorn from another angle.

Seven threw herself on top of Thorn, just as Valley cried out, "Alto!" and the needles jerked back, shaking violently before falling to the ground. Valley collapsed on the ground herself, wiping sweat from her forehead.

"It's over," coughed Valley. "I think you can get off Thorn now."

"Thorn, are you okay?" asked Seven. She got up and helped Thorn sit.

"I am," Thorn said. "You could've gotten hurt, Seven."

"I'm an Uncle, my skin has the strength of bark," Seven recited automatically. Maybe the lessons *were* sinking in.

"All right, what in the hex was that?" asked Valley.

As they watched, a purple mist rose from the needles, the same hazy light they'd seen during the stone hex and that had crackled around the Cursed Toads when they revealed their true form during their battle with the Witchlings.

Archaic magic.

Thorn ran over to her sewing kit, to the case where her needles had been. The same purple haze was slowly fading from it.

"Who could've done this to your kit, Thorn? Has anyone had access to it?" Seven asked.

Thorn shook her head, bringing her hand to her chest.

"I don't know." She turned back to Valley and Seven, her eyes brimming with tears.

Seven felt helpless, but there was one thing she was sure of: After seeing Wren scurrying away from the direction of Thorn's tent moments before a stack of needles attacked them, Seven had to find out what the Shadowmend sisters knew.

CHAPTER NINETEEN
UNDERCOVER MOTHS

SEVEN AND FIGGS walked up the cemetery hill to Moth House and went over their plan.

"So, we're breaking into their rooms?" Figgs said.

"And looking for anything suspicious: a book on archaic hexes, or parts of Thorn's sewing kit, anything singed by purple fire . . . anything that might give us clear answers," Seven responded. She had clues, sure, but none of them lined up. First, there was Graves lying about the Moth House origins of the hex, then both Graves and Wren being in the perfect line of sight to attack Alaric, and Wren coming from the direction of the tent right before the needle attack. Those things seemed to point to the Shadowmend sisters, sure, but then there was that gray hair in Thorn's cursed sewing kit, which Seven kept circling back to. Was it a clue? "If so, it pointed to an older witch—not Graves and Wren."

Seven needed something definitive about Wren and Graves being behind the hex before she went to the Gran.

"What if they're in their rooms?" Figgs asked.

"They won't be. I checked their location on the trackers."

"This better work. I can't look this good for nothing." He flipped his straight black hair to the side dramatically.

Seven covered her mouth and held in a giggle. "It'll work, we look *just* like them."

She'd had some practice with disguises last year, but Seven and Figgs had gone to Crimson for help with their Moth House transformations.

"What do you need all this for again?" Crimson had asked as he handed black eyeliner to Seven.

"School project!" Seven had said. "It's for a play on the history of Ravenskill; we are playing Moth House witches."

"Hmm, okay," Crimson had said, and helped them with some of his clothing and a temporary enchant-dye for Seven's hair. By the time they'd finished, both Seven and Figgs looked sallow, Seven was raven-haired, they had bangs that swooped over one eye and, most importantly, projected mystery, thanks to the many, many layers of eyeliner and black lipstick.

"Have you got your rosebuds in?" Seven asked, and Figgs gestured to his ears and gave her a thumbs-up.

"Perfect. Let's go pretend to be creepy." Seven pushed her

straightened black hair out of her eyes and walked up to the Moth House door.

Thankfully someone was leaving just as they entered, so they didn't have to contend with how to get in. Now, to find Graves's and Wren's rooms. Seven huddled with Figgs near a fireplace and tried not to look suspicious.

"I know that the fifth- and sixth-year witches are on the first floor since they're new. Wren is tenth year so she should be on the third floor. But that's as far as my knowledge goes." Seven cringed. "This might be harder than I thought."

Figgs scoffed. "For us? No sweat. We'll find them." Figgs winked and Seven's stomach fluttered. "What if we split up? I'll go to the third floor to Wren's room and you check Graves's room on the first. We have our rosebuds in case of anything," he suggested.

"Good plan. If anything happens, just say, 'I forgot to get Edgar his flies,'" Seven said.

"Got it," Figgs said.

"You know, I haven't had spicy flies in too long," Edgar said from Seven's pocket.

"Not now, Edgar. Don't come out either. Your mustache is too recognizable."

"It's difficult being this famous," Edgar sighed, and Seven shook her head as she and Figgs split up.

Seven passed a group of Moth House witches baking in

their massive ground-floor kitchen. The smell of fresh-baked goods was almost enough to make her stop and grab a few muffins. She went up the stairs and made her way to the first floor where the dorms were.

The dorm doors each had small, golden paper frogs, adorned with the names of the witches who lived within. Seven imagined they made new ones for every season and wished, not for the first time, that Spares could have their own coven house. It would be nice to hang out with other Spares and, more importantly, for Spares who were still in school to have a safe, happy place to live.

She passed a few Moth witches who didn't notice her. This would be a piece of cake. She reached a door with a particularly large golden frog and read the names: *Barlow* and *Graves*.

"Flingo." Seven pressed her rosebud and whispered, "Figgs, I found Graves's room."

"Great, because I still haven't found Wren's."

"I'm going in. Keep your rosebud engaged."

"You got it."

Seven took a deep breath. She would knock first, just in case, then pretend to be lost if anyone was in there.

She knocked once, twice, three times, pressed her ear against the door, but nothing.

"I found Wren's room," Figgs said. "Rats, there are voices coming from inside. Her roommates maybe?"

"Maybe. Is there any place for you to, like, wait and see if someone comes out?"

"There's a small bench in an alcove a few toadstools down."

"All right, sit there and pretend to write sad poetry or something if you have your notebook with you. Blend in."

Figgs snorted, then added seriously, "What do you mean pretend?"

Seven shook her head and smiled as she tried the doorknob to Graves's room, but it was, as she expected, locked. Seven looked around. Nobody was in the hallway at least, so she raised the sleeves of her black shirt and aimed her palms at the doorknob.

Suddenly the door flew open, and a sleepy-looking witch about Thorn's height peered up at Seven.

"Can I help you?"

"Oh, um, yeah, I was looking for Graves actually, we're . . . friends," Seven said.

"I was napping. And I was having a dream about Witches of Heartbreak Cove. The Wicked One was in it!" The witch, who Seven guessed must be Barlow, spun inside her room and flopped onto her bed. Seven took a cautious step inside and looked around. The room was covered in posters from popular Twelve Townian musicians and from telecast programs. There were two witch-sized beds, each tucked into a corner of the room, two matching desks with books stacked neatly on them, and a black fluffy rug in the center of the room.

"Was it a nightmare?" Seven asked.

"Are you kidding me? It was the most beautiful dream." Barlow hugged her pillow and looked up with a starry-eyed stare. "I was Bianca and the Wicked One was about to ask me to marry him. And then your knocking woke me up." Barlow covered her face with her pillow and screamed as Seven walked around the room trying to snoop discreetly.

"Sorry about that," she said. "Do you know when Graves is coming back?"

Barlow threw the pillow on the floor and got up. "No. Probably not for a while though." She gave Seven a curious look. "Did you say you were a friend of hers?"

Seven laughed nervously. "Yeah, you could say that. I'm from Crones Cliff Manor."

"Ah, makes sense why you look so weird, then," Barlow said.

"Excuse me?" Seven said.

"You can wait here. I'm gonna go get some sleepy bear tea and see if I can go back to the same dream." Barlow put her slippers on and left. Seven was in Graves's room alone.

She got to work quickly, going through her desk, looking under the bed and in the closet. Sweat dotted Seven's forehead as she frantically searched, hoping to the Stars that Barlow didn't walk in and find her looking through Graves's things. A few minutes passed, but aside from some schoolbooks, pictures, and a lot of black clothing, Seven hadn't found a single piece of evidence.

She shoved everything back in its place just as Barlow walked in with a big, steaming cup of tea.

"Still no Graves, huh?" Barlow asked.

Seven opened her mouth to answer, but just then, something vibrated softly within her pocket. And it wasn't Edgar. Seven chanced a look: Graves's silhouette was lit up on her tracker!

"Um, I mean, excuse me, I have to go. Thanks for your help!" She began to leave as Barlow called out.

"Wait, what's your name? What should I tell Graves?"

"Se—" Seven began, but then remembered she was in disguise. "Serpentine."

"Wow, cool name," Barlow said.

"Thanks, see ya!" Seven closed the door as quickly as she could and pressed the side of her twenty-sided crystal with Graves's silhouette.

"We must not fail this time," said a voice.

"Will it be safe?" said another low, gravelly voice . . . Graves's voice, Seven was sure of it!

"Do you still doubt me?" The unfamiliar voice laughed.

"I would never," Graves said—but just then Seven was interrupted by someone coming down the hall.

Graves was right in front of her.

"Good," said the other voice in her ear.

"What?" Seven asked, bewildered.

"Hi," Graves said with a curious look. "Did you need help finding something?"

"What is our next move?" asked Graves's voice in her ear, but the Graves right in front of her was still looking at her expectantly. Not speaking. What kind of magic was this?

"I . . . have to go . . . I'm . . . I'm sorry!" Seven said.

"Okay?" Graves said, clearly confused.

Seven couldn't keep talking though. She couldn't focus, not when the Graves in her ear continued to speak.

"I'll be ready," said Graves.

Seven took off running down the hall, shouting into her rosebud at Figgs, "I forgot to get Edgar his flies! I forgot to get Edgar his flies!"

CHAPTER TWENTY
WALTER AND GEORGIE

"AND NOW, LIFTING TWO BROWN bears, for a combined weight of four hundred loaves, is Rol Malum for the town of Crow Spring," said the announcer softly as Rol walked up to the bear-lifting stage.

The crowd clapped politely as the champion took her place behind a metal bar with two red seats on either end. They were in the Goody Garlick Academy gymnasium the next morning, and Seven was on bear-liaison duty.

From the right wing of the stage, Seven looked at the group of bears in the backstage waiting area, then down at her clipboard. "All right, Walter, Georgie, you're up, paired with Rol Malum."

Walter and Georgie got up from their squishy chairs and waddled over to Seven.

"Will we get a snack after?" Walter, a brown bear, asked.

"Yup. A snack, then . . ." Seven referred to the schedule on her clipboard. ". . . one more match for today."

"Thank you, Uncle Seven. You've been most helpful," said Georgie.

"She is quite nice, if a bit small," said Walter.

"It can't be helped with witches," Georgie said.

The two enormous bears then walked on their hind legs onto the stage, positioned themselves in front of the red chairs on either end of the metal bar, and sat. Seven was on a mandatory rest from training—Gran's orders—while she figured out why the Nightbeast had been summoned to the stadium during the Uncle trials. In the meantime though, Seven could still help with smaller tasks like this one and take some of the work off the other Uncles' shoulders. Talking to bears was easy. They were all very nice.

"Are you comfortable?" Seven called out to the bears onstage from her list of questions. The small crowd, who could also hear Seven, laughed good-naturedly.

"Quite," said Georgie. Seven looked out into the audience. Thorn and her mother were in the front row, a Guard pacing the aisle beside them. Thorn had been assigned a private escort from the Gran's Guard, but Seven had seen how easily the hex had gotten past all the extra security during the last fashion trial. Just one Guard wasn't gonna do much. Thankfully, Thorn had someone else looking out for her. Tia Stardust sat beside Thorn and her mother, her eyes darting around the room attentively. If there was one witch Seven trusted to keep her friend safe, it was the famous Hyacinth champion. As an added precaution, Seven had asked one of her raccoons to slip a note under the Gran's door about her Shadowmend suspicions. It couldn't hurt to have the Gran's eyes on her only suspects too.

Rol clapped her hands together and prepared to lift. This was a big moment for Crow Spring. If Rol managed to lift these bears cleanly and get the bar over her head, they might be able to pull ahead of Boggs Ferry for top points.

Rol bent down, gripping the bar with both hands, and with one fluid motion lifted it up to her chin. The bears shifted a bit, but the seats were deep enough that they were snugly tucked in and would not fall out. Rol then took one, two, three deep breaths and spread her legs apart with a little jump, trying to lift the bears above her head as she did.

"She's almost there," the announcer said.

The crowd watched on in silence. This was a lot less rowdy than costura or toad racing. The seconds counted down on a screen above Rol's head, and she began to wobble as she tried to straighten her arms above her.

"We seem to have some turbulence," said the announcer, and the crowd leaned in collectively, small gasps coming from every corner of the gymnasium.

Rol's face was bright red, but Walter and Georgie looked unconcerned. There was a special bouncy magic on the mats beneath them, after all. Even if they were dropped, they wouldn't feel a thing.

Rol could hold the bears no more, and she dropped the bar down in front of her with a loud grunt. The bar bounced softly, and Walter and Georgie looked over at Seven in the wings. Walter waved.

Rol looked disappointed, but she still had two more attempts. While she went over to her coach for water and a pep talk, Seven pulled her twenty-sided crystal from her cloak and considered it. Had it been glitching yesterday when she heard Graves's voice? She couldn't be sure how reliable it was, but the whole ordeal had only served to make Graves look even squirrelier. She placed the small rosebud speaker into her ear and put her hand over the sides of the crystal to see if anything new had been captured from Graves or Wren. She went through a few captured recordings, but neither sister seemed to be saying much over the past few hours. Seven switched over to the other champions, in case they had seen something interesting, but after a few moments, it was clear that it was mostly the same thing: gossip.

The Hastings-on-Pumpkins champions were having a total meltdown, there was a love triangle brewing on the Sleepy Hollow spaceball team, and the toad racers from Stormville had lost their most poisonous toad. There was nothing of note from the other fashion champions or the Moth House witches. Seven sighed and put the crystal back in her cloak, disappointed that she hadn't been able to find any more leads.

Rol walked back to her bar and made a second lift attempt. This time, she lifted the bears to her chin, then after a small hop where she went into a sort of lunge motion, she heaved them over her head with tremendous effort. The crowd clapped, the Boggs Ferry team in the other wing of the stage looked concerned, and Rol dropped the bears once more.

Her second attempt had been froggin' good. From a table in front of the stage, the judges scribbled furiously and conferred.

"Hmm, I don't think she's gonna pull it off," said a familiar voice in Seven's ear.

Huh? Had she forgotten to shut off the crystal? She took it out of her pocket but it was not lit up. She shouldn't still be hearing voices.

"Walter and Georgie also look very hungry if you ask me—are you positive they don't eat the weight lifters?"

Seven smirked and tapped her rosebud to speak. "I don't know how you got access to my rosebuds, but cut it out, Figgs." She looked out into the audience and there he was, in the very back of the gym, his silver earrings sparkling as he tugged on his ear to show he had his own set of rosebuds in.

"You had no protective magic so I was able to connect to it easily. You look cool up there, by the way."

Seven blushed and Georgie and Walter waved her down.

"May we get up?" Walter asked.

"Oh rats, sorry, yes, you're all done," Seven said.

Georgie got up, then helped Walter up from his chair, and they both waddled offstage. Seven ran to get them icy cold salmon-flavored water and dried mango.

"Anything from the twenty-sided crystal?" Figgs asked.

"Ugh, no, nothing. Just a million mini-crises. I couldn't get anything about Wren or Graves. And I'm still completely stumped about the double-Graves thing. How could she be talking in my ear and also be right in front of me? It doesn't make any sense," Seven said, pouring the water into a giant bowl for each bear and dumping mango slices onto plates.

"Maybe she got rid of her tracker somehow," Figgs said. "Or maybe you put it on the wrong witch?"

"She's the only teal-haired witch I tracked, I'm sure of it," Seven said.

"We saw a teal-haired witch yesterday, didn't we, Georgie?" Walter asked.

"We did, we did indeed. I remember because her hair was the color of that morning moss tea I so love!" Georgie began to clap. "Uncle Cymric was walking us to dinner and we saw her coming from Starlight Cottage, didn't we?"

"Wait, you saw her coming from the Gran's house?" Seven asked the bears.

"Yes, indeed. She was with three other older witches. She called one of them . . ."

"Wren," said Walter.

"Yes, Wren! And the others she called Mom, and Papa," said Georgie.

So the Shadowmend sisters and their parents were with the Gran around dinnertime. Around the same time Seven had seen Wren coming from the tents . . . or was it someone else pretending to be Wren?

"Do you remember what time it was? Exactly?" Seven asked.

Georgie tapped his chin in thought.

"It was six oh five. We were five minutes late to dinner and I never forget dinner," said Walter as he sipped his salmon ice water.

Flingo!

"You hear that, Figgs?" Seven said. "Another double, Wren this time!"

"Someone is impersonating the Shadowmends! Do you think that means they're guilty . . . or innocent?" Figgs asked.

Seven furrowed her brow. "I'm not sure, to be honest. But I would bet anything the witches the bears saw were the real thing, if they were with their parents and the Gran."

"That sounds right," Figgs said, but then Seven saw her crystal light up again. Someone was speaking.

"Okay," the unfamiliar voice said. "Plan C."

"Tell me what to do, and I'll be there," said Graves.

"We strike at midnight. At the maze," said the voice.

"Figgs," Seven said once the voices cut off, "I think I know what we have to do next."

CHAPTER TWENTY-ONE
THE MIDNIGHT MAZE

THE MIDNIGHT TOAD RACE was probably the most exciting match of all the Golden Frog Games. It would take place in a garden maze, with Boggs Ferry up against Castle Point. But there was only one thing on the Witchlings' mind: the hexer.

After the events at the bear-lifting competition that morning, Seven, Valley, and Thorn had scrambled to make sense of the two Graveses. Seven hadn't completely discounted the Shadowmend sisters as the hexers, but she wasn't as sure as she had been that they were involved. She just couldn't figure out who was behind it all. She did know that whoever the hexer was had a lot more tricks up their sleeve than they had realized. And after the conversations she'd overheard on her rosebud, she was almost certain there were two witches working together.

They were sitting on wooden bleachers overlooking the

Midnight Maze in North Ravenskill. There were copper lamp-posts faded rusty green along the perimeter. They were styled to look like the vines of a curling plant, a soft white glow coming from their globular lights. They cast pockets of light along the maze, but for the most part it was shrouded in darkness. That was part of the challenge, and excitement, of this toad race. It wasn't just about speed, or dance ability, or even the racers' connections to their toads—like other toad races—but about cunning, mental fortitude, and bravery. The Midnight Maze was treacherous by design.

"I'm telling you, Graves is innocent," Valley said.

"I never said she wasn't. Just that she was hiding something," Seven said. "And to be honest, we still don't know for sure if she's innocent."

"Well, I have a way to prove she's got nothing to do with the hexes," Valley said. She pointed at Graves and Wren, who were walking in their direction.

"What's going on?" Thorn asked.

"If something happens tonight, Graves and Wren will be sitting right next to us. Either way, we'll know," Valley said.

Seven had to admit, it was a good idea, and she smiled at the Shadowmend sisters as they slid into the seats beside them.

The Witchlings had decided to go to the Midnight Maze race and find out who the mysterious witches from Seven's rosebuds were. She hoped being able to keep an eye on the

Shadowmend sisters would help discount them completely, once and for all.

Edgar popped his head and arms outside Seven's pocket and got comfortable. "We see colors perfectly in the dark. If the racers are smart, they'll find a way to exploit that," he said. Normally he slept in there, but even he was excited for the race.

"I'm sure Tia knows that," Seven said. "It's not like I could give her insider information anyway; that would be cheating."

"Be less nerdy, Seven," Edgar said.

"It's still so weird that you can talk to him," Valley said, waving a finger at Edgar as if he were a baby.

"I'm kinda used to it." Seven yawned.

"Ask him if he likes me," Valley said.

"Edgar, Valley wants to know if you like her," Seven said.

"She's acceptable. As is Thorn. Truthfully, you are my least favorite of the three." Edgar made a deep croak of a laugh in his throat.

Seven shook her head. "He said yes."

"He said something mean, didn't he?" Valley asked.

"I don't wanna talk about it," Seven said, and all three Witchlings dissolved into laughter. Not just because Edgar was an endless source of fun, but because if they felt anything like Seven did, she knew they were electric with fear.

Anything could happen tonight. She had warned the Gran too, of course, but had not told her *how* she knew. If the many Gran's Guards standing everywhere were any indication, Knox had taken her seriously.

Valley was talking to Graves and they were both smiling softly at each other. It was clear how well they got along, and Seven felt guilty all over again.

"They're obsessed with one another," Wren said from beside Seven with a chuckle.

"They are," Seven said.

"I'm Wren, by the way, I don't think we've ever met formally."

"Hey," Seven said, her cheeks going hot.

"Graves told me she lied about the whole Moth House hex thing, and I get it looked fishy. But people always think Moth House witches are up to no good. They're always judging us and blaming us for things, so Graves has a hard time with stuff like this," Wren said.

Seven nodded. "That makes sense. I'm sorry for ever implying you were involved. I was just worried about Thorn and trying to follow the clues."

Wren nodded. "Noted. And no hard feelings. I would've done the same for my sister." Wren held her hand out and Seven shook it, glad that they had gotten the chance to actually talk. Even if it was froggin' awkward.

The race was about to begin. The crowd was restless from

the wait, and the air was thick with excitement and a crisp breeze from the Boggy Crone River.

"Witches! Welcome to the Midnight Maze!" Enve Lopes said into a green microphone that had grown from the ground like a giant plant. She was wearing a gold bodysuit under a dress fashioned to resemble the globe lamps above the maze. A soft glow emanated from lights that had been enchanted to look like dancing fireflies inside the translucent outer layer of the garment. Her wig was the highlight of the night's ensemble, however—it was a giant shimmering toad made of glitter-dipped moss. "Tonight the Boggs Ferry Raccoons will battle the Castle Point Trolls in what is sure to be a rousing match!"

Everyone clapped loudly as the teams came out and stood at their respective maze entrances.

"Now, this will work almost like a normal toad relay race, with some exceptions. We will have five toads instead of ten, the length of the race is halved from 131 toadstools to 65.5 toadstools, and instead of batons, the toads will use an enchanted sunflower to avoid injury."

The audience clapped in appreciation. Witches really loved the racing toads. Some of them even had official T-shirts and buttons. Seven thought she spotted one witch wearing an Edgar Allan Toad sweatshirt as well; if he noticed she'd never hear the end of it.

"One thing that will not change is, of course, the music!

And to make tonight extra special, we have members of the Ravenskill Philharmonic here to play our designated racing song for the night, "Danse Macabre" by Camille Saint-Saëns!"

"Oh, that song is creepy!" Thorn said, pulling closer to Seven.

"I like it," Valley said.

"Me too, but it *is* creepy. Not like we have a serial hexer on the loose or anything," Seven said.

"The race will begin in just a few more minutes!" Enve said, and retreated to speak to the racers.

"Seven!" Miss Dewey waved at the girls and they waved her over. They were saving her and Ambert a seat.

"We got here just in time," Miss Dewey said.

"Hi, girls," Ambert said. "Who are you hoping wins tonight?"

"No hoping necessary. Tia's got this," Seven said.

"And she deserves to win extra-especially after being Thorn's personal bodyguard the past few days," Valley said.

Thorn nodded appreciatively.

"I heard Castle Point's team has been training hard. A few patrons in the library today said they were much better in a few of their last matches. I'm a bit worried," Miss Dewey said.

"Nah, they're toast," Valley said. "The only racers that can beat Tia are Holo Vexx and his toad Lorenzo."

"Don't start this again!" Thorn said.

"She's right," Seven said.

"Nobody can beat Tia," Thorn insisted.

"Hmm, not according to the toad-racing championships last year," Valley said.

"That was a fluke." Thorn crossed her arms.

"We should probably stop arguing and focus. The hexer is probably already here," Seven whispered.

Thorn and Valley nodded and straightened up.

"Hey!" Figgs said, sitting in an empty seat right in front of Seven.

He leaned back, signaling for Seven to come closer. "Ready to catch the hexer?" he whispered conspiratorially.

"Froggin' ready," Seven said. "I hope we can stop them once and for all."

"We will. I promise I won't let them hurt you," Figgs said.

Seven sat back in her seat and tried really hard to wipe the giant grin off her face.

"They're starting," Thorn said, pointing at the starting line of the race.

The toads would begin from two separate entrances, but eventually the maze melded into one big hedge labyrinth.

"Hold on to your seats, witches, the race is about to begin!" Enve said just as the wooden stands around the maze began to shift, and witches cried out. The once-flat seating area was hoisted up and slightly over the maze so it looked like the audience was inside a giant bowl.

"On your mark, get set, TOAD!"

The crowd roared as the first racers took off and "Danse Macabre" began to play.

They both ran at a steady, rapid pace for the first few toadstools, before Boggs Ferry's toad dove right into a hedge after a particularly ambitious leap and got stuck.

"Come on!!!" Thorn yelled as Castle Point pulled farther and farther ahead.

Finally the sunflower batons were passed to the last two toads. Bob, Tia's toad, was at a huge disadvantage. But Tia wasn't the most famous toad racer in the Twelve Towns for nothing.

"Bob, let's go!" Tia bellowed from her end of the maze, her voice so powerful that the hairs on the back of Seven's neck stood up.

Racers and their toads had to work hard, not just by training, but by forging a connection through magic. When Tia called out commands, when she encouraged Bob, it wasn't just words . . . it was enchantment. The stronger the magic, the stronger the connection, the better the racer. So even though Bob was the one physically on the track, Tia's magic made them a team. It was the closest anyone who wasn't an Uncle got to speaking to animals, Seven realized. If only Edgar liked to race, she might be a champion herself.

Bob began to gain ground, and soon he was a mere three or four toadstools behind the Castle Point toad.

Seven, Thorn, and Valley were on their feet with the rest of the crowd, cheering and screaming.

"Uncle." Seven heard, and looked down.

Cheese was emerging from under the seat.

"Look." He stood on his hind legs and pointed toward another raccoon. Fish was on a hedge, facing a corner just off the maze exit, which was shrouded in darkness. There was a figure there, lingering suspiciously in the shadows.

"Bob and Tia are rounding the final corner! Only a few gills behind! Will he be able to pull this off? Will Boggs Ferry advance to the next round?"

"Uncle Seven, a witch," Cheese said again. Seven looked and the figure seemed to have its hands up, as if they were about to strike.

"It's the hexer," said Seven.

"What?!" yelled Valley, who was engrossed in the race and not paying attention.

"Where, Seven?" Thorn asked.

"They were just . . ." Seven pointed toward the place where she'd seen the shadow, but it was gone.

"BOGGS FERRY TAKES THE WIN!" the announcer yelled, and the crowd was roaring.

"We have to stop them, before something happens!" Seven got up from her seat and made her way toward the shrouded exit.

"Wait up." Valley and Thorn followed her, and the three

Witchlings weaved through the unruly audience. When she looked back, Seven saw both Wren and Graves had gotten up with them, and were running not far behind.

The closer she got, the more fear crept in.

As they neared the finish line, where all the champions were gathered, something furry and heavy ran across Seven's feet and she nearly shrieked before she realized what it was.

"Hello," said Cheese.

"It's too hard for us to get through the crowd—can you go ahead and see who it is?" Seven said.

"We will help," Cheese said, then he chittered loudly. Fish chittered back from his hedge, then held his paws up and flexed its claws.

"The rest of the raccoons are here; we will help," said Cheese.

Seven nodded and kept scrambling around the crowd to reach the shadow, when a shriek pierced the night air like a dagger.

Thorn, Seven, Valley, and the Shadowmend sisters stopped short, nearly bumping into one another as they turned in the direction of the shriek.

"Oh no, look!" Graves pointed at a witch bounding through the maze. It was October. She was running toward the end of the maze, her hands in her hair as she dropped to the ground in front of someone. The Witchlings weren't very far from October and changed course in her direction as if they were one. Seven's heart felt as if it were in her throat. She could hear the raccoons chittering, the voices of the birds above wailing, and witches calling to one another in a panic.

She reached the opening where the finish line was, and the world spun around her. There, in the middle of a swarm of witches, with October kneeling in front of her, was a statue.

Tia Stardust had been turned to stone.

"No . . ." Thorn's voice caught in her throat.

"Tia, Tia!" October cried out as everyone watched on in horror.

"Someone, get the Gran!" called the announcer.

Seven filled with rage. Her fists clenched and she wanted to scream.

She spun back toward the hedge where she had seen the figure, just in time to catch a glimpse of someone running back into the shadows, an emerald-green cloak trailing behind them.

CHAPTER TWENTY-TWO
THE GREEN-CLOAKED WITCH

THE GRAN'S GUARD began securing the area and questioning witches near the hexing. They asked Seven, Valley, Thorn, and the Shadowmend sisters where they'd been and what they'd seen, and moved on. Seven mentioned the suspicious figure in the corner, but they didn't seem to take it seriously when she wasn't able to provide more detail. She would have to mention it to the Gran.

Graves and Wren were picked up by their parents, but the Witchlings were instructed to stay put. Tia was covered with a wool blanket and would be wheeled out to the Bluewing Infirmary to be worked on by healers, like the other hex victims. October had been given a valerian tonic to help her calm down, then taken to House Hyacinth to rest. Seven's heart ached for her and Tia and Alaric and Mayhem. What was taking the healers so long?

"And of course, *they're* here again!" a familiar voice called out. Rafflesia Dimblewit, with Aphra beside her, strode right up to the Witchlings.

"*You* three are always at the scene of the crime," she said, waving a finger in Seven's face. There was sweat on her upper lip, and when she spoke, a vein in her forehead popped out.

"You're here too," Seven said. "How do we know it wasn't you?"

"You spoiled little—"

"They were watching the race like the rest of us," Miss Dewey said, as Ambert held her hand in support.

"We were sitting beside them the whole match," he said.

"Who knows what wicked magic they used to get to Tia. That Thorn designed tap shoes to walk on water; she could've made ones that teleported her!" Aphra said to angry murmurs from the crowd.

"It was part of the competition. You can't hold that against her now!" Valley said.

"We should take them to the Tombs. They should be locked away!" said a witch in the crowd.

"They're children." Miss Dewey stood in front of the Witchlings. "You're supposed to protect them, not make their lives more miserable."

"They're dangerous and unruly and it's time someone showed them a bit of discipline," Mrs. Dimblewit said.

"I'm afraid my aunt here is correct. We should, at the very

least, let the Gran's Guard escort them out and take them to the dungeons . . ." Aphra addressed the crowd, her long cape fluttering in the wind behind her. While some witches seemed to agree, stepping forward to help him stop the Witchlings, others in the crowd protested and stood in their way. Some of them, Seven noticed, were Spares.

Don't get in trouble because of us, she tried to tell them through her pleading look, but they didn't back down.

"Shouldn't we take every precaution to stop the hexer? If these Witchlings are always at the scene of every crime, shouldn't we take that seriously? I am simply asking questions." Aphra smiled.

"Hey, butt-toad, why don't you stop that trash talk before I make you stop?" Valley had her hand on her waist, right in the place where she kept her blades, and Thorn reached out to stop her. She shook her head no, and Valley nodded, putting her hand down, however reluctantly.

"Resorting to violence? It's no surprise you would say something so distasteful. Considering the family you come from . . ." Aphra said, repeating the words she'd said on Tiordan's telecast program.

Valley clenched her fists and leaned forward, Thorn barely restraining her.

"Let her," Seven whispered, the Nightbeast's growl ringing in her mind. "She deserves it."

"Your *father* did at least one thing right, and it was to

suggest that Spares be sent to the Tombs," Mrs. Dimblewit said. Her eyes were alight with malice as she gave Valley a withering look.

"We will take them home. You have already questioned them, correct?" Ambert asked one of the Guards, who nodded a solemn yes.

"So we're free to go," said Seven, and she began to walk past the crowd.

Aphra grabbed her arm and immediately all ten raccoons flanked Seven, teeth bared.

Mrs. Dimblewit pushed Aphra behind her. "She's only a child!" she screamed, shaking with rage. Then Mrs. Dimblewit raised her hands in a fighting stance and, faster than anyone expected, she actually shot at Seven.

"PALIZA!" she screamed, but her attack did not hit.

Ambert stepped in front of Seven, quicker than lightning, and threw his own hands up. Without a word, a burst of the brightest light Seven had ever seen exploded all around them. But instead of sending Mrs. Dimblewit careening back, it pulled her in toward Ambert. When they were nose to nose, the librarian whispered, "Termita fundida," and got the witch square in the jaw with a crackle of fire.

Mrs. Dimblewit stumbled but got up quickly, and this time Aphra backed her up, attacking Ambert with a cannon spell and sending him tumbling into Miss Dewey.

Mrs. Dimblewit once again struck out, this time directing

her anger at Thorn and Valley. Valley whipped her blades out and deflected the spell, guarding Thorn. Seven could take no more. She felt the rage of the Nightbeast explode within her and let the full force of her magic free in a brutal attack.

"Machete!" she shrieked, hitting Mrs. Dimblewit in the chest and knocking her over.

"Zarpazo!" She attacked again, this time at Aphra. The other witches in the crowd stepped back in horror as Seven unleashed every ember of fury she had at them.

"Seven, stop!" Miss Dewey cried out, putting one hand on Seven's shoulder. Seven paused, her breathing ragged and exhausted from the magic.

She walked up to Aphra, and Mrs. Dimblewit and sneered. "Don't think you can treat us however you want because we're Spares and you're from the Hill. I am your future Uncle!" Seven's face was red with rage as she leaned in. "And you should get used to that idea. Because we're not going anywhere."

The Spares in the crowd looked at one another with poorly disguised glee. Seven was surprised they didn't break out in applause. Even Ambert and Miss Dewey exchanged surprised looks as Seven turned and walked away from the crowd.

With Valley, Thorn, Miss Dewey, and Ambert right behind her, and her raccoons hissing and walking backward behind their party, they got away safely. But despite the brave face she'd put on, and her head being held high the entire time as she walked away, Seven's thoughts raced with what she had seen in the shadows, and the soft cackling of the Nightbeast in her mind.

An hour later, the Witchlings' parents sat in Valley's living room, speaking to Knox in hushed whispers.

"Can you hear them?" Thorn asked.

She and Valley were crouched down, halfway out of Valley's bedroom door. Seven lay on the bed, reading the latest draft of Witches of Heartbreak Cove (Valley best friend privileges).

"You could do that, or you could just . . ." Seven flicked her wrist and whispered, "Chisme."

A breeze swooshed into Valley's room and carried their parents' voices with it—it was like they were right in the room with them.

Seven scrambled off the bed and they all sat on the floor together, listening.

"We must do something to keep them safe," Leaf Laroux said.

"Cancel the games! That's what we should've done from the beginning," Fox said.

Thorn shook her head no and covered her mouth. The games meant everything to her right now, Seven knew, but she couldn't help but agree with her mom.

Someone sighed.

"I have brought that up to the Circle of Grans. We held a vote, but there were more people for the games than against," the Gran said.

"How can we let this continue? Don't they care about the victims?" Talis asked.

"They don't. They believe that Thorn is the target and"— Quill lowered her voice even more and the Witchlings leaned forward so their heads were nearly touching—"many of them want the hexer to succeed."

A shiver ran down Seven's spine, but truthfully, she already knew this. Judging by Valley and Thorn's non-reactions, they knew it too. They were used to being unwanted by now, no matter how many expectations they'd surpassed. It seemed no matter what they did, or how hard they worked, no matter how many laps they ran around their peers, witches only ever saw them as one thing: Spares. But Seven would prove that even Spares were worth rooting for. Maybe together, they could change what it meant to be a Spare.

"The first magic duels match is tomorrow . . . well, today really," said Thimble. "It's one of the more volatile sports, as we all know, and we need to be certain the champions are safe."

"Measures are being put into place," said the Gran. "But this hex is unlike anything we've ever encountered. It moves quickly but affects the atmosphere and, in turn, my Guards. They cannot react in time and . . . I do not know how to fight it."

"I am worried about them—about all the champions of course, but especially our three girls," said Talis. Seven, Valley, and Thorn smiled.

"I am *just* as worried. I assure you I am doing my very best to find the serial hexer. I've spoken to a few of the witches of interest and was able to clear their names at least," the Gran said.

"Graves?" Quill asked softly.

"Yes, I spoke to her family myself just a few days ago. They were in my cottage and I made sure to strip the area of any deceptive magic or illusion," the Gran said. "It's just a precaution, but my guard is keeping an extra eye on them as well. The hexer might be targeting witches who are helping them or close to them in some way, and if that's the case, Graves might be a target."

"What?!" Valley yelled, startling Seven and Thorn, and causing their heads to collide in the middle of their circle.

The adults went silent, and the sound of footsteps swiftly approached Valley's door. The three witches scrambled: Seven back on the bed, Thorn on a chair, and Valley, panicking last minute, jumped inside her own closet, her legs so long her feet stuck out.

"You wouldn't be trying to eavesdrop, now would you?"

The Gran waved her hand in the air, gathering the residue of magic from Seven's spell.

Seven chuckled nervously. "Weeeeee were not! Just talking about . . . schoolwork?"

The Gran shot her an unconvinced look. "You know that rumor about me hexing that one Witchling's eyebrows to grow uncontrollably?"

Seven and Thorn nodded. Valley gulped from inside the closet.

"Well, it's not so much a rumor as a half truth. I made his eyebrows *and* his nose hairs grow. Don't let me catch you spying again or you'll be next." Knox winked, then closed the door.

"Valley, don't frog out, I'm sure Graves will be okay," Seven said.

Valley was shaking her head. "If the hexer even tries to come near her . . ."

"They won't. We'll make sure of it. Plus, you heard what the Gran said, she has extra security looking out for Graves. And she has Wren, a literal wand dueler," Thorn said.

That fact seemed to calm Valley down a bit. If anyone could protect Graves, it would be someone skilled enough to be a wand duel champion.

"The best way to keep Graves, Thorn, and everyone else safe is to figure out who the serial hexer is. So who's on our suspect list?" Seven asked, taking out her trusty faux dragon-scale notebook. It was nearly out of paper, she realized. She'd need to get a new one.

"The Dimblewits for sure. Aphra and Mrs. Dimblewit seemed really invested in all of it back at the maze," Valley said.

"Right." Seven put stars next to their names.

"I wish we could figure out the whole double-Graves and -Wren thing. At first I thought my tracker malfunctioned, but I saw Wren with my own eyes when she was definitely with the Gran on the other side of town," Seven said. "Someone must've been trying to frame them."

"What are the things we *do* know?" Thorn asked.

"Our clues are: a gray hair in Thorn's sewing kit, weird double-witch sightings, and a witch acting suspiciously during the toad race tonight," Seven said, reading from her notebook.

"There's probably also two witches behind this, since you heard two voices in your rosebud," Valley pointed out.

Seven nodded, and suddenly something dawned on her. It had been really dark at the maze, but while Seven was *almost* positive she had seen a witch in a green cloak escaping from the maze, she knew someone with excellent eyesight who would know for sure.

"Edgar," Seven said, peeking into her rucksack.

Thorn and Valley exchanged curious looks.

"What now?" Edgar asked.

"The witch who ran from the maze, the one who we

thought was the hexer, did you happen to see the color of their cloak?" Seven asked.

Edgar yawned. "It was a very emerald green. Looked like my color back when I was younger."

"Thanks," Seven said, then turned to her coven.

"What did he say?" Thorn asked.

"An emerald green, he said," Seven said, something suddenly occuring to her. "Goats, what if the hair from Thorn's sewing kit wasn't gray? What if it was *silver*?"

They looked at one another for a few moments, Seven's heart beating.

Thorn's eyes spilled over with tears. "River," Thorn said. "River has silver hair and, famously, an emerald green cloak. You don't really think it could be her though, do you?"

"Whoever the hexer is has always been one step ahead of us . . . And River would've known everything we were up to, would've been able to feed into Graves being a suspect, and to attack Tia, because we told Figgs everything," Valley said.

Seven's stomach dropped. If Figgs was in on this, she would never forgive him. And she would turn him into a toad herself. She had to admit, though, that the theory made a lot of sense.

"What do we do now?" Valley and Thorn both looked at Seven, and the pressure of it made her chest constrict.

"We have to look into River, get solid proof to bring to the Gran so we don't fudge this up again," Seven said.

"We can sneak into her room, check to see if we find anything like you and Figgs did in Moth House," Valley suggested. "There's a wand duel tomorrow in Frog House. Maybe if we went, it would give us an excuse to snoop."

"We can't get in though. Those are only for important town figures and older witches since it's so dangerous . . ." Thorn said, shifting her gaze to Seven.

"But *I* can. That's exactly what I'm gonna do."

She turned to the suspect list in her notebook, and above where Graves's name was crossed out, she wrote another name in red, circling it many times: River Moonfall.

"How are you going to sneak into River's room without being noticed?" Thorn asked. "Those matches are really strict about people going in and out. You might not be able to get away."

"I have an idea of how you can do it." Valley smirked. "And you're gonna need my rat."

CHAPTER TWENTY-THREE
COTTON SWAB THE RAT

COTTON SWAB THE RAT was very upset with Seven Salazar. A few years back, when Valley had misguidedly put him in Seven's rucksack, intending for him to be a gift, Seven had thrown the rucksack clear across the spaceball field and run all the way home. But not before telling Valley off for it.

It was one of the many reasons Seven had considered Valley her mortal enemy, but she hadn't thought about the rat in many months. Now that she could literally understand animals, Cotton Swab had some words of his own for her.

"Not a rat, not that one especially," said Seven, shaking her head at Valley.

"You owe him an apology!" Valley held her rucksack open, revealing—Seven shivered—Cotton Swab.

They were hidden in a small grove of trees, as Seven prepared to infiltrate Frog House with Valley's rat. How she'd convinced her this was a good idea, Seven would never know. Cotton Swab squeaked and Seven recoiled.

"Can you please move back? I didn't mean to hurt him! I was just shocked and I'm sorry I threw him, but you scared me," Seven said.

"Okay, well, say sorry," Valley said. "You're going to have to talk to him anyway! I can't understand rat."

"Suddenly I wish I couldn't either," Seven grumbled.

"Rats have excellent hearing," said a soft little voice from within Valley's open rucksack.

Seven dared to look a bit closer at the dark interior of the bag. Two little eyes blinked back at her. Cotton Swab the rat climbed out slowly, his little pink nose twitching in the air.

Seven took a small step back when Cotton Swab smiled at her. He had round pink ears and his face looked . . . almost like a little bear's.

"I— Hi, I'm Seven," Seven said, her arms still held close to her chest in fear.

"I am Cotton Swab," said the rat in a cute little voice. "Hello, Seven dear."

Valley opened her eyes wide at Seven. "Go on," she mouthed.

"I'm sorry for throwing you that one time. I hope you weren't hurt," Seven said cautiously.

Cotton Swab smiled again. "I wasn't. Valley dear is quick and used a cushion spell to break my fall. It was quite comfortable."

"Oh, I'm glad," Seven said.

"Valley dear tells me you need my help. I'm happy to help a friend and honored to help the Uncle." Cotton Swab bowed reverentially.

"Don't bow, don't bow." Seven waved her hands. "I do need your help though."

Seven took her faux dragon-scale notebook from her rucksack and slipped out the map Poppy had made from memory since one of her new best pals was in Frog House, and showed it to Cotton Swab.

"See this door here." Seven pointed with her pen, then made a circle around a door with an *R* on it. "That's the room we need you to snoop in."

Because Cotton Swab was Valley's pet rat, he had a very particular set of skills: He was well versed in mazes and maps, he could sniff out monstruo tracks, and most importantly for today's mission, he could detect the smell of archaic magic. Valley had kept a small piece of broken necklace from the Cursed Toads the year before and had been training Cotton Swab with it ever since.

"You never know when you'll need an evil-detecting rat," she had explained to Seven.

Cotton Swab nodded and Seven made the paper into a little scroll. Without thinking, she handed it to Cotton Swab and he took it in his little hands, touching Seven's fingers in the process. She tried not to shiver, because it would be rude, but she was still deathly afraid of rats. Even if Cotton Swab was, she admitted to herself begrudgingly, kinda cute.

"I will do my best. I will not get caught. I have lookie-looed around with Valley dear through your locker many times and was never caught—"

"You used to snoop in my locker?" Seven asked, eyes wide at Valley.

"Ha ha, all right, Cotton Swab, enough of those jokes," Valley chuckled nervously.

Seven shook her head and smirked. It was always strange to think how far their friendship had come from the days when Valley was her actual bully.

"Okay, I'm heading over," Seven said. "Once we go inside, I will leave my cloak in the hallway. When the coast is clear, you'll make your way to River's room. Okay?" she said to Cotton Swab.

Cotton Swab held one little paw up.

Seven raised an eyebrow.

"He wants a high five," Valley said.

"Oh," Seven said, before bracing herself and tapping his paw.

She had touched a rat twice and hadn't died!

"I will complete my mission and hope for cheese, Seven dear," said Cotton Swab before diving into the cloak pocket where Seven normally kept Edgar. She shivered, but found the rat's warmth a bit comforting.

"See you on the other side," Valley said. "Don't get killed."

"I'll try my best," Seven said, and then she made her way to Frog House.

CHAPTER TWENTY-FOUR
TRUTHFUL TO THE LAST

MAGIC DUELS WERE THE MOST dangerous and ancient of all the Golden Frog Games, and unlike the rest of the sports in the tournament, not everyone was invited to see the matches. A guide brought groups of attendees down an enormous hallway, deep into Frog House, for the match. As Seven followed along, she wondered if she'd be able to get to River's room herself.

The halls of Frog House were elegant and grand, and the walls were adorned with the framed portraits of famous Frog House witches of days past, old class photos, and tapestries.

"This here is our founder, Oak Peridot, on Colors Day," the guide said, pointing to a portrait where Oak had their face painted green and pink as was customary during the Twelve Town Colors Day tradition.

"This hallway is the only remaining part of the original

Frog Coven House, which was built, as legend has it, in just one day." The guide smiled proudly.

"Yes, using expensive magic, no doubt," said the older witch in purple robes beside Seven with an indignant harrumph. House Hyacinth witches and Frog House were forever in a rivalry for coven supremacy.

"This here is the famed Hat of Truth," the guide said, gesturing toward a picture of a regal-looking woman with a pointy nose and deep brown skin. She was wearing a deep pink witch's hat with a wide, floppy brim. It was adorned in hundreds of sparkling crystals of all colors, delicate teardrop pearls hanging from each side. "This hat was created by our Frog House ancestors, and though not much information remains about the identity of the creator, it is known that it comes from a line of witches who were said to be exceedingly skillful at the art of costura. It was said that wearing this hat would reveal the wearer's true self. It could also extract the truth from anyone the wearer questioned and could break through any sort of deceptive enchantment or illusion. Like many powerful spells, enchantments, and even hexes, the hat is believed to have been passed down through the same family for many years, sometimes landing in Frog House, sometimes not."

"So cool." Seven marveled at the elaborate-looking hat, and when the group had moved on, she snapped a quick picture with her portaphone so she could show Thorn later.

The guide led them to the entrance of the dueling hall. "We hope you have a pleasant evening in Frog House and, please, do not ask anything more of me. I have an arachnid final exam to study for!" the guide said before running away. Maybe Valley had a point, and Seven *should've* been a Frog House witch.

Seven lingered toward the end of the line, looking for an opportunity to sneak off. There didn't seem to be any Guards around—maybe she would be able to help Cotton Swab search River's room after all. She walked swiftly away, then turned a corner in the direction of River's room, when from out of nowhere two tall, armored Gran's Guards appeared before her.

"No witches beyond this point during the match," they both said in thundering voices.

"Ha ha, right," Seven said. "Sorry!"

Those witches were scary. Seven walked back toward the line, and on her way, casually draped her cloak on a fancy table.

"Good luck," she whispered to Cotton Swab as he leapt out. It was up to him now.

Seven hurried to find a good seat, nervous for Cotton Swab and hoping the rat didn't get caught.

"Welcome, good witches of the Twelve Towns, to a test of magic, wit, and steel," said Enve, dressed in a white-and-green military-style suit in the fashion of Frog House witches of old. Each house used to have its own Guard, until they became one unit under the Gran. Enve's interpretation was, of course, glittery from head to toe, with golden tassels hanging from the epaulettes, a cinched waist adorned with a utility belt, and high green boots to match the details on the sleeves. Pastel pink hair peeked out from beneath her white-and-gold helmet, and she held a golden walkie-talkie, which had been enchanted to work like a microphone.

"Tonight we are in for an elitist—I mean exclusive—treat." She winked. "As Crones Cliff Manor takes on Ravenskill in one of the most anticipated wand duel matches of this year's games!"

There was polite clapping from the crowd and Seven looked around to take in her surroundings. The room was a bit bigger than one of her classrooms and long and high enough to accommodate mahogany risers. At the center of the room was a runway of sorts with yellow lines drawn every few toadstools.

"For Crones Cliff Manor we have Crimson Riddle of Moth House against Bonecross champion Killian Frost of House Hyacinth!"

"I hope this doesn't drag on like the last time," said one of the witches in front of Seven, shaking her head.

"Killian will make swift work of that Crimson witch, have no doubt," said the other.

Crimson sauntered out in a suit of black, shimmering scale-mail armor and Killian appeared on the opposite end of the runway in purple armor. They smiled and waved to the applauding audience before closing their masks and getting into position.

"The rules for the match are simple: Each witch gets three spells to disarm their opponent. They must use spells from an approved list. No killing spells, obviously, or overly violent spells will be tolerated. In addition, each witch has chosen one unknown enchantment for their armor. Ready, begin!"

Enve Lopes was floated up and away from the stage in a flourish of lights.

"Spared no magic, did they?" asked one of the chatty witches in front of Seven.

"Rayo!" said Killian, sending a stream of crackling light toward Crimson, who blocked it easily with a parry.

The champions reset into position, and it was Crimson's turn.

"Seven, I feel weak."

The Nightbeast.

Seven looked around the room, suddenly overcome with paranoia.

Crimson got into position and struck out. "Látigo!"

A cord made of light swung at Killian and connected with her shoulder with a loud *CRACK*. The crowd gasped, and Killian lost her balance, the pain clearly visible on her face despite the armor and protective spells. This was why magic duels were so dangerous; no matter how much you prepared, modern witches just were not used to the power of using wands. It was why they were outlawed, save for use by Town Grans and the games.

Killian held on to her wand, but was rubbing her shoulder. She went into her corner and took a moment to regroup before getting into position again.

Killian thrust forward with her wand-bearing hand and screamed, "Alma vacía!"

A gray light shot straight at Crimson and hit him square in the chest, and he dropped his wand. The crowd got up and some began to clap. Others were disappointed, but then, from behind Killian, a voice called out, "Estocada!"

Crimson was not where he had been originally, Seven realized, but behind Killian somehow.

"How in the world?!" asked a witch beside Seven, and then Crimson struck the final, winning blow. "Diezmar!"

Killian tried to turn around and block in time, but it was impossible. She dropped her wand and, with a look of defeat, bowed to Crimson. The Moth House witch had won. They shook hands and stood on the runway, nodding and clapping at the cheering crowd.

"That was thrilling!" Enve Lopes said, coming back onstage. "A masterful use of the armor enchantment spell, Crimson."

The crowd murmured in agreement.

"I merely used the magic of my Moth House forebears," an out-of-breath Crimson said.

"Hmm," said Enve Lopes, "I know an espejos protection spell when I see one! Bravo and well done—and well done, Killian, brilliant effort!"

The crowd clapped politely and settled down for the next match while others lined up to congratulate Crimson at the far end of the room. Seven should maybe give Cotton Swab one more match, but she was too worried about him to just sit, so Seven made her way through the crowd and toward the exit.

"Seven!" Crimson called out. Seven turned and gave him a small wave as he smirked, rustling his flame-red hair. "I didn't know you'd be here." Seven shuffled closer to Crimson reluctantly. He was River's teammate; he could very well know what she was up to, or worse, be her hexer in crime.

"Ha, yeah, congrats on the win," Seven said.

"Thanks," Crimson said, then took a big swig of his water. He was really very sweaty, Seven realized.

"I've gotta get going," Seven said. "Good luck on your next match!"

"Thanks, and Seven, be careful out there. There's a hexer on the loose." Crimson winked and turned back to his fans. Seven walked away, dazed. Had that been a threat, or was she just paranoid?

Worry for Cotton Swab overtook her, and Seven ran to the hallway, arriving just as the rat was jumping back into her cloak.

"Cotton Swab!" Seven whispered as she hustled out of Frog House. "Was there archaic magic in River's room?"

Cotton Swab waved his little paws in front of his nose. "Seven dear, I've never smelled so much archaic magic in my life."

"So it *was* River," Seven whispered triumphantly.

"Well, perhaps," Cotton Swab said carefully.

"What do you mean?" Seven asked.

"The room, it was ginormous. Ten beds, many things. River's things were there, yes, but also the things of nine other witches. I cannot be sure she is the hexer, because everyone's things were tainted."

CHAPTER TWENTY-FIVE
ILLUSIONS

SEVEN WAS UNEASY about River Moonfall. All signs were pointing to her, and Seven had more than enough evidence to bring to the Gran, but . . . something felt off. For starters, River had been onstage during every stonification, so she wasn't working alone. But who was the other hexer? And then there was the mystery of the second Graves—who had snuck into Thorn and Gunnar's tent? Who had Seven heard in her rosebud speaker? It all felt too easy, too neat to pin River for the stonifications, when there were still so many loose ends to tie up. Seven wasn't supposed to be investigating, and she knew she'd be in huge trouble once she finally told the Gran. She'd probably be assigned a twenty-four-hour Gran's Guard to keep an eye on her, so she had to be sure before she said anything.

It was two days after the wand duel and the start of the

Springtide holiday break. Because the holiday usually fell right in the middle of the games, it was a chance for everyone to get a small rest from the competitions, and many witches took the opportunity to travel home for a few days. Normally, Seven would be snoring away in her room until noon during her break. Beefy would be climbing into her bed and blowing raspberries on her cheek. The smell of pancakes would finally get her up, and her parents would make bad jokes as she sat down to eat with them. Instead, she was with the Gran on her way to Crones Cliff Manor by train. The Gran thought Seven would enjoy a trip out of town and could ease back into her training with some light practice on her tracking skills. Seven was an Uncle-in-training now, so she'd have to get used to early-morning train rides in the fanciest car with the eldest and most powerful witch in town instead of spending time with her family. Even if she did miss them terribly.

There was someone else she missed. Seven did not want to admit *that* even to herself, but she had not heard the Nightbeast in almost a full day, and her heart lurched with worry. She really was doing her best not to think about it, but that was hard to do when she knew the Gran was investigating her magic. Did she somehow know about her connection to the monstruo? Had she found a way to cut it off? And why hadn't she updated Seven? What if she had found something bad and told the other Grans or the council, and they were thinking of a way to deal with Seven right that second?

"Is everything okay, Seven?" the Gran asked as they waited to get off the train.

Seven pushed past her fear and asked what she really wanted to know. "I am a bit worried about the investigation into my magic. Anything new?"

Seven's chest tightened as the Gran looked out the window. "We've yet to find anything amiss, but it could be that there is something we've never encountered before. It might take a while, but whatever it is, you will be okay. You do not need to worry."

Seven supposed it was a good thing they hadn't found anything, but the truth still stood: She could communicate with monstruos. She had to get her powers under control and pass her Uncle trials this autumnal equinox so she wouldn't meet the same fate as Delphinium. Seven was sure that once she officially had the Uncle power, then nobody could hurt her even if they did find out what she could do.

"I'm worried I'm falling behind. Maybe we could ramp my training back up all the way after this trip? After all, I have my Uncle trials soon and I've already taken a lot of days off," Seven said.

"And as I've reminded you, you have until your eighteenth birthday to take on the Uncle powers if you so choose. *Choose*, Seven; you have a choice in this," the Gran said.

Seven looked down. She knew the Gran was being generous, and that the other Uncles were stretched thin because three Uncles had been lost at once. She was the only new Uncle chosen so far; if she didn't assume her powers now, she'd be letting everyone down.

"Barbatos became the Uncle at just thirteen," Seven said softly.

The Gran looked cross now. "Barbatos was a scoundrel who didn't actually care for the animals he was tasked with protecting. He was never a true Uncle, he stole that power from poor Rulean. You are not like him, Seven. You are responsible and caring and hardworking. Don't compare yourself, or your abilities, to anyone who is not you. Do you understand what I mean?"

"Like . . . I should only focus on myself, kind of?"

"Yes, in respect to your abilities and your accomplishments. You should only try and be better than you were yesterday, and even then, it is okay to fall short of what you expect of yourself. You are more than your work, Seven. Those in constant competition with their peers, who resent them for doing better, become bitter bats with only their jealousy left to fuel their heartbeat."

Seven shrank in her seat a bit. "What if I don't make it?"

Seven didn't just mean not making her Uncle trials; she meant not making it, period. She wished she could just tell the Gran, but fear kept her from it. Like not going to the doctor because you're scared they'll tell you something's really wrong. Part of Seven hoped she was overreacting. A big part of her. But she had read and reread the passages in Delphinium's diary and there could be no mistaking that she had trusted her Gran, and had been sentenced to death because of it.

"If you don't pass by your eighteenth birthday, you will still be a brilliant, important witch. And if you choose not to be an Uncle, that is your right too. Seven, do you know how I became the Gran?"

Seven nodded. "The Stars chose you."

"Yes, but did you know I was only seventeen when I was chosen? And it took me another twenty-five years to become the Gran. Partly because of the training, but also because I wanted to *live*. It is a great responsibility to be the head of a Twelve Town. There is no shame in taking your time with things, with life. And do you know what the very first thing I tried to do was when I became the Gran?"

"No," Seven said.

The Gran was quiet for a long while, but when she finally spoke, she said something Seven was not expecting. "I asked if we could abolish the Spare coven," the Gran said, looking out the window again.

"What? But where would Spares go? Would they be sent away?"

"No, no, Seven." The Gran looked at her with kind eyes. "I

wanted to alter the magic of the Black Moon Ceremony so that a Spare coven wouldn't be needed at all. I wanted every Witchling to belong, and to have a choice . . . but it wasn't possible. I was young, and didn't know that such magic can't be broken. I wanted so badly to change that, to rewrite things how I thought they should be. You have that chance for your own life, and I never want you to forget it. The power to rewrite your story will *always* belong to you. Nobody can tell you who you are; that knowledge is in your heart alone. Okay?"

Seven wasn't one hundred percent sure she knew what the Gran meant to tell her, but she nodded anyway. Something did occur to her though.

"What if I choose not to be an Uncle now?" Seven asked.

"You could do that. But nature will not choose another Uncle until you are eighteen, or once you've passed on. We would stop your training, but your powers would still live in you until then. You would still hear the animals, I'm afraid."

And hear the monstruos, Seven thought.

The train slowed to a stop, and Seven heard the sounds of passengers shuffling around and gathering their things. A car would be picking the Gran up to take her to Antares Calarook's cottage and Seven would be off to Whispering Grove, the forest of Crones Cliff Manor, to check on the animals she had supposedly tracked.

"Good luck with your assignment today. I hope you find your tagged animals safe and well," the Gran said.

Seven nodded nervously, hoping to the Stars that the Gran didn't ask her to show her the twenty-sided crystal that currently had the silhouette of twenty witch champions and zero animals.

"Do you need some help? I helped train poor Rulean when he was very young." The Gran had a sad look in her eyes, remembering the Ravenskill Uncle who had been toadified. "Let's take a look." The Gran gestured at Seven's rucksack, perking up. "I used to be quite good at the twenty-sided-crystal when I was younger. Though I used it for less than savory reasons." The Gran cackled, and Seven swallowed hard.

"Um," Seven said. Her face was hot, and her palms were slick with sweat as she tried to come up with an excuse, fast.

Just then their car door opened. "We're ready for you, Gran." One of the Gran's Guards popped his head in their car, saving Seven.

"I'll be right out, Sol," the Gran said, then turned back to Seven. "Seven, I want you to know that anytime you need to talk to someone about these things, I'm here. It's not easy to be a leader, much less one chosen against her will, but know I will always, always support you. So long as you are always honest with me," the Gran said softly. Seven felt a pang of guilt take hold of her heart.

"Yes, Gran," she said, and the old witch smiled kindly at Seven.

"Gran?" Sol poked his head in again.

"Yes, yes, I'm coming, I'm coming. Seven, I will meet you at Gran Antares's house for lunch. If you don't know the way, ask the animals. They'll know." The Gran winked as she got up and left the train, and Seven made her own way to the Whispering Grove.

"Now, where is that bunny?" Seven asked herself as she walked through the forest, looking for the animals she had tagged on her last trip here. She had found six of them so far, and was able to restore their tags on her twenty-sided crystal.

"Excuse me, sir? Have you seen Popcorn the bunny any-where around here?" she asked a deer.

"Popcorn? No, I think he's on vacation," said the deer before running off.

"Rats," Seven said, crossing Popcorn's name off her list.

Seven strolled through the lush grove. Seven must've been too far from any monstruos to hear them right now, so the only voices were the chattering of the small wood-land creatures. A flowery path led to a small pond, where she hoped to find a particular furfish, when she heard a twig snap just a few toadstools behind her. Seven spun around, and a shadow dove behind a tree. Someone was following her. She crept as quietly as she could toward the witch, because it *was* a witch—and one she had seen trailing her twice before. When Seven reached the tree he was hiding behind, she jumped at him, but the witch dashed out of reach so quickly it took her by surprise. She chased him through the grove and to the edge of the forest.

"Seven!"

Seven stopped cold and turned toward the voice: the Gran.

"Why are you running? Is everything okay?" The Gran ran toward her with a worried expression on her face.

"I'm . . . all right," Seven panted. She looked out in the direction the witch from the woods had run, and scowled. She'd had her suspicions before, but now she was sure that the witch she'd seen following her before, lurking in the shadows, and now in the Whispering Grove, was someone she knew. But why was he following her?

"Are you certain?" the Gran asked, still clearly concerned.

Seven looked at her and smiled. "Promise. Let's go, I'm starved!"

The Gran laughed and they walked together to Gran Antares's house to eat and review Seven's progress with the twenty-sided crystal.

Seven was up before the sun the next morning. She tagged a few more animals in the woods but didn't get rid of all the witch trackers, just in case. Then she made her way toward the beach. That's where Spares lived, she remembered, and there was a particular Spare she needed to find.

It turned out she didn't have to look very long, because the witch came out of a bakery a few toadstools down from Seven, who slipped behind a mailbox, watching him. He looked out into the sky beyond the cliff, the sun shining on his face. He swung his shiny black hair back from his face and closed his eyes, letting the sun warm his skin. Seven's heart skipped a beat.

She clutched her chest and looked down. "Stop it, betrayer."

The witch tucked the freshly baked bread beneath his arm and began to walk. Seven had become worryingly good at following people. It wasn't exactly a skill a twelve-year-old witch should have, she knew, but it had come in handy more than once. The witch made his way down the winding cliff-side stairs, and Seven kept a safe distance as he walked toward the shore. She would get him alone and get some froggin' answers.

The witch reached the row of neat little houseboats by the water. There were mangrove trees along the shore enclosing the area to make a cozy little cove. He looked to his left, then right, before walking through . . . yes, *through* a tree. Seven rubbed her eyes. Was she seeing things?

She took off after him. If this was some sort of secret

passage, it could lead anywhere—to the hexer themself, even—or maybe she'd get a face full of trunk. Either way, Seven had to give it a shot. You don't just see a witch walk through a tree and not try to follow. Seven looked around and found a few bright blue seashells shaped a little like hearts. She picked them up and threw one in the direction of the tree. It went all the way through and then disappeared.

"Oh my goats," she whispered, stuffing the rest of the sea-shells into her pocket.

Seven took a deep breath, closed her eyes, then stepped one foot into the tree. It went inside. She looked down and there were wavering lines all around her leg that looked kind of like . . .

"A holograph illusion," Seven realized. She stepped all the way inside and emerged in a very different scene.

The idyllic houseboats painted in bright colors were gone, and in their places were badly burnt remains. What was this magic?

Ahead she saw the witch entering one of the burnt houses. Unlike moments before, when all Seven could smell was the salty, fresh scent of the ocean, now the air was heavy with the stench of charred wood. It took her a few seconds to gather her courage, but she followed him onto the deck of the boat. It creaked loudly, swaying on the water danger-ously. She stood frozen in place, waiting for someone to run out and catch her, but nobody did. As Seven stepped inside the houseboat, she realized it was bigger than she had expected. It was also nicer than she'd expected from the outward burnt appearance. It had been beautiful once, but it was still dry, and warm, and decorated lovingly. There were a few boxes scattered throughout, as if someone was moving or doing a Springtide cleaning. Seven made her way toward the sounds of breakfast being made and someone humming happily.

As she entered the small kitchen, the witch spun around and dropped the delicate white cup in his hands. It shattered. "Seven? What are you— How did you . . . ?"

"Hey, Figgs," Seven said, and then she raised her hands and blasted him with a freezing spell.

CHAPTER TWENTY-SIX
QUESTIONS AND CAFECITOS

SHE JUST KNEW it was him. Outside of Frog House, disappearing behind the tree the morning she'd gone to Moth House, he had been creeping around for weeks, and now he was going through holographic trees. Figgs was up to something and Seven was going to find out what it was.

Figgs was frozen in place, his hands up, his face one of shock. Seven circled him, making sure the spell had gotten his whole body.

"Cuerda," Seven said, making a pulling motion like she had a rope between her hands. A rope made of red light appeared and Seven wrapped Figgs up tight before putting her hand up close to his face and using the derretir spell to melt the magic ice just enough so he could see and talk.

"Seven," Figgs gasped. "What are you doing here?"

"What am I doing here? What have you been doing

following me all over the place? Why are all these houses hidden behind some sort of holograph?"

Figgs sighed. "I'm sorry, I just . . ."

Seven tightened the cord around his body. "Don't think about lying because I won't hesitate to hurt you," Seven lied. "The truth, now."

"Okay, okay," Figgs said. "It's illusion magic."

"What?"

"This spell hurts. You don't need to freeze me *and* tie me up, do you?"

Seven bit her lip. Figgs worked for River, and River was most likely the hexer, but Seven tried to think back to the times witches had been stonified: At the champion unveiling, Figgs had been sitting a few rows behind the Witchlings and nowhere near the stage; he had been right next to Seven when Alaric had been stonified; and he had been talking to her while the two voices were going off in her rosebud in Moth House. He had also been sitting right in front of them during the maze race. The chances of Figgs being the second hexer were pretty slim, especially since he was a Spare, but that didn't mean she could trust him completely. "Fine, but if you try anything funny, I will do worse than the freezing spell."

"I won't do anything, promise," Figgs said, and Seven melted the rest of the freezing spell away, though the magic rope still held him in place.

Figgs rolled his neck and squeezed his eyes. "That was

awful. Remind me to never get in a fight with you again."

Seven suddenly felt terrible about hurting Figgs. Maybe it was silly, but she slackened the magical rope. A look of relief spread across his face. It still sat loosely around his shoulders and with just one false move, Seven would tighten the rope till his eyeballs popped out.

"There's more where that came from if you don't come clean."

"I don't know where to start."

"How about telling me why these houses are hidden like this and why you have been following me."

Figgs let out a breath and sat down on a rickety wooden stool. "The houses *used* to be nice. But a few days before the games, they were all set on fire."

Seven gasped. It wasn't, for whatever reason, what she expected to hear. But there had been violence spreading against Spares for weeks, and it made sense that Spares having something, anything, nice wouldn't be tolerated right now.

"I'm really sorry, Figgs," Seven said.

"I'm fine." Figgs gave her a sideways grin, and Seven's heart fluttered.

"I know this is awkward, but . . . would you like some tea or mudbean milk? I feel rude not offering," Figgs said shyly.

"All right, I'll have some mudbean milk," Seven said, hoping to the Stars her cheeks weren't red. "But don't think you're off the hook." Seven flicked her wrist, showing she still had her end of the magic rope engaged.

Figgs held his hands up as he got to work. "Nope, I'll keep confessing." Using magic, since he couldn't reach above his head, Figgs pulled his supplies from a cupboard above the sink and poured water into a metal mudbean pot. "I was actually one of the lucky ones in the fire. Some houses were just a pile of rubble once they finally managed to put it out."

"You'd think being near water would help," Seven said.

Figgs shook his head as he placed a strainer into a glass carafe and filled it with ground mudbeans. "It wasn't . . . normal fire."

Seven sat down. "What do you mean not normal?"

Figgs poured water over the ground mudbeans and the glass filled with piping hot dark brown liquid. The small houseboat filled with a rich, comforting aroma that reminded Seven of rainy mornings and her mother's warm hugs.

"It was purple and gray, and it crackled quicker than normal fire. Come to think of it, it looked sort of like . . ."

"The hex?" Seven asked.

Figgs poured steaming milk into ceramic cups, then poured just a splash of mudbean juice in each. It was normal for Witchlings to drink mudbean juice from a young age, even in their bottles. But it was always mostly milk.

"Yeah, like the hex." Figgs passed Seven a cup and she took a slow sip. It was creamy and perfect.

So, whoever set the fires was probably the same witch behind the hexes, she thought.

"Our Town Gran panicked after the fire and cast this illusion to keep any visitors from seeing the state of our houses," Figgs said, leaning against a counter with his own cup. "They were planning on rebuilding, but there was too much pushback from some of the rich witches in town, so they've been stuck arguing. The town is actually always fighting about us. Half of the witches want us to keep having better living conditions than Spares in other towns, and the other half probably wouldn't care if our houseboats sank."

How could Crones Cliff Manor do this? While everyone was going around praising them for being fair to their Spares, they were leaving them in these unsafe homes. What a butt-toad move.

Seven took a long sip of her mudbean milk and looked straight into Figgs's eyes. "Why have you been following me?"

Figgs looked uncomfortable. He took a deep breath and spoke. "It wasn't because I wanted to. River asked me to keep tabs on you Witchlings. She asked me to report back every day on what you were doing and where you'd be the next day. I was supposed to watch all three of you, but you weren't together very much, so I just followed you." Figgs's face went red.

Seven felt sick, and she had to blink back tears. She had no doubt River was the hexer. The silver strand of hair, the green cloak, the archaic magic infesting her room, and now this. Figgs had been following her around, had been near her, because of the hexer out to get Thorn. Seven was a jumble of emotions, none of them good. She felt angry, sad, betrayed. She had thought, maybe, that Figgs just happened to save her seats, and smile at her shyly, because he liked her the way . . . Seven's stomach writhed . . . the way she liked him. But now she had to wonder, had Figgs ever really liked her, or was he just keeping an eye on her? The thoughts were sobering, and Seven waited till Figgs took a sip of his mudbean milk and put the cup down before tightening the magic rope around his shoulders. Figgs winced.

"Sorry, but how do I even know I can trust you?"

Figgs just shrugged, his cheeks turning even redder. "River wanted me to spy on Thorn's preparations for the games," he said hurriedly. And you might not believe me, but I would never do anything to hurt you three, ever. You mean more to Spares than . . . anything. Especially you, Seven."

Seven narrowed her eyes. This was exactly what the Wicked One did in Witches of Heartbreak Cove: pretend to like Bianca before turning on her. *Well, not on my watch.*

"This was all about winning the games?"

Figgs nodded. "She's really competitive."

Seven wrestled with her next words. Anything she said to Figgs, he would tell River. It would be best to tread lightly, but maybe after literally freezing Figgs and tying him up, the time for that had passed. Might as well ask the questions that mattered. "Is she hexing people?"

"River!? No way she'd do something like that." If she is, I haven't seen her doing it and I would *never* help her, no matter how loyal I am."

"But you'll help her spy," Seven said.

"I don't have much of a choice, Seven. I'm a Spare, but I'm not an Uncle like you. River is the closest I can get to having a decent life; you can't blame me for doing everything I can to protect that."

Seven felt guilty for not considering that before, but it wasn't like she could trust everything he said. Still, Seven had never made mudbean milk for herself, because she'd never had to. Figgs knew how to make it because he lived alone and had no one to take care of him. She really couldn't fault him for trying to hold on to the bit of protection and love he had in his life. She would probably do the same.

"I'll be fourteen this fall. Four years after that I'll be done with school, unless I somehow come up with enough money to go to advanced witch school, which . . . my only hope for that is River. No matter how you look at it, I depend on her. She's the only person I have."

"What happened to your family?" Seven said.

"I lived with my aunt and uncle; my parents died when I was young. We lived in our equivalent to the Hill, big houses and all that. I was the first in my family to become a Spare, and they tried to fight it at first. When they realized there was nothing they could do . . ." Figgs wiped his eyes and Seven got a sinking feeling.

"I came home from school one day and they were gone. They took their things and just left. Put the house up for sale and everything." Figgs let out a bitter laugh. "I don't know where they went, and they never contacted me again. I came down here to the Spare housing, because for all its faults, at least this town gives us a place to live, I suppose. That's when River's family found me, and I've been working with them ever since. River has always treated me like family, and I couldn't possibly betray her, especially when she told me you goats might be up to no good. I thought I was doing the right thing."

"I'm sorry, Figgs. For the freezing spell and for hurting you and for all of it."

Figgs shook his head. "No, you had every right not to trust me. I was following you, after all."

"You weren't very good at it." Seven smiled.

"I know." Figgs laughed.

"What now? Will you tell River I found out?"

"I won't. I promise."

Could Seven really trust him? River was the hexer, and she was using Figgs to help her scope out the competition. But what choice did Seven have? It wasn't like she could wipe his memory. She didn't have that sort of power.

"I know you don't want to believe she's the hexer, so

maybe you can help me prove she isn't. Because if she is, Figgs, we could both get really hurt."

Figgs nodded. "You'll see you've got it wrong about River. She would never do anything like that."

Seven looked down at the table and considered what she knew of River. She was smart, great at magic, rich, beautiful. Sometimes people thought those things equaled good too. But being likable or popular didn't equate to being a good witch. River had also helped Thorn; she had defended her, encouraged her during the games. She had been there for Thorn when Seven couldn't be. Seven considered this for a moment, then looked up at Figgs.

"If she's so good to you, what are you still doing in this half-burnt house?"

"If it were up to River, I'd live with her, but her family is another story. The Moonfalls are a Frog House legacy family. Every Moonfall has been sorted into Frog House for generations, and they're obsessed with balance. They believe that if there are going to be wealthy witches there must also be poor witches, and that Spares are necessary for their way of life."

Seven shook her head. "That's a butt-toad thing to think."

"It's not very different from what a lot of wealthy witches believe. My old family included."

Seven nodded, her mind whirring with a million different things. Something that Figgs had said had tickled something in the very back of her brain . . . but she couldn't figure out why it was nagging her just yet.

"By the way," Figgs said, pulling Seven out of her thoughts. "This is probably the wrong time to ask, but . . . are you going to the Frog Ball?"

Seven's eyes went wide. She hadn't even thought about the Frog Ball. It was a big party that everyone went to on the night before the final trials.

"I suppose I have to go, being a future Uncle and all," Seven said shyly to a still-tied-up Figgs.

"If you need someone, I mean if you don't wanna go alone. I just figured, I could go with you, only if you really wanted to of course. What I mean is—"

"I'll go with you, Figgs," Seven said. If Figgs was a betrayer, she would keep an eye on him, and if he wasn't . . . well, then it might be fun.

"Oh, yay. I mean cool." Figgs made a serious face and leaned back, but almost toppled over since he was still tied up. Seven held back a laugh.

"I've gotta go, the Gran is waiting for me." Seven flourished her hand at the magic rope. "That'll come off in ten minutes. In case you decide to be a warlock."

"All right. And Seven, I'm sorry I've been lying to you."

"So long as you don't do it again, I forgive you," Seven said.

"I won't," Figgs said with a sideways smile. "Promise."

Seven smiled, and on her way out, she left a blue heart seashell on Figgs's kitchen table.

CHAPTER TWENTY-SEVEN
THE FLICKERING PENDANT

A STRONG WIND BEGAN to blow as Seven walked up the cliffside stairs. The stairs swayed and shook, and Seven clung to the rails. She couldn't stop thinking about the things Figgs had said, about River, about his family abandoning him, about the Frog Ball. Her face went hot and she couldn't help but smile. She knew she was being an absolute goose, and that she shouldn't trust Figgs, but she wanted to so badly and promised herself she wouldn't get too lost in her feelings.

"Seven!" a voice called out, and Seven looked up to find River standing just above her. Her green cloak flapped in the wind, her long silver hair dancing above it and her purple pendant glinting in the sun.

"Hi, River. Just on my way to see the Gran," Seven said, so that River would know she wasn't alone.

River nodded. "I see. Enjoyed the beach?"

She nodded brightly, trying to tap into the thing Thorn did to fool people: be cute.

"I love the beach! I was collecting some of these to make a necklace." She pulled the rest of the blue seashells from her pocket and showed them to River.

River smiled and took a step down. Seven fought the instinct to flinch or step back.

"Who were you going to give it to?" River asked.

"Probably . . . Thorn," Seven said.

River nodded. "She's doing quite well in the contest. Is she here in Crones Cliff Manor?"

"No, she's not here," Seven said. She inadvertently took a step back, almost losing her balance.

River took another step in her direction. "How's everything been going, with your training and all?"

"It's been . . . all right," Seven said.

"Just all right? It's a big deal that you're an Uncle!"

"Well, not quite yet. An Uncle-in-training," Seven said.

"Even so, it's quite an accomplishment." River stepped closer, the sun winking off her pendant as it flickered from purple to green, then back to purple again.

Purple, Seven realized suddenly, and had to keep herself from running as Figgs's words came back to her.

The Moonfalls are a Frog House legacy family. Every Moonfall has been sorted into Frog House for generations, and they're obsessed with balance.

River was famously a Frog House witch, but her coven pendant was shining the bright, glowing purple of House Hyacinth. Something was not right.

"I'm late to meet the Gran," Seven said, trying to squeeze by River and preparing to run for her life.

"You know if you need anything, you can come to me, right? I just want to help, Seven." River smiled widely.

"I know," Seven said.

River reached out to grab her hand, quicker than Seven could react. "Are you sure everything is okay?" she asked. Her eyes seemed sincere, her voice sweet, but Seven felt ill. She was ready to fight if she had to.

"Are you in danger?" she heard the Nightbeast whisper in her mind, and she closed her eyes in relief. She was not alone. Seven was never alone. She opened her eyes and looked up, crows circling above and cawing. On the shore, a bald sea dog waddled to the beach, looking up at them; from the edge of the cliff, a fox looked down.

River noticed as well, and let go. She smoothed her dress. "Have a nice time with the Gran."

But Seven was already running, the animals making a grand commotion as she did, getting the attention of the other witches in the street the moment Seven made it off the stairs. She did not stop running; she ran and ran, getting as far away from the ocean as she could. Because now she was sure that River had not been River at all.

CHAPTER TWENTY-EIGHT
BALANCE

THE MOMENT SHE got home, Seven ran to meet her coven and tell them what she'd discovered at Crones Cliff Manor. It had been storming all day and the raccoons, despite Seven's insistence that they take cover, were crowded beneath Seven's green umbrella on Thorn's stoop.

"I don't think they'll let you in," she told them regretfully.

"It's not a problem. We will take our showers," said Mozzarella Stick, who Seven had learned was Breadstick's twin brother.

"You shower in the rain?"

"It is delightful!" The raccoons began to clap just as the door opened.

"Come on in, Seven." Mr. Laroux gestured inside.

"We will see you tonight!" the raccoons called out as they ran away. Some of them had already begun rubbing their little faces and armpits with their paws (creating suds with soap they'd gotten from Stars knew where), eyes closed as they took their rain shower. Seven shook her head and smiled.

"They're funny." Mr. Laroux winked as they walked inside the house. It always smelled nice at Thorn's place, like expensive perfume and fresh flowers, and it looked like the inside of a fancy magazine for witchy interior design.

"Thorn and Valley are in Thorn's room. I'll be down here if you girls need anything," Mr. Laroux said, and sat down with a loud grunt. The sofa creaked under the tall, muscular witch's weight. It was no surprise Leaf Laroux had been a bear-lifter, one of the best in Boggs Ferry history. With the size of his arms, Seven believed it. She bounded up the steps to the second floor, where she could already hear Valley and Thorn talking loudly about something.

"If Seraphina dies in this book, I will never forgive you," Thorn said.

"I can't control what my mom does!" Valley threw her hands up. "She's her own woman!"

"I don't think Quill would do something like that," Seven said, plopping onto Thorn's bed. "It wouldn't make sense for the story."

"Yeah, but it would make us all cry, and you know how she just *looooves* to do that." Thorn narrowed her eyes at Valley.

"Again, my mom, not me, writes the WOHBC books."

"You're her only daughter! You can convince her," Thorn said.

Seven smirked. When she had first met Thorn, she was much shyer than she was now. But with time, she'd come out of her shell, or maybe it was Valley's influence, but she was different. Still sweet and caring, still Thorn, just with a touch of added Goose House about her.

"Well, what happened in Crones Cliff Manor?" Valley asked, hugging a pillow to her chest.

Seven got up and closed the door but left it open just a crack, as was the rule in Thorn's house. "I couldn't chance portaphoning you. I don't know what kind of weird magic the hexer has anymore."

Valley was sprawled across the bed. Thorn was sitting at her sewing station and working away on her final presentation piece for the games, a glittering cloak. Seven perched on a giant cushion as she recounted what had happened with Figgs. She told them about running into River—or someone who'd looked like River—on the stairs leading to the Spare houses, and about her pendant being purple instead of Frog House green.

"Wait, why would she be wearing someone else's pendant?" Thorn asked. "Witches never do that—it's not allowed, right?"

"Right." Seven nodded. "That's why I think the witch I saw wasn't actually River. Remember what happened in Moth

House too—I saw someone who looked like Graves at the same time that I heard someone who sounded like Graves. Then I saw Wren at the tents when she was actually with the Gran."

"Does that mean River isn't really the hexer?" Thorn asked.

"That's right—I don't think she is. It looks like our serial hexer is also impersonating witches."

"Whoa, you think the hexer has been using some sort of enchantment?" Valley asked.

Seven shook her head no. "An enchantment would need to be, I don't know, otherworldly good to make you look that much like another witch. And imitation magic isn't practiced in the Twelve Towns, you know that. We can alter our looks, but not to look like one another. I think there's something else behind this."

"There's something I haven't been able to stop thinking about since my run-in with River. During the ghost clothing challenge, when you all had to make garments according to the Rule of Mirrors . . ." Seven said.

"Yeah?" Thorn asked.

"What if there's a magical garment that could create the illusion the hexer used to look like other witches?" Seven asked.

"Hmmm, it would need to be very powerful and probably super old. Made before the multi-covens were outlawed, but back then I suppose it would've been possible, yes," Thorn said.

"That's what I was thinking," Seven said, then she held up her phone, to show them the picture that she'd snapped at Frog House. "This is the Hat of Truth," she said.

"Oh my goodness, you don't think . . . there's a mirrored hat! Of course!" Thorn hopped up and ran to her closet.

"Uh, I still don't get it," Valley said.

"When I went to Frog House for the magic duels, a guide said the Hat of Truth could uncover a witch's true self. When I was trying to figure out what magic could allow someone to look like someone else, I remembered the Rule of Mirrors. If there was a hat that *uncovered* the truth, wouldn't there have to be one that hid it?"

Thorn pulled a box down from her neatly organized closet. She opened it up and started going through what looked like old clothing sketches, until finally she found the one she was looking for.

"Look!" Thorn said, holding up a sketch of a hat that looked just like the Hat of Truth except everything was on the opposite side. Like it was a reflection. An actual mirrored image. "This is the Hat of Deceit! I tried researching this ages ago in Intro to Peculiar Costura class, but it was nearly impossible since there is very limited information about it on the witchernet or in our schoolbooks. Anything we knew was all based on rumor. But in that very same class, they told us that the wearer could carry out all sorts of deceptions— including visage."

"That looks just like the hat from this picture, remember?" Seven showed them the picture of the witches holding foxes that she'd seen in the Crones Cliff Manor Museum. She zoomed in to the witch wearing the floppy, crystal-encrusted hat in the background—it looked just like Thorn's sketch.

"Oh my goats," Valley said.

"The Hat of Truth has been passed down within one family," Seven said. "Maybe the Hat of Deceit has been as well. If we can find out who is wearing it in this picture, maybe we can find out who is using it now."

Thorn bit her lip. "I have no idea who that witch is, but I know who might!"

Thorn left the room, and moments later she returned with her mother and Grandma Lilou.

Thorn's mother, Thimble, looked, as always, like she was on a runway. Even in her house clothes. She wore a beautiful flowing dress made of expensive-looking fabric, with tassels down the front and gold embroidery on the sleeves. Her short aquamarine hair was slicked back, and she wore furry slippers that were all the rage in town, thanks to her boutique.

Grandma Lilou was in one of her floral cotton housedresses, and she smiled sweetly at the Witchlings as they said hello.

"What did you want to show us, darling?" Thimble asked.

Thorn handed over Seven's phone with the museum

picture zoomed in. Thimble and Grandma Lilou looked at it, eyes wide.

Grandma Lilou sat on the bed. "That is the Hat of Deceit."

Thimble cocked her head to the side. "A relic that hasn't been seen in many, many years."

"It was forged in the very first Golden Frog Games and used by a few champions to cheat their way to victory," Grandma Lilou said.

"Do you know the name of the witch wearing the hat?" Seven asked.

Grandma Lilou looked closer, squinting. "No, I don't. I'm sorry."

"Thanks, Mrs. Laroux," Seven said.

"Any time . . ." Mrs. Laroux paused on her way out of the room. "You girls aren't getting into any trouble, are you?"

"Us? Never," Valley said with a smirk.

"We're just curious about the history of the games, is all. Since this is the first time any of us has been so involved," Seven said.

Mrs. Laroux raised an eyebrow. "Okay. But I'll have my eyes on you."

Thorn's mother and grandmother left and the Witchlings exchanged knowing looks.

"The hexer is definitely using the hat to disguise themselves as other witches," said Valley.

"And if the hat allows a witch to perform visage, it's even more worrisome," Thorn said, a nervous look on her face.

"Yeah, what is visage? I've never heard of that," Seven said.

"Visage is taking another witch's appearance and making it your own," Thorn explained. "With visage you will embody a witch completely; everything from their face to their voice to their walk will be yours."

"Well, if that's true, how are we supposed to trust anyone?" Seven asked.

"We can't." Thorn looked down. "We can't trust anyone at all."

Just then, something rapped on the window three times, startling the witches. They all turned to look, and a crow with a scroll tied to its little leg stared back at them from the rain.

"Probably for you," Valley said.

Seven carefully opened the window. "Are you okay?"

"Quite all right. The letter is for Thorn," the crow said.

Seven untied it. "Who is it from?" she asked, but the crow flew away, cawing in the night.

"He said it's for you." Seven handed the scroll to Thorn.

Thorn unfurled the small scroll and read, "'Quit before it's too late, or the worst attack is still yet to come.'"

She looked up at Valley and Seven, eyes wide with fear, just as the scroll went up in flames.

"Thorn!" Seven cried, not thinking as she grabbed the

scroll from her friend's hands. The fire went out as soon as she did . . . but Thorn was still on fire.

"Agua!" Valley cried, sending a burst of water over her hands.

Thorn cried out in pain, her hands singed by the flames, as Seven ran to the window and cried out for the animals to find the crow who had come to Thorn's window. Birds exploded from the trees and flew out into the night, and a familiar voice growled in Seven's mind.

"I will find the crow," said the Nightbeast. "And I will make him pay."

19th January 1790

I will confess, I am frightened. It worries me that I do not want them to stop. With every passing day I welcome the monstruo voices. They are like a lullaby to me, and I can only hope that in my death, they will comfort me.

—From the diary of Delphinium Larkspur, the Monstruo Uncle

CHAPTER TWENTY-NINE
TO SUMMON A NIGHTBEAST

THAT NIGHT, the Nightbeast would not let Seven rest.

She turned over in her bed for what felt like the billionth time and smushed her face into her pillows.

"Seven. Meet me in the forest."

"No," Seven said.

"Is the beasty at it again?" Edgar asked from his mushroom tank.

"Sorry, Edgar, I didn't mean to wake you."

"You didn't. I was awake, contemplating flies."

Seven sighed and got up from the bed. *Might as well get Edgar a midnight snack or . . . a witching-hour snack,* she realized, looking at the clock. It was already a whole hour past midnight. She trudged over to her Edgar supplies area to get him his favorite spicy flies. All around her room were articles and books she was using to research visage and anything she could find about the Hat of Truth. There was almost nothing on record about the Hat of Deceit, and she was no closer to finding who could be using it now. Seven scooped out a big helping of flies from a container and walked over to Edgar.

"Here you go," Seven said, putting the flies inside his tank.

"Thanks," Edgar said, and began to eat happily.

Seven smiled, patting her toad's head gently, before a yawn took over. She stretched her arms over her head and waited to hear the Nightbeast again, but all was quiet. Maybe it had finally fallen asleep.

She made her way back to her bed and slid under her covers. They were warm and soft, and just as she began to drift off to sleep, a growl echoed in her mind.

"I would not insist if it were not important."

Seven put the pillow over her face and muffled a scream. *Fine.* She would get up. And she'd just have to pray to the Stars the Nightbeast wasn't luring her to dinner—a dinner where Seven was the meal. She threw on a black cape over her flowery purple sleeping clothes and took a small bite of a shushroom to make sure nobody heard her sneak out.

Her bedroom was technically the attic of their house, so it was high up, but Seven had not been training for hours each morning to let something as small as height defeat her. She expertly slid down the slanted roof beside her window, swinging to the adjacent wall and shimmying down the trellis gingerly. Finally, she jumped the five or so toadstools to the ground, landing in a roll, then looking up to make sure nobody had seen her. Seven smiled and flipped her hood over her head before setting out for town.

"Okay, where are you?" she asked in her mind.

"I do not know how to explain."

"So how am I supposed to find you?" Seven slipped behind Babbette's Bubble Tea Shop.

"Maybe . . . you can call me to you."

Seven rubbed her face. The last thing she wanted to do was summon a Nightbeast into downtown Ravenskill, or anywhere outside its protected area, to be honest. But if it wasn't going to let her sleep, or rest from its incessant pleading, she would have to do it. Besides, what if it really did need her?

Seven stepped out from behind the brick building and quickened her pace down the cobblestone streets of town, keeping an eye out for anyone lurking in the shadows.

"Okay, wait for my signal. I'm finding a good spot."

The Nightbeast grunted in assent and Seven headed in the direction of Oso Mountain. She walked past Birdsall Tavern, where she could see a fire roaring in the large windows. Witches sat around having warm drinks in ceramic cups and eating cheesy toasted breads as they laughed. A four-piece band played a calming amargue instrumental Seven recognized. It was her father's favorite.

She walked on until she reached the Cursed Forest, and

found she was not afraid to enter. The voices of the monstruos exploded in her mind the moment she stepped foot inside. She recalled the passages from Delphinium's diary where she entered the Cursed Forest and ran out, distressed, every time. But Seven would not allow herself to panic. Instead of pushing their voices away like she had before, she would stay calm and actually listen to them.

And so she began to answer them as their terrifying, bloodcurdling voices flooded her mind.

"I will see what I can do about more pine needles for your bath, yes." And, "If you don't bite him, perhaps he'll be more agreeable toward you?" And, "I promise the ghosts mean you no harm, it's just uncomfortable when they pass through you sometimes, but it won't affect you if you don't let it." At last she was on the other side of the path and on a hill near Oso Mountain. Seven was surprised. Monstruos, and their needs, didn't differ all that much from animals. All they wanted was to be listened to.

The moon shone high overhead, and as she looked around, she confirmed this place was shielded enough from the rest of town that she should be able to summon the Nightbeast without being seen. Something rustled in the trees behind her and Seven whipped around, hands up.

"Tell me who you are or I'm going to send a fireball right at your face!" Seven said, when the witch ran out, hands in her open cloak pockets.

"Stop, stop, it's me!" said Valley.

Seven put her hands down and let out a breath of relief before remembering . . . this could be anyone. She put her hands back up, inspecting Valley's pendant: red.

"Tell me something only you know about me," Seven said.

"Wha—ohhhh. I'm not some imposter witch, but fine. I know you kissed Edgar Allan Toad once because you were so relieved he was okay, but before that there was a rumor in school you were a toad kisser and, okay, maybe I helped spread it a bit, but you have to admit it was funny." Valley chuckled and Seven shook her head.

"Okay, okay, it's you." Seven put her hands down. "What are you doing here?"

"I . . . um . . . want to come with you to whatever you're doing." Valley pulled on the collar of her distressed black sweater nervously.

"No way," Seven said.

"Why?"

"It's . . . it's Uncle stuff," Seven lied.

Valley crossed her arms in front of her chest. "I don't believe you."

Seven scoffed. "You don't have to believe me. But you can't come and that's that. Gran's orders."

"The Gran is not here," Valley said smugly.

"Uncle's orders, then." Seven smiled.

Valley took a step forward. "Seven, please?"

"There is nothing you can say to convince me. I won't put you in danger! Even being out here is too far. Please, Valley. Go home."

Valley walked to Seven and grabbed her arm gently. "Seven, I'm begging you."

Seven shook her head in confusion and stepped back. "You're acting weird. Are you sure you're Valley?"

"I know my mom is the secret author of Witches of Heartbreak Cove, and if you really want proof, I'll spoil part of the next book!"

"Nope, nope!" Seven covered her ears.

"So can I come?"

"Still no. And I'm not gonna argue with you anymore," Seven said, turning away and walking toward Oso Mountain. She'd just have to find another hill to summon the Nightbeast on.

"Seven, why won't you just listen to me?" Valley pleaded, following close behind.

"Why are *you* being so pushy about this?"

They kept walking down the hill.

"You're going to see the Nightbeast, aren't you?" Valley asked.

Seven was silent a second too long, unable to get a lie out in time.

"I knew it!"

"All the more reason why you can't come," Seven said.

"Please?" Valley tried again.

But Seven did not stop walking. She would freeze Valley in place if she had to; she refused to put her friend in harm's way.

"I know you're brave and that you're a fighter, but this is the Nightbeast. Remember how big it is? There's no way I'm gonna let you come see it with me. Just go home," Seven said. Then she whispered, "Veloz," and her steps sped up, leaving Valley in her dust.

"I can hear the Nightbeast!" Valley cried out, and Seven stopped cold. She turned around and zoomed back so she was facing her friend.

"What?"

Valley closed her eyes and turned her face up toward the sky, as if she had been waiting awhile to say what she had just said. She looked back down at Seven.

"I hear the Nightbeast almost every day. It calls to me to come help, it pleads. I've tried to find it more than once, but I'm not an Uncle and I can't do what you do, Seven."

"How can you hear it?" Seven asked, shocked.

Valley shrugged. "I'm not sure, but I know it's hurting somehow."

There was no way in hex Valley would know this if she wasn't hearing the Nightbeast, but how?

"It's been torture not being able to do anything. I feel useless, and powerless, and . . ." Valley was crying now, and Seven reached for her hand. Valley held her hand out and kept crying. "Everything is so messed up, and no matter how hard I try, there's nothing I can do to make it better."

This was why Valley wouldn't stop asking about the Nightbeast, why she was willing to risk her friendship with Thorn to help it. Because the Nightbeast had been talking to her too. If Seven had just trusted her friend from the beginning, maybe they wouldn't have had to go through this alone.

"You're not useless," Seven said. "Don't ever say that about yourself again. You are stronger, and cooler, than I could ever be. And . . . you can hear it. Not everyone can, Valley, but you can. That's gotta mean something. It trusted you enough to ask for help."

A shiver ran down Seven's spine—because this put Valley in danger too.

"You haven't told anyone, have you?"

"No way." Valley pulled her hand away from Seven and wiped her eyes. "Do I look like a warlock to you? I was just scared to tell you because I wasn't sure if you could hear it too. But it told me you were here tonight so I figured you could."

"Traitor," Seven said to the Nightbeast. "Can you talk back to it?"

Valley shook her head no. "One-way chats, I'm afraid."

"All right, let's go, then," Seven said, trudging back up the hill.

"Really?"

Seven turned around and held her hand out. "Yeah,

butt-toad. Let's do things together from now on." Seven smiled and Valley smiled back, and in that small pocket of time, everything felt like it would be all right.

"And are you sure this is gonna work?" Valley asked.

"I dunno, but we're about to find out," Seven said.

When they reached the top of the hill, a crisp breeze rustled through their capes as Seven prepared to call the Nightbeast.

"Are you scared?" Seven asked.

"Not when I'm with you," Valley said.

"Okay, here goes nothing."

Seven closed her eyes and called the Nightbeast to her. "I'm here."

She imagined it running through the woods quicker than lightning, she felt her magic pull it toward her, and suddenly the ground around them shook, and when Seven opened her eyes, two enormous ones were staring back at her. Energy coursed through Seven's body. The strength and energy she felt after healing the baby skeleton bird came back, intensified. She had not felt this invigorated or awake in months. She had summoned the Nightbeast and she wasn't scared at all, she was electrified.

"Oh my goats," said Valley.

Let it lead the way, she remembered from her lessons, and she gave the Nightbeast a small nod and a gesture she hoped it understood to mean *"the floor is yours."*

"Seven," the Nightbeast croaked, and let something like a cough out. It looked unwell.

"Are you okay?" Seven asked.

Valley stood frozen at her side, and Seven looked at her with a reassuring gaze.

"I have been sickly for weeks," the Nightbeast said.

"Can you understand it now?" Seven asked Valley.

Valley shook her head no. "I can't. I could only hear it in my mind. Not when it speaks aloud." Valley looked disappointed.

"Do you know why Valley can hear you?" Seven asked the Nightbeast.

"I do not know. I only know that I am drawn to you both, as well as the one with the dark hair."

"Thorn?" Seven asked. She could not imagine and didn't want to think how horrible and afraid Thorn would feel if the Nightbeast spoke to her.

The creature nodded. "I have not spoken to her because . . . I sense she fears me. I did not mean to hurt her mirrored self. The witch forced me." The Nightbeast coughed again. "Through evilness."

"What witch?" Seven asked, wrapping her arms around her body in fear.

The Nightbeast shook its enormous head. "I cannot remember."

Seven translated for Valley and added, "Whoever forced

the Nightbeast to do those things is the witch who taught the Cursed Toads archaic magic in the first place, and could be who the hexer is now."

Valley nodded, and Seven turned back to the Nightbeast. "Do you know how the witch controlled you? Is there anything you can remember?" Seven asked.

The Nightbeast considered. It cocked its head to the side, like a dog might, and Seven felt a pang of affection for it.

With every passing day I welcome the monstruo voices. The passage from Delphinium's diary rang true for the first time, and Seven was glad to have Valley beside her. Her friend, who gave her courage.

The Nightbeast growled. "The Cursed Toads were putrid. Rotting. Especially when they became their true selves. They did not always look like the false Uncles. Sometimes they slipped out of those forms. I believe to rest from the evilness."

"The archaic magic," Seven said, before explaining to Valley.

The Nightbeast nudged Seven with its nose, startling her. "I remember a second thing," it said.

"Go on," Seven said kindly.

"The Cursed Toads said many things in my presence. Mainly nonsense; however, there was one thing that stood out to me. One evening, I overheard them speaking. They said, not all magic comes from nature or the stars."

"What?" Seven said, baffled. The laws of magic stated all their abilities were derived from nature or from the stars. But maybe the Cursed Toads' magic came from elsewhere, somewhere nefarious? Seven thought of her own abilities to speak to monstruos, her connection to the Nightbeast, and wondered if her magic came from another place as well. Was it even possible?

The Nightbeast lay down, the hill shaking as it put its enormous head on the ground. It licked a spot on its belly and groaned. Valley dropped to her knees beside it, as did Seven.

"What's the matter with it?" Valley asked.

"I'm not sure," Seven said. "Is this why you've been insisting on speaking to me? Because you are unwell?" she asked the beast.

It nodded slowly. "I do not trust other witches. If they know I am ill, perhaps they'll end my life. Or just let whatever my disease is take me. I knew you would help heal me if you could."

The Nightbeast was breathing heavily and quickly, its eyes watery and red. It was in pain, that much was clear. Seven set her mouth in a line and stood up. It was her responsibility to care for this creature. Monstruo or not. She pushed up the sleeves of her cloak up and then threw her hands toward the forest. Seven closed her eyes and tried to connect with the grass beneath her feet, with the wind rustling through the breeze, with the voices of her raccoons, chittering at her from afar.

"Hongos!" she yelled, and waited. In just moments, a batch of cura-shrooms came flying from the forest and formed a circle around Seven's hands. She pushed the healing hongos toward the Nightbeast and released her hold. They exploded in a cloud of colors over the Nightbeast's stomach.

The creature's breath became less jagged and it seemed to calm down a bit.

They sat in silence, stroking the beast's fur, when finally the Nightbeast got up and shook the cura-shroom dust off.

"I am better," it said. "I can take you to my home now."

"What?" Seven asked.

"So that you know where to go to see me and help me with that good and wonderful healing Uncle magic. Or to come and bring me meats," the Nightbeast said, and Seven smiled.

It crouched down and gestured with its enormous muzzle for Seven to get on. Seven hesitated. This was the Nightbeast. The legendary beast from the old Twelve Towns tales. The beast that ate children and terrorized witches. And now it was asking her to get on its back. But what had Seven seen of this monstruo? It had killed Petal and attacked her, Thorn, and Valley. But it had been under the control of forbidden magic. Could she really blame it for something it did against its will? Now that it was free from that magic, it could've killed Seven and Valley at any moment. In the area here atop this hill where nobody would see them, it could've ended her life in an instant. And it hadn't. And then there was the pull Seven felt toward the monstruo. As an Uncle, her emotions were intertwined with the animals', and she couldn't help feeling sadness and happiness for them, depending on the moment, but . . . it was different with the Nightbeast. She felt *pulled* to it. Like they were connected somehow, and it had told her it felt the same.

Seven put one hand on the Nightbeast's back and, without a second thought, she jumped.

CHAPTER THIRTY
ENCHANTED GLADE

IT WAS SOFT and warm on the beast's back. Seven rubbed her cheeks against it and smiled. And again, like the day she had passed out in the Cursed Forest, Seven felt strangely power- ful, and she wondered if the Nightbeast had something to do with it.

"Seven! Don't!" Valley cried out.

"It won't hurt me, Valley. I'll be okay," Seven said.

"No! I mean don't go without me!" Valley screamed, her face one of desperation.

"Can Valley come too?" Seven whispered in the Night- beast's ear.

"Yes," the Nightbeast's low voice rumbled.

Seven reached down and, with enormous effort, helped Valley up behind her. With Seven gripping the Nightbeast's fur, the monstruo took off in the direction of the forest.

Ravenskill whipped past Seven and Valley. From up here, they could see the Boggy Crone River, the tops of houses, and the colorful flowers that adorned their town. Birds flew overhead, and Seven could hear their concern.

"Be careful, Seven," they sang.

Her heart swelled with the affection she knew not just the birds but all the animals felt for her. They wanted to keep her safe, just as she wanted to keep them safe. As the wind rushed through her hair and Valley held on to her, Seven realized she could not lose these powers. She needed to stay alive and truly become the Uncle. The birds reminded Seven of the crow that had brought Thorn the burning message. She leaned in close to the Nightbeast.

"Did you ever find the crow?"

The Nightbeast grunted. "I did. But I ate it by accident."

Seven sighed. "Thanks for trying."

Thorn's hand was healed, thanks to some calendula oil Seven had in her rucksack, but a purple scar ran across her hand, and Seven wasn't sure if it would ever go away. The crow had been a good reminder that not all animals were on her side. It would have been helpful to try and question it though, and now they wouldn't get the chance.

They rode on the Nightbeast's back through thickets and glades, through mud and dirt and stone. Seven was overwhelmed with a feeling she couldn't find the right words for. It was a feeling like rain on a hot day, like a clear blue sky and a dip in the cool river, like a hug from her mother, a word of encouragement from her dad. It felt like happiness.

Behind her, Valley sighed, and Seven wondered if she was thinking about all her troubles. "How have you been feeling about the whole thing with your parents?" Seven asked Valley.

"I've been okay," Valley said softly.

"Are you *sure* you've been okay?" Seven asked, looking back.

"She hasn't, Seven dear." Cotton Swab climbed up from Seven's cloak and rested on her shoulder.

"Oh, you brought Cotton Swab?" Seven asked. She wasn't as scared of the rat anymore. In fact, she kinda liked him. A lot.

"Yeah, what did he say?"

"He said you're a big fibber," Seven said.

Cotton Swab ran up and sat on a furry tuft on the Nightbeast's neck, so he was directly in front of Seven.

"Valley dear has been crying a lot more than usual. I am worried about her. Please, will you help her?" Cotton Swab asked.

Seven smiled. "Of course I will. Get back in Valley's cloak. I don't want you getting hurt. It's a long fall down for a little pal like you."

Cotton Swab nodded and scurried back to Valley.

"He's worried about you, Valley. He said you've been

crying a lot!" Seven looked back at Valley and there were, in fact, tears streaming down her face.

"He's worried about me?"

Seven nodded. "Are you crying because of Cotton Swab?"

"I dunno, it's just thinking of Cotton Swab talking to you makes me feel all weird inside. In a good way. Happy. It's just really neat that I know this stuff about him I never knew before, and I *live* with the guy. It's nice to know someone is worried about me."

Seven had never thought of her powers being a source of strong emotion for someone in this way, but it made sense. It probably was quite impactful to know for the first time what a part of your family was thinking. What they sounded like or the nicknames they had for you. There were so many things that Seven had, in this short time, gotten used to knowing that nobody else except other Uncles could know. It was a great privilege, she was beginning to learn. And for the second time that night, she promised herself that if her powers didn't literally get her killed, she would make sure to never forget it.

"I will be okay, I promise," Valley said. "I think I just need some time. And maybe to see Dr. Blackwood again."

"I think that's a toadmendous idea," Seven said, and Valley held on to her even tighter.

"Thanks for being such a good friend to me, Seven. Even when I was being a butt-toad."

Seven smiled, tears welling in her own eyes. "Wait, when have you not been a butt-toad?"

Valley and Seven laughed as the Nightbeast began to slow its pace.

Deep in the Blue Mountain Forest they reached an inconspicuous canopy of trees when the Nightbeast stopped and said, "Here."

Seven held both hands up and tried to channel the magic the other Uncles had sealed this place off with. Her arms trembled with the effort, her stomach turned, and she felt moments when she might pass out, but she was able to open the entrance to the glade and the Nightbeast walked in. The habitat they'd created for it was beautiful and lush, with a small freshwater pond and a stockpile of meat. There was what looked like a bed made from hay and moss, and even the remnants of jelly bean fish, a favorite snack of the Nightbeast.

"This is incredible," Valley said, looking around.

"Are you okay here?" Seven asked the Nightbeast.

"It is comfortable but too small." The Nightbeast crouched to let them off and both of them dismounted. "I cannot run the way I am accustomed to."

Seven remembered reading that Nightbeasts needed large expanses of land to run and roam free. It was their nature, and though this enchanted glade was beautiful and safe, it was still a prison.

"As soon as I can, I will find a way to get you out," Seven said.

"For now . . . I am safest here," the Nightbeast said as it curled into a ball much like a puppy would, and its eyes began to close.

"Ask it what's wrong with it before it falls asleep," Valley said.

Seven did.

"My body hurts, and I cannot sleep. I am not sure why, or what is wrong with me, I only know I am unwell." The Nightbeast yawned. "I must rest now. But do not forget to check on me."

"We won't," said Seven, and both Witchlings stayed beside the Nightbeast until it fell into a deep sleep.

CHAPTER THIRTY-ONE
THE FROG BALL

IT WAS THE NIGHT before the final day of the games, and that meant one thing: the Frog Ball. Ravenskill was buzzing with excitement; even the animals seemed delighted as Seven walked through the fairgrounds encircling House of Stars on her way to the party. Each champion had their own tent, and Thorn would be in hers for a while answering interview questions. Seven looked around for Figgs, not seeing him anywhere. She had felt like a butt-toad about accepting his invitation tonight, but now that River was most likely innocent, which meant Figgs was as well, Seven let herself be excited. The night felt electric, filled with possibility, despite all the bad happening around them. Witches always found a way back to hope, no matter how dire the times.

"If he stands you up, I'm gonna ruin his life," Valley said. She and Graves were walking around with Seven, and although it made her feel kinda like a third wheel, it was nice of them not to leave her on her own.

Everyone at the Frog Ball always made sure to look their best. Valley was in an all-black, sharply cut suit, with pink socks, and a pink handkerchief in her jacket pocket, while Seven wore a glittering blue dress with a cape attached, that used to belong to her mom when she was Seven's age. They had seen Thorn briefly before she disappeared into her tent. She was wearing a puffy yellow dress that made her look like a flower, that she had, of course, designed herself.

"That looks like Figgs over there," Graves said, and sure enough, he was standing at the entrance to House of Stars. Seven turned around, horrified.

"Is my face red? Do I smell? Is my breath bad?"

Valley smirked. "You look fine and you smell like you normally do."

"What does that *mean*?" Seven asked.

"Like, your plants and that vanilla stuff you put in your potions so they taste nice," Valley said.

"All right." Seven took a deep breath. "Don't leave me alone for even one second though."

"Got it," Graves said with a smile. She wore a black dress trimmed in teal beadwork that complemented her hair and looked froggin' cool. Every time Seven saw how happy Valley looked, she was glad all over again that Graves had ended up not being behind the stone hex.

"Seven." Figgs lit up when he saw her. He was wearing a blue velvet suit with glittering blue accents to match Seven's. He wore his signature silver earrings, with one addition—a dangly earring in the shape of a clear opal-hawathoria plant, Seven's favorite. She noticed immediately and it made her heart flutter.

"Hi. You're lucky you're here," Valley said.

"Huh?" Figgs gave her a confused look.

"Don't mind her," Seven said, guiding Figgs away. "Let's go inside."

"Oh, okay," Figgs said.

They entered the ballroom, which was decorated with thousands of flowers and twinkling lights. A gauzy, iridescent silver fabric hung from the ceiling in giant, dramatic swoops, giving the room a cozy, ethereal feeling. Soft, mellow music played as witches talked and ate from the giant table of food, holding everything from salty bacon wrapped around sweet plantains to buttery yucca and fizzy red drinks. A few Goose House witches were scrutinizing absolutely everything, still bitter about losing out to House of Stars in hosting the party. And of course, House of Stars witches took every opportunity they could to gloat, gliding around the ballroom and smiling brightly at every Goose House witch they met. Seven had to admit, House of Stars had done an incredible job with the party. Everything from the food to the decorations was perfect, and House of Stars had every right to be proud of their work. Even if Goose House tried to blow them up for it later.

"Let's dance!" Graves said excitedly to Valley.

"Now?"

Graves rolled her eyes and smiled. "Yes, now! We are at a ball." Graves held one gloved hand out and Valley blushed before taking it and going to the dance floor with Graves.

"We can dance too, if you want?" Figgs said nervously.

"Okay!" Seven grabbed Figgs's hand and they all went to the dance floor as a quick merengue song began to play.

Seven had been training for this moment her whole life.

They began to dance, the normal side-to-side step, hands clasped. Then the music sped up and Figgs, who was a pretty good dancer himself, began spinning Seven. They moved expertly to the music, laughing and sweating as they glided across the dance floor. Their hips swayed back and forth, shoulders rolling smoothly as their heads moved side to side. The dance floor was filled with witches, and soon they began switching dance partners. Figgs spun Seven and she danced with her dad, then Valley, and even the Oracle. Eventually she made her way back to Figgs and they were red and sweating and happy, their hearts thumping along with the beat of the tambora. The twinkling lights of the room spun around them as they danced quicker and quicker, and Seven felt like she was flying. They danced until the song ended, and Seven wished it could go on forever.

"Okay, okay. I need a break," Figgs said, out of breath, both hands on his knees.

Seven laughed and held her hand out. "Want to go sit?" She raised an eyebrow and Figgs straightened up and took Seven's hand as they walked to their table.

They were holding hands.

Seven had never held hands with someone she liked. She looked around for Valley, and she was already at the table with Graves. They were each having one of the elaborate juices with fancy cut-up fruit and whipped cream.

"Do you want one?" Figgs asked Seven, eyes wide.

"One what . . . oh, a drink? Yes, I'm so thirsty and they look great." Seven smiled.

"Be right back." Figgs nearly tripped as he ran to get Seven a fruit juice.

"I was so sure it would be River, but no," Valley was saying.

"You goats talking about the hexer?" Seven asked as she slid into her seat.

Graves nodded. "We're trying to brainstorm who else it could be."

Seven rested her chin on her fist and thought. She was almost positive the hexer was using the Hat of Deceit, but she had no way of proving it or tracing it. She pulled out her porta-phone and stared at the picture from the museum.

Figgs returned with a large maracuya shake for Seven and she quickly filled him in on their hunt.

"So you think that picture has some sort of clue?" he asked Seven, pointing to her portaphone.

"Yeah . . . there's something familiar about it, but I can't figure out what." Seven bit her lip. "Thanks." She smiled at Figgs and took a big, refreshing sip of the creamy fruit drink, putting her portaphone away.

"Getting more snacks," Valley said, and she left with Graves as Seven took in the scene around her.

It seemed *everyone* was at the ball tonight. Jonafren danced dramatically at the center of the dance floor. Leaf Laroux struggled to keep up with his wife's intricate moves. Seven's parents waved at her discreetly as they danced, her mother giving her an amused look when she spotted Figgs. *Mortifying.* Beefy was asleep, lying across a few chairs, a jacket covering his body.

Lotus swept into the ballroom area with a sparkling silver gown. Beside her, River looked stunning in a sleek gown in gradients of green. Crimson trailed them, wearing a shimmering red-and-black suit. Seven realized that everyone she had suspected at one point or another was in this room, and yet she had no leads as to who the hexer was. Who could've used that horrible magic on two witches and a ghost? None of the victims had been healed, and day by day the hex snaked closer to their hearts. She spotted October sitting at a table on the other side of the dance floor looking forlorn. She must be so worried about Tia, Seven thought.

Seven caught her eye and waved her over, but October mouthed, "I'm fine," and stayed where she was.

The Gran walked through the ballroom with a few of the other Town Grans beside her. They were talking to witches and smiling calmly, probably trying to instill the most jittery witches with a sense of calm.

Grandma Lilou waddled over to their table, Beefy holding her hand and yawning beside her.

"Baby Beefy is tired, and those chairs are uncomfortable," Grandma Lilou said to Seven. "We are heading to my house and I will put him to sleep. I told your parents, so don't worry."

"All right. Did you eat? Do you need me to bring you a plate?" Seven asked, but Grandma Lilou waved her away.

"No, no. I will tell Thorn to bring me some on her way home. And some cake," Grandma Lilou said.

"Beefy, cake," Beefy said, rubbing his eyes.

"Of course, I'll save you some too." Seven walked over and kissed her little brother's cheeks. "Do you want help with him? He's really heavy."

"Pfft," Grandma Lilou said. "He is a big boy. He can help me, right, Beefy?"

Beefy nodded, his adorable round cheeks a bright red.

"Okay!" Seven said. "See ya!"

As they walked away, Valley and Graves returned with little bags in hand and sat down, smiling and out of breath.

"What's that?" Figgs asked.

"Party favors," Valley said, before dumping everything out on the table unceremoniously.

"Careful, there might be something fragile in there." Seven shook her head.

"Yeah, yeah." Valley riffled through her gifts and Seven craned her neck to look.

"Oh, it's the pictures from Creeping Phlox Hill," Graves said, looking at a stack of small cards from her own bag.

Valley picked up a picture from the pile of trinkets and sweets, and smiled.

"Look, this one turned out nice." Valley handed the picture to Seven; it was of the three Spares. Thorn in the middle, a smile so big she seemed to light up the whole world around her; Valley right beside her, with one arm over her shoulder and a small smirk on her face; Seven on Thorn's other side, her head tilted as she smiled warmly at the camera. They looked so happy and proud and . . . familiar.

"Wait," Seven said, taking her portaphone from her dress pocket. She pulled up the picture from the museum, put it beside Valley's picture, and looked closely.

"This looks like it might've been taken on Creeping Phlox Hill," Seven said, showing Figgs.

"Hmm, it kind of does, but there are no flowers," Figgs said.

"That's because they're on the other side of the hill. Look." Valley pointed. "If you look closely, there are champion tents in the distance. It was a Golden Frog Games!"

"Of course! We should've realized this sooner!," Seven said. "Thorn's grandmother said that the hat was used in the Golden Frog Games to cheat. The witch wearing the hat might have been a champion, or at the very least someone who was helping a champion win! And if they were, they might have signed their name in the ledger of champions."

"Oh my goats, you're right," Figgs said.

"But how will we know which signature belongs to the hat witch?" Graves asked.

"There are pictures," Thorn said brightly. "When I signed my name, the portrait they took of me on the hill appeared beside it automatically."

"That book might be our last hope," Valley said.

"I know who can help us locate it." Seven gestured over to the punch bowl, where Jonafren was admonishing someone for spilling some red liquid on the white tablecloth.

Seven got up from the table and went over to pretend she was getting a drink. As she filled her cup, she glanced at Jonafren from the corner of her eye. She poured a bit too much punch, nearly causing another spill.

Jonafren let out an exasperated sigh. "Don't pour too much. My *Stars*, can't anyone serve a drink properly in this town?" He grabbed the ladle from Seven's hand and poured her a neat cup of red fizzy drink and put a slice of purple limon on the side of the cup, making it look fancy.

"Thanks." Seven took a sip. "You must be tired doing

double the work for the games without poor Alaric, *and* doing announcer duties."

Jonafren sniffed haughtily. "I can handle it quite well on my own, thank you."

"Oh, I know. I just mean you've been doing an excellent job. All your Enve Lopes looks have been incredible."

"Well, thank you. I worked very hard on them. Sewed them myself." Jonafren winked.

"Has anyone even been helping you? Normally there are lots of Hall of Elders employees working the games." Seven took another sip of her drink and Jonafren seemed to get more worked up.

"You would think they'd provide some assistance for me, but it appears 'poor Alaric,' as you called him, did a lot more work on his own than any of us realized. And he never even complained," Jonafren said softly, before clearing his throat and straightening up. "What with that and this absolute goose of a games season, many of my coworkers have been pulled away to help in other areas."

"That must be challenging," Seven said.

"Hardly," Jonafren said. "Nothing I cannot handle."

"If you ever need help, I'm great at cataloging! I helped my dad organize his magical insurance files one year so I've had lots of practice. There must be hundreds of signatures in the ledger of champions for you to go through, for instance," Seven said, trying to keep the nerves out of her voice.

Jonafren waved her away. "That is the least of my worries. The book takes care of itself. Once all the champions sign it, I just take it back to the Hall of Elders, lock it up, and leave it be till the next games."

Flingo.

"Do people ever ask to see it?" Seven asked, pushing her luck.

"Sometimes, but it is customary to only take the book out during the games every four years. So that really is the only time people are allowed to look through it. It is a very delicate and important book. Did you know it was forged—"

Seven downed the rest of her red fizzy drink and smiled. "Thanks for the chat, Jonafren. See ya."

Jonafren deflated a bit. "Yes, see you."

Seven ran back to her table. "Okay, who wants to break into the Hall of Elders with me?"

CHAPTER THIRTY-TWO
THE LEDGER OF CHAMPIONS

DOWNTOWN RAVENSKILL was a ghost town. With everyone at the ball, the streets were eerily quiet except for the faint music in the distance. Lights from the ball twinkled like glittering stars in the night sky as Seven, Valley, Graves, and Figgs crept up to the Hall of Elders.

"How can we get in?" Figgs asked.

"Leave that to Seven. She's practically a picklock," Valley said.

"I can't break in here as easily as I do at school," Seven said, running her hands along the door. She turned back to the others. "There are valuable things in the Hall of Elders. This door is heavily fortified with protection magic, and I won't be able to use my normal lock-breaking spell."

"Does sound like you do know an awful lot about breaking into places." Graves quirked an eyebrow.

Seven laughed nervously. "A little."

"So what are we gonna do?" Valley asked.

"It's too bad I don't have my rucksack, because I have some pretty corrosive magical plant sap in there, but I will have to make do. Valley, once I break in, I need you to disarm the alarm with the acallar spell, pointed right . . ." Seven searched for the metal bell where she knew the alarm spell was kept, then pointed. ". . . there."

Valley pushed up the sleeves of her jacket. "Got it."

"I think the most important thing is that we do this quietly and leave no damage—" Figgs began.

"There's no use in trying to get her to do things calmly," Valley tried.

"I'll have to break the door," Seven said decidedly.

"See?" Valley said, and Graves laughed.

"Here goes nothing." Seven raised her hands.

"Seven, don't!" Figgs said.

"Quebrar!" Seven threw her hands toward the door as Valley silenced the alarm so quickly it barely beeped.

The door snapped open, one half crumbling to rubble on the ground as the other stayed up somehow.

"How can she—?" Graves asked, bewildered. "That's a level-six spell!" Some twelfth-year students couldn't even do level-six spells, let alone a Spare.

Seven dusted her hands off and smiled. *Simple.*

"Come on," Valley said as she helped Seven over the

rubble of the door. "Jonafren is gonna *kill* us," she said.

They split up to look for the ledger in various areas of the enormous hall, but Seven had a feeling the book would not be far from Jonafren's desk. She riffled through the carefully organized files and books and moved boxes aside, until finally she found it. The ledger of champions.

"You goats, I found it!" Seven said, her voice echoing through the hall. Footsteps ran in her direction, and they all gathered above the heavy-looking book.

Up close, it was more ornate than Seven imagined, the cover made of what looked like pure gold, etched with leaves and flourishes. The paper was thick and soft, almost fabric-like. She was careful as she turned the pages, going through the dozens and dozens of champion signatures, from ten, twenty, thirty years past until they reached the year they were looking for, the year on the picture: 1790. They went through the hundreds of champion names there.

They cross-referenced the museum photo against each champion entry, and finally they found her, wearing the Hat of Deceit. The same witch from the picture.

"This must be her," said Seven. "It says her name was Fortuna Crypt."

"Wait, what?" Figgs cried in alarm.

"Fortuna Crypt," said Seven. "Do you know her?"

"Yes," Figgs said wearily. "I know her well. Fortuna is Lotus Evenstar's great-great-grandmother."

CHAPTER THIRTY-THREE
ARCHAIC MAGIC

LOTUS. SHE HAD BEEN THERE, under their noses the entire time, but Seven had never even considered her as a suspect. Her words from Creeping Phlox Hill came back to Seven then: *"The best way to make them eat their words is to win no matter what."* She had even mentioned her great-great-grandmother Fortuna! But they'd had no way of knowing she was the cheating witch from the 1790s Golden Frog Games, and that now her great-great-granddaughter was doing the very same thing.

As Seven and her friends ran back from the Hall of Elders to warn Thorn and tell the Gran, smoke began to rise from the Golden Frog Games fairgrounds surrounding the House of Stars. And then she saw what she had been dreading—crackling purple magic. Although she was too far away to actually feel the heat of the purple flames, something about it made her feel like she was running a dangerous fever. Sweat began to drip from her forehead, her mouth was dry, and her throat was scratchy. Yet she couldn't look away.

In fact, they were *all* frozen in place, as if the fire had somehow hypnotized them. The moment felt unreal, like a nightmare. This couldn't be happening. Not when all their families, all their friends, were there.

"Uncle Seven." A voice broke through the haze. "Uncle!" it said again, and Seven took a desperate breath of air, as if she had been underwater for a long time.

"Uncle Seven, there is a fire." It was the raccoons, and they were trying to snap the witches out of whatever spell they were under.

"Come on," Seven yelled to her friends, now fully awake and desperate to get to the fairgrounds. "Valley! Figgs, Graves, let's go!"

Soon they were running at full speed, the raccoons by their side, right toward the fire. The entire way, Seven saw the faces of her mom, her dad, Miss Dewey, Poppy, and Thorn in her mind. She knew that they would be the first ones out of the party and trying to help put out the flames. That they wouldn't care for their own safety as much as others'. They were probably looking for her, she realized, her chest constricting with an awful, piercing pain. They had to be okay, they just had to be, or Seven would burn the entire town down herself.

They saw Valley's mother first. Quill was covered in soot, the bottom of her dress singeing as she ran toward them.

"Valley!" She dropped to her knees and hugged her daughter. "Are you okay? Oh my Stars, Valley." Quill was crying now and Valley was desperately trying to tell her she was fine.

"I have to go find my family, and Thorn," Seven said.

"I'm coming with you," Valley said.

"No!" Valley's mother held on to her.

"Mom, it's my coven. I can't let Thorn die, and this fire—whoever did this is probably after her!"

Quill was shaking, but she nodded and took Valley's hand. "Then I'm going too."

And then they ran straight into the mouth of chaos. Witches were screaming, calling out for family members, coughing and escaping, or trying without any success to put the fire out using various spells. Seven ran straight to Thorn and Gunnar's tent, nearly catching fire herself a few times and blasting it back with a wind spell. Finally they reached the champion tents, and Seven's heart fell. The world around her spun and spun like a top and she had to lean against Figgs not to fall over. Thorn's champion tent was fully engulfed in flames. All the champion tents were. And there were piercing screams coming from inside. House of Stars witches were working hard to keep the fire from the actual party, where hundreds of witches looked out, trapped. But Seven knew it was only a matter of time before it got them too. In just moments, if something wasn't done, the flames would level everything.

Through the small window in Thorn's closed tent flap, Seven could see someone's face inside: Gunnar! He was red and crying, screaming, his hands out, probably trying desperately to quell the flames around him. If something wasn't done, they would consume him, and if Thorn was in there with him, she would die too.

"Oh, oh, Thorn! Gunnar!" Valley screamed and tried to run to the tent, but her mother held her back.

"I can't let Thorn die!" Seven said, and she took off toward the tent, her raccoons by her side.

"Extinguir," Seven tried, her hands up against the fire so close that they blistered from the heat, but it was no use.

"We will help, Uncle," the raccoons said, before Seven could stop them, Cheese led them straight into the flames.

"NO!" A scream ripped through Seven. In just an instant all ten raccoons had leapt into the fire, and Seven couldn't breathe. The scorching air smothered her, and she was suddenly frozen in place again, staring at the fire. And something was telling her to walk right into it herself. Why did it have a hold on her like this? What kind of hex *was* this? Seven clenched her fists and set her jaw. She would not let this happen. Not without a fight.

A hand landed on her shoulder. Valley. "I'm here," she said. "Tell me what we have to do."

"Just don't go," Seven said softly. "Don't leave me alone."

"I never will," Valley said.

A chittering noise drifted back toward her and Seven saw the faces of her raccoons from within the flames. They were unharmed.

"We will help. We won't let the flames get the witch," they cried out, and suddenly Seven understood. This fire was hexed. It was cursed fire so it could not hurt the raccoons, who were half animal, half *monstruo*. She knew now what she had to do.

Seven closed her eyes and raised her hands. This was the only thing she could think of, her only shot at saving her friends and her town.

"Come," she called to the skeleton birds in her mind. "I need you."

Wind picked up, whipping Seven's hair around her face and making it almost impossible to see. But then, through the haze of the purple flame, the flapping of the skeleton birds click-clacked through the sky toward Seven.

"The tent. Pick them up and get them out of the fire."

The skeleton birds changed course and made a sharp U-turn up into the air and back down, surrounding the various tents and, with their beaks, picking them up and out of the fire.

"Please, bring water from the Cursed Forest," Seven called out to any animal, any monstruo from the Cursed Forest that would listen. "Help us put the fire out, please. Before it's too late."

The earth around them shook, and Valley looked at Seven, bewildered. "What's happening?" she asked.

"Just a bit longer," Seven said, pulling every bit of magic from the woods surrounding them as she could. She didn't care if she exploded, so long as this worked.

And then Seven dropped to her knees from the exertion and Valley picked her up and dragged her out of the path of the fire, which was getting closer every moment. In the next instant, all manner of flying beast erupted from the Cursed Forest. Enormous wings of beasts that never let themselves be seen flapped above them, and mercifully, streams of water fell from their mouths. They poured water over the flying tents first, then swooped down and showered the fairgrounds with Cursed Forest water. They were putting the fire out bit by bit, as Seven used a wind spell to push it all in the direction of the Cursed Forest, which would not burn, and where the fire could not hurt any creature within.

"Come on," Seven said, forging a path toward the place where her skeleton birds had taken Thorn and Gunnar's tent.

There were still small fires around them, though slowly, the monstruos were helping to put them out, with the help of witches who had caught on and were now using magic to bring streams of water from the Cursed Forest.

"Thorn!" Seven cried out when she reached the tent, but she wasn't there.

The raccoons had ripped through the tent entrance and were just now getting up from Gunnar's body. They had shielded him with their own small furry forms, and Gunnar was alive, but not unharmed. There were burns on his body, and he was passed out.

"Healers! Please!" screamed Valley as Seven pulled a batch of cura-shrooms and soothed the burns all over Gunnar's body. Immediately, his jagged breathing normalized, but he still did not wake.

Seven was trembling. "Where is Thorn?" she asked the raccoons.

"She was not inside, Uncle Seven," said Sopa.

"We checked thoroughly," said Puddin.

"Seven!" Figgs's voice called out. He ran up to them, panting, Graves by his side.

"Thorn is . . . Thorn is . . ." Figgs tried.

"What, what?!" Valley asked.

Graves looked distraught. "She went home before the fires began. To bring Grandma Lilou and Beefy cake. What if the hexer followed her?"

As the healers arrived to carry Gunnar away, Seven realized she knew how to find the hexer. She pulled the twenty-sided crystal from her cape and located Lotus Evenstar.

CHAPTER THIRTY-FOUR
RIVER MOONFALL

THE CLOUDS HUNG low over the moonlit water as Seven, Valley, Graves, and Figgs ran along the Boggy Crone River. The crystal showed them Lotus was on the shore, close to the train station and on the way to Thorn's house. A figure appeared, and Valley pulled Seven's arm.

"Get down," Valley whispered; they all crouched behind the nearby shrubbery.

"Who is it?" whispered Seven.

"Hold on." Valley held one hand up and peeked over the hedge, her dagger already in her other hand.

"I can't tell, it's too dark."

"I know you're back there, and I know what you did. I know everything!" they heard someone call out.

"I think it's River," Seven said.

Figgs took a look, then hid again. "It is her, but I can't see who she's talking to."

"I know you sent Figgs to spy on them, he told me everything. I *thought* you had taken my robe, but when I saw you set the fire, I knew for sure. I saw you with my own eyes, so don't try to deny it!" River said, and then she screamed.

The hiding witches ran out and found River splayed on the ground. There was no one else in sight.

"River!" Figgs said, kneeling down on the ground beside her.

She had been hit with some sort of flame spell, her dress was scorched right at her stomach. But she was alive, just hurt.

"Aliviar," Seven said, running her hands above River's body, and a bright light emitted from her palms, warming the air between her and the older witch. River's eyes fluttered but did not open.

Moments later, Thorn emerged, running from the direction of her house. She was out of breath. Seven and Valley threw themselves on her, hugging their friend in relief.

"Thorn! Are you all right?" Valley asked as they pulled away.

"Yeah, I was just on my way back to the ball. What happened to River?!"

"Someone attacked her," Graves said.

"Oh my goats. Should we spread out and look for them?" Thorn asked.

"No, it's too dangerous. It's probably the hexer—there was a fire—we have a better chance if we stick together," said Valley.

"River, please, wake up," Seven said, tapping her cheek softly. "Valley, call our parents and let them know Beefy and Grandma Lilou might be in trouble. We need to send someone over to Thorn's."

"On it," Valley said, taking her portaphone from her pants pocket.

"What should we do?" Thorn asked.

Seven considered. She didn't want to leave River here, and she didn't think it was safe for them to split up, but she was worried about Grandma Lilou and Beefy.

"Thorn, why don't you, Valley, and Graves go to your house and make sure everything's okay, at least till our parents get there, then you can come back here. Figgs, you can stay with me just in case."

"All right," Valley said.

River began to cough then, blood dripping from her mouth.

Thorn covered her mouth with her hands in horror as River's eyes fluttered open and then went wide.

"No," River said, shaking her head. "Get away from us!" She was pointing up at someone, and when Seven followed her gaze, it went right to Thorn.

Thorn brought her hand away from her face slowly, baring her teeth as a slow, deep laugh came from her lips. She threw her head back, the light of the moon shining on her, as she cackled loudly and then fixed her glare on River.

"You should've stayed *asleep*, witch!" she shrieked, her hands up. But before she could attack, Valley slashed a cut in her hand with her blade.

"AH!" Thorn cried out, bringing her hand to her mouth as River scrambled to her feet and the other witches scrambled away from Thorn.

What was this? What was happening? Seven was disoriented, until she noticed Thorn's pendant flickering from red to purple.

"It's not our Thorn!" Valley cried, just as the Thorn imposter hurled a hex at Valley.

"Veneno!" she screamed.

"Desviar!" Seven rerouted the spell. The spell changed course and crashed into the Boggy Crone River, sizzling and letting out a putrid, dead-thing smell on impact.

River staggered to her feet, and Figgs, Graves, Valley, and Seven all stood up against the witch in front of them.

"We won't let you get away," Figgs said.

"Watch me, *Spare*." The witch with Thorn's face spat the word *Spare* out as if it were rotten, and attacked again.

"Incendio!" she screamed.

Instead of a singular stream of fire, an enormous blaze roared toward them all at the same time. They shuffled back, and River easily put the fire out with a flick of her hand, her other hand holding her injured stomach. It helped to have an older witch on their side.

"Give it up," River said. "You're caught and outnumbered."

"This *is* hardly fair," said the witch, making an undulating motion with her hands before pulling at the magic surrounding her. When she was finished, the illusion had fallen away and it was Lotus Evenstar, wearing the Hat of Deceit. "Five against one? I expected more of a challenge!"

"Don't worry," Seven said as they got into formation. "I can handle you myself."

Seven pulled the magic from the wind around her and sent a powerful cyclone of air right at Lotus's chest. It took the older witch by surprise, as her eyes bulged from her head and she fell flat on her back. But in a moment, she was up again, smirking.

"I forget you are more powerful than you're meant to be. Don't worry, that will change soon." Lotus waved her hands in Valley's direction. "Seven is your enemy. Kill her or she will kill you."

Lotus stumbled slightly. Then something snatched Seven by the cape of her dress, and she was suddenly on her back. Valley was above her, her twin daggers at her neck.

"Valley, stop!" Thorn—the real Thorn—cried out as she appeared, running toward them and covered in soot.

Lotus began to throw spells at them, but River, Graves, and Figgs held her off.

"Detener!" Thorn shot at Valley and she flipped back, her wrists pinned to the ground.

"You focus on Valley, I will handle Lotus," Seven said.

"Don't let me go," screamed Valley, her legs kicking wildly. Her mind was corrupted by the archaic magic, but not completely.

Lotus shot a freezing spell at Thorn and she was trapped in place next to Valley.

"I'll save the best for last, after I kill the future Uncle," Lotus shrieked, her powder-blue hair blowing in the wind.

Seven shot a stream of fire at Lotus, but she quickly shifted out of the way, shooting back at Seven and hitting her shoulder with an acid hex. A guttural scream came from Seven as she was thrown back by the spell and lay incapacitated on the ground. Figgs and Graves attacked Lotus then, but she flicked Figgs aside like a bug. He crashed hard against a tree and lost consciousness immediately.

"Figgs." Seven tried to call his name, but only a whimper came from her. The hex was burning her shoulder and spreading to her neck. It was a pain like Seven had never felt before.

Graves ran at Lotus, her hands up, her skeleton rings gleaming in the moonlight.

"Sombraaaaaaa, sombraaaaaa," she sang, her voice echoing as she pulled the shadows from every corner. The shadows descended on Lotus, biting at her skin and pushing her back.

Graves picked the shadows up, one by one, and shot them

at Lotus like poison darts. Lotus was hit once, twice, three times, stumbling back as Graves gave her everything she had. But Seven knew she would not be able to beat her alone. River, still badly hurt, ran to Graves's side and began shooting paliza spells at Lotus in between the shadow magic.

Seven gathered what little strength she had and did the only thing she could think of. "Hongos," she croaked. At first nothing happened, but after a few seconds of waiting, the colorful mushrooms came hurtling at her from the woods and exploded over Seven. She rubbed the chalk-like curative on her shoulder and took a deep breath of relief. Soon she was up and fighting beside River and Graves. Lotus sent Graves flying through the air, landing with a sickening crack on the ground.

Lotus sneered, secured the hat on her head. "I should've done this from the beginning."

She shot the purple archaic magic at Seven, who tumbled backward, the wind knocked out of her. Seven coughed up blood, her body weak as she struggled to stand. River held her hands up, screaming as she tried to hold Lotus back. Blood began to drip from River's nose, and her knees buckled beneath her. River fell to the ground, unconscious. Quicker than lightning, Lotus moved both hands in unison, a burst of the purple archaic light picking River up off the ground.

"Viento!" Seven yelled, throwing Lotus off-balance and sending her tumbling backward. Seven saw her opportunity and unfroze Thorn. Her friend ran to her side immediately, hands up and ready.

"Do you still want to kill me?!" Seven yelled at Valley.

"No!" Valley screamed. "Let me at her!"

Seven waved her hands at Valley's restraints and she ran straight at Lotus with her blades. Lotus was just getting to her feet as Valley struck her once on the left, then on the right.

"Ahhh!" Lotus screamed, falling to one knee but recovering quicker than should have been possible. She moved like the wind and landed a powerful blow on Valley in the form of a lightning bolt. Valley shuffled back, and it gave Lotus just enough time to turn her wrath on River, who was running toward her, ready to attack. With both hands up in the air, Lotus shot out toward River, picking her up and then releasing her into the choppy waters of the Boggy Crone River.

"No, no!" Seven ran toward the water. If she didn't help her, River would drown. *River.* No, her name prophecy couldn't be this!

Lotus laughed cruelly.

Thorn tried to pull River from the water, but she could not. The water was too turbulent, and every attempt at a spell to get her out failed. The waves were pulling Thorn in, threatening to drown her too.

"Get back, Thorn, it's too dangerous!"

"River!" Thorn cried.

Seven shot her hands out toward the water, trying to call

on the fish and any other creature who could help her, when Lotus screamed behind her.

"Lápida sepulcral!" Lotus threw the spell in Seven's direction. At her back, like a coward. Seven did not have time to turn or even to be afraid. She was going to be stonified. As quickly as she could, Seven crouched down and sent a silent wish into the air that her friends would make it out okay, and braced herself for impact.

But the hit never came.

Seven stood up slowly and spun around to find Valley . . . her friend. One of her very best friends, with her skin the color of ash. Valley Pepperhorn had been turned into stone.

"No!" Thorn screamed in agony. "Nooooo, Valley, Valley!" Thorn was sobbing.

"Valley?" Seven's voice caught in her throat.

Valley's face was frozen not in shock, but determination. She had put herself between Seven and the stone hex. Tears spilled down Seven's face, and a rage that had been building for weeks, no, for months, now bubbled over like a potion in a cauldron. Every color bled from the night, so Seven could only see one, the same as the brilliant gem around her neck: red.

The screams of her friends brought the world back into focus, and Seven ran straight at Lotus. Figgs and Graves had both been knocked out, and it was only Thorn and Seven against the Hyacinth witch. But not for long. Seven closed her eyes and called on the animals surrounding them. She could feel their heartbeats, their worry for her, their anger. She could feel their desire, their willingness to fight, but they would not do so without her orders, and now she had given them the go-ahead.

Her raccoons appeared then, claws up and hissing, and from the forest the sounds of animals running in their direction filled the air. Birds circled overhead, and a bear, an actual wild bear, stood up behind Seven and her friends. They would not be alone. They had the power of nature on their side.

"Paliza!" Thorn cried, and Lotus blocked her spell, but she could not block Seven. Not right now.

"You hexed Valley!" Seven screamed. Her rage poured into the animals and they dove at Lotus. The bear swatted at her with its enormous paws, the raccoons slashed and bit, but even with all their help, she would not go down.

"I am not one of those Cursed Toads," Lotus said cruelly. "I am smarter and more powerful than they were. You and your little animals can't beat me."

Seven's breathing was ragged, she was covered in sweat and soot from the fire, and there was a pain in her heart unlike anything she'd ever felt before. Deep, desperate sobs were trapped inside her, and she knew that if she survived, they would erupt and take over her body. Seven looked at Thorn, whose eyes told her she was in just as much pain as she was, but that right now, they had to fight. Right now, the only thing they needed to do was end Lotus Evenstar for good.

"La muerte!" Lotus bellowed, using one of the most defiled ancient killing spells.

But Seven stood by Thorn's side and they thrust their hands up, blocking Lotus's onslaught of killing spells.

"Go back," Seven told her animals. They had done enough, and she did not want them to get hurt because of her. But they would not move. They continued to circle Lotus, throwing her off-balance and buying the Witchlings time to block and strike back.

"She's too strong," said Thorn desperately.

"We can tire her out. Don't give up," Seven said, but her hands were trembling with exhaustion. If she passed out again, Thorn would be on her own and Lotus would get what she had been looking for all along. To kill her. And with the Hat of Deceit she'd be able to throw the blame on anyone else, and still get her pointless victory.

"All this for a trophy!" Seven screamed. "Why don't you quit now and stay alive while you still can?"

"You *fool*! You think all I want is a trophy? The winner of the games gets much more than that. Use your head! I thought *you* were supposed to be the smart one!" Lotus said.

What else did champions get besides . . . the Golden Frog? thought Seven. But could gaining knowledge of the future really be that important? Not unless . . . there was something she didn't want Thorn to see. Seven's legs wobbled beneath her. The hex on her shoulder was spreading, and she wouldn't last much longer.

"I want to touch the Golden Frog. You of all witches should know how powerful knowledge is, secrets! If little Thorn had not been so good at costura, none of this needed to happen. River, Crimson, and I would've won, as we were meant to, and the vision would've belonged to us. But you just had to defy expectations, didn't you?" Lotus spat. "I tried to scare you off, to get you to quit," she yelled at Thorn. "But you refused!"

Thorn shook her head. "It's not my fault, I didn't know. I was just competing like everyone else!"

"It doesn't matter now. I *will* complete my mission, at any cost!" Lotus waved her hands over her head, gathering wind from around her to shoot a spell at them, but Seven was faster.

"Volcán!" Seven threw a steady stream of fire at Lotus, her hands up to maintain the flames as she spoke to Thorn. "Thorn, I'm gonna do something. Don't be scared, and trust me, okay?"

"Okay," Thorn said.

Seven opened her mouth, turning her face toward the full moon, and howled like a wolf, like the Monstruo Uncle that she was becoming, and called for the Nightbeast.

CHAPTER THIRTY-FIVE
MONSTRUO UNCLE

A ROAR LOUD enough to wake the Twelve Towns echoed through the night, and even Lotus stopped her attacks to marvel at the Nightbeast. It seemed bigger than the last time Seven had seen it—maybe it had finally begun eating more—maybe it was healthy enough to fight. Something else had happened the moment Seven called to the Nightbeast: The world became clearer; her energy spiked. Somehow, every time she had summoned the Nightbeast, every time she spoke to monstruos, her powers had opened up more and more, and perhaps if Seven gave in fully to what she could do, if she accepted her ability to speak to monstruos, she could get a handle on her Uncle magic.

"Seven." The Nightbeast nodded.

Thorn took a step back, a look of terror overtaking her face.

"We don't want to kill her, just stop her," Seven said.

"I will help you," the Nightbeast said, and turned on Lotus, baring its enormous teeth. "Because I do not care for her."

"Back!" Lotus screamed, scrambling to get away from the Nightbeast. "Terrestre!" The ground shifted and moved around them, blocking the enormous creature and creating a barrier of rock all around Lotus.

A groggy Figgs ran over to them, rubbing his head. "What's going on?"

"Figgs, go get help. Go for the Gran, tell her to come. Quick!"

"On it!" Figgs limped toward House of Stars, looking back in worry as he did. Seven met his gaze and gave a small smile. She hadn't even gotten to slow dance with him. But if she survived tonight, she would. And maybe she'd even hug him.

The Nightbeast growled and Seven turned back around.

"She is emerging from the rocks," it said.

"Okay, ready?"

"Ready," said Thorn, her small gloved hands making fists, her tearstained face determined.

"Let's go. For Valley," said Seven, and together she, Thorn, and the Nightbeast began to attack.

Lotus was a formidable opponent, holding her own against Seven's high-level fire spells and Thorn's wind spells, and holding back the enormous creature on her tail.

"Just a bit more," Seven said.

Lotus turned around, rage in her eyes, and struck out.

"Machete!" She slashed across the sky. The hefty spell

threw Seven and Thorn back, slashing the Nightbeast's face.

It roared loudly, and the ground shook as it took off in Lotus's direction. She could not hide her fear of the animal. With wide eyes she screamed, scrambling away from it. She looked like what she was, still a teenager. Someone young enough to go to Seven's school. Maybe it didn't have to be this way. Maybe, if they could convince Lotus to help them, she would know how to heal Valley and the rest of her victims. Maybe she could tell them who had been behind it all. The witch who'd taught the Cursed Toads archaic magic, and now her. The true villain of the Twelve Towns.

"Lotus, if you would just tell us why." Seven got to her feet and stood behind the Nightbeast as Lotus held up a wall of light for protection.

"We just want to know who taught you archaic magic. Why did you hurt the champions? If you tell me, I'll call off the Nightbeast."

Lotus looked into Seven's eyes. She was shaking. "I learned the art from my grandmother, who learned it from her mother. I do not know who taught her and that is the truth."

"But why did you hurt the champions?" Thorn asked.

"I was after you, of course. Because I did not want you to touch the Golden Frog."

Seven and Thorn exchanged looks. Lotus was trying hard to sound confident, but Seven could tell that she was afraid, and it was almost like her words weren't her own. There was no malice there, only fear.

"Why?" Thorn asked.

"I don't . . ." Lotus shook her head.

"Who are you working with?" Seven asked. "We know you didn't cast the hexes at the matches, you couldn't have— you were onstage—"

"I do not need to explain myself to you!" Lotus screamed.

"We can talk to the Gran and make sure you're not thrown in the Tombs. If this wasn't your doing, if someone made you do these things, we can help you," Seven tried. She remembered that Lotus's family had lost everything, that she was the laughingstock of her town. Seven knew how much that hurt. She knew how being hurt and letting it fester could drive you to do terrible, inexcusable things.

Lotus shook her head over and over. She looked so desperate and lost.

"Lotus," Thorn said softly. "We don't want anything bad to happen to you, but you have to help us heal those witches you hurt. You have a good heart. I know it."

Lotus looked up, her eyes filled with tears. For a moment, Seven thought she might agree and walk calmly with them to find the Gran, that Valley would be healed that very night.

"I won't believe a thing you say. There are things that you do not deserve to know. The Golden Frog is a gift only for the deserving, only for those who know what to do with the gifts it grants. You are *Spares* . . ." Lotus's voice shook with rage. "Disgusting, lowly Spares. That knowledge should only go to witches like my family. Who've earned it! You are beneath me, and I will carry out my mission like the others before me. I will make sure that you do not forget your place!" She screamed and threw her hands back up. "La muerte!" she bellowed, and sent a killing spell right at them.

Seven and Thorn did not have time to react, when the Nightbeast jumped toward Lotus.

"NO!" Seven screamed as the spell careened toward the Nightbeast, but it pushed Lotus up into the air with its enormous snout and the spell shot into the sky, harming no one. Lotus landed on the ground with an awful, cracking thud.

Seven and Thorn ran over to her, and though there was blood around her, she was alive. Seven fell over then, the adrenaline that had been keeping her going depleted as she realized that they had stopped Lotus, but they had lost so much more. They had lost Valley.

The Witchlings returned to the place where River had drowned and pulled her out. She was frigid and blue, but she looked peaceful, as if she were sleeping. She was gone, Seven knew. Her hair fanned around her, spotted with tiny pink flowers. *Lotus* flowers. Two name prophecies had been revealed that night, both intertwined with tragedy.

CHAPTER THIRTY-SIX
THE FINAL COSTURA TRIAL

THE VERY LAST thing Thorn Laroux wanted was to go onstage.

"I don't care about this anymore. I only care about healing Valley," she whispered to Seven.

They were standing in the wings of the Spegg, waiting for Thorn's turn to present her cloak. It should have been a happy moment: the youngest champion, and a Spare no less, reaching the final round of the costura trials with two other teams. Instead, all Thorn and Seven could talk about was Valley and the battle from last night. And the mood was anything but celebratory. The crowd was subdued, an unease in the air. Despite that, there were almost no empty seats, with everyone wanting to witness a Spare in the final trial. A Spare who had defeated the hexer, no less. There had been protests from some residents to stop the final day of the games, but they went on all the same. Just like everything always went on, because the wealthiest witches demanded it. They did not care about grief, or fear, or weariness. Their only care was for coins.

Crones Cliff Manor had been eliminated, of course, so Thorn was up against Crow Spring, and Irvingstar. The two teams presented their cloaks. One the color of frothy hot chocolate that hid an infinite number of items, which got good but not great scores when a grandfather clock fell out of it. And the other, a stunning ivory cloak that controlled the weather around the wearer—blocking rain, melting snow, and providing cool gusts of air in the heat. It was the sure favorite to win unless Thorn could really stun the judges.

"What does your cloak do?" Seven asked.

Thorn perked up just a bit, giving Seven a small smile. "You'll see."

Seven looked closely at her friend. Thorn had worked *so* hard for this; this was her dream. Gunnar was still badly injured and unable to participate, so Thorn had to do this on her own. Maybe it wasn't happening at the best time, but Seven had learned that there was no way to know what twists life would throw your way and when. They would do everything they could to help Valley, Seven was sure of that, but right now they had to keep on living. Besides, if Thorn won, if she did get to touch the Golden Frog, perhaps it held the cure to the hex. It's what Seven and Thorn were hoping for, even if it was far-fetched.

"I can't wait to see it," Seven said, returning Thorn's smile.

"It must be hard to compete when everything is so awful, but what would Valley tell you right now?"

Thorn looked down, her eyes filled with tears, and then she raised her chin up, like Valley had taught her to do. "She'd say don't let those butt-toads win."

Seven let out a laugh, and tears streamed down her face. "So don't. Don't let them win, Thorn. This is *your* moment. Your time. Don't let them steal it from you." Seven put her hands on Thorn's face, trying to pour every ounce of strength, of bravery, of love she had into her friend.

Thorn nodded, her eyes red and brimming with tears, and then her name was called.

Finally, it was Thorn's turn.

Seven watched her friend walk out to the middle of the Spegg alone. There was heightened security everywhere, even though Lotus was in the Gran's custody. But Seven knew that though the threat had been quelled, it was temporary. Someone had taught the Evenstar family archaic magic, someone had helped Lotus hex Mayhem, and Alaric and Tia. And Valley. And that someone was still out there.

Thorn pulled her cloak from her dress form and put it on. Seven leaned in as Thorn closed her eyes and opened her hands. Light shone from the cloak; the crowd was silent as they watched, waiting to see what her entry would do. And then something extraordinary happened.

Thorn began to fly.

Now the crowd gasped in unison as Thorn flew just a few feet above the ground, circling the stage, and then rose a bit higher, until she was level with the middle-section seats. The inside of her cloak glittered with thousands of tiny crystals and light. It was the most beautiful garment Seven had ever seen. A few witches clapped, the buzz of conversation filling the Spegg, but mostly they were all bewildered.

Witches *could not fly without brooms*. It went against their laws of magic. It should not be possible, especially not for a Spare. But if her coven had taught the witches of Ravenskill anything, it was that nothing was impossible. Nobody knew about Seven's monstruo abilities, but her Uncle powers were enough to let people know that two Spares could do what they were not meant to do.

Seven clapped and screamed as loud as she could, but the lack of applause was noticeable. Everyone was in shock. Except . . . for the Spare section. They cheered as loudly as their small group could, and Seven looked up at them appreciatively. The Spares had never been a unified coven before, but maybe that was changing. Thorn landed, gave a small bow, and then joined the other champions to the side of the stage to await the winner announcement.

After a few minutes Enve Lopes came back onstage.

"Thank you for your patience, all. We have the results!" Enve was wearing a subdued black dress, covered in feathers, to match the mood.

The crowd cheered, and the tension was high. Seven rubbed her hands on her jeans and whispered over and over again, "Come on, Thorn, come on."

"The winner of this year's costura trials is . . ."

The moments stretched out and felt like forever. Seven would not take her eyes off Thorn, and Thorn, looking incredibly nervous, was staring right back at her. *You've got this, Thorn,* Seven wished she could tell her. *No matter what happens, you've got this.*

"THORN LAROUX!"

"Yes!" Seven jumped up and began screaming. She had to keep herself from running out onto the stage and hugging Thorn.

Thorn looked stunned as she was handed the costura trophy and enchanted to be dressed in the cape she had made, with the shoes she had made, the gloves she had made, everything Thorn had created throughout the trials.

While many witches in the audience clapped, some people didn't, many of whom walked out, leaving the Spegg altogether. The Spare section was thunderously loud, and Seven spotted Thorn's family and her own, cheering wildly from their seats.

"Thorn Laroux has made history as the first Spare *and* the youngest witch to win a Golden Frog Games sport, and as of just moments ago, we have the overall Golden Frog Games winner as well . . . RAVENSKILL!"

Now the crowd erupted in wild cheering, some witches even running back in to join the celebration. And Seven had to hold herself up against the wall, exhausted and stunned, because, according to the scoreboard overhead, Thorn had won not just the fashion trials, but the entire games. She had pulled ahead in public sentiment points, making her the costura champion and the MVW.

Thorn Laroux had won. She had done the impossible and now she would get to see the future.

CHAPTER THIRTY-SEVEN
VISIONS

THAT VERY NIGHT, Thorn touched the Golden Frog. She went into a lit-up booth that had been erected on the roof of the Hall of Elders. Her family and friends were allowed to wait outside, but only she could enter. She was nervous, and hugged Seven and her family before she went in.

"I don't know why, but this is scarier than fighting Lotus," Thorn said.

"Maybe it will tell you how we can help Valley," Seven said.

"That's what I'm hoping for too."

Seven squeezed Thorn's hand. "Good luck."

Thorn squeezed back and walked into the booth.

Seven wasn't supposed to see the vision, but somehow, the moment Thorn touched the Golden Frog, Seven's mind went with hers. A scene flashed before her: a peculiar house in Ravenskill she did not recognize, the symbol of a large animal on the front door, a group of witches meeting in secret, the three witches holding the foxes that Seven had seen in the Crones Cliff Manor Museum. Ravenskill, engulfed in flames. A bright, enchanting light underwater. When Thorn emerged from the booth, she stared at Seven. She was pale, and her hands were shaking. Neither of them knew what the vision could mean, but one thing was for certain: It wasn't anything good.

CHAPTER THIRTY-EIGHT
DOWN WITH SPARES

TWO WEEKS HAD PASSED since the games, and the investigation of the Cursed Toads and the stone hex had hit a wall. The only definitive conclusion they'd come to was that Lotus was involved.

"No kidding!" said Seven as she read the *Squawking Crow* article. Seven and Thorn were in Seven's room, the windows wide open to let the fresh spring breeze and sunshine in.

In Lotus's room they had found River's green cloak, a missing poisonous toad ("Who *knows* what she was going to use *that* for," Seven told Thorn), one of Thorn's needles, Graves's ring, and a paper singed with purple flame. All signs pointed to Lotus trying to frame River, and that in order to impersonate a witch, she had needed something that belonged to them.

There was a memorial page set up for River and for the

victims of the stone hex, who had still not been healed. Seven and Thorn visited Valley in the Bluewing Infirmary every day and every night, and Seven tried to come up with a cure on her own using plants and potions. If she could communicate with monstruos, if she could roam the Cursed Forest unharmed, then she would use it to her benefit. Graves also visited Valley often, and had put a small bracelet on her stone wrist, the words *My Pumpkin* carved into a delicate copper plate held together by a brown cord.

Thanks to Seven's and Thorn's information, they knew Lotus wanted more than anything to touch the Golden Frog herself. Why she wanted the knowledge so badly, they still did not know. The Committee on Magical Misdeeds concluded that Lotus had been lying about her grandmother and great-great-grandmother teaching her archaic magic, since they had both died before she was born. Indeed, they had died even before the Cursed Toads became Spares, so it was impossible they taught them archaic magic, and the mystery behind who had been orchestrating all the chaos in the Twelve Towns would remain unsolved. For now. But not forever, if Seven had anything to do with it.

The Golden Frog was safely housed in the House of Elders, where it would remain for the next four years. Seven had nightly dreams about the vision she had seen, and she and Thorn wondered to each other why they both were able to see it.

"It's like the way I am connected to the animals, in a sense," Seven said. "I don't see what they see but I can speak to them with my mind. Maybe you were telling me without realizing it."

"Or maybe our coven connection is really strong," Thorn said. "There have been cases where covens shared special powers depending on their bond."

"Maybe," said Seven, but she couldn't help thinking it was more complicated than that.

"Did they ever give you your cloak back?" Seven asked.

"No." Thorn was sitting on Seven's bed, hugging a pillow to her chest. "They said it was an abomination! I think they're going to burn it."

"We can't let them," Seven said, already scheming a way to steal it back.

"No more capers. Please, not for at least a week?" Thorn groaned.

"Okay, okay," Seven said, but she was still planning a scheme in her brain. Just in case.

Seven had resumed training for her official Uncle trials, but now that she had gotten a handle on her monstruo abilities, she was less nervous and not so sure she would participate this coming autumnal equinox. She had until she was eighteen, the Gran had said, so as long as nobody else found out, she would be okay. Suspicions about why the Cursed Forest monstruos had helped douse the fire were circling, though

Knox had assured the town that sometimes that happened out of self-preservation. Seven thought she might be covering for her, and if she somehow knew about her monstruo abilities since Seven had decided to still keep that a secret.

The tests on her magic had not revealed anything about her abilities either, thank the Stars. The Gran had chalked it up to Seven's extraordinary abilities as a Spare—an anomaly that they had no experience with so far. Seven wanted to slow down a bit, spend more time with Thorn, Graves, and Poppy and write to her friends in Crones Cliff Manor, Figgs and Crimson.

She had finally reached the end of Delphinium's diary a few days back, and it had left her, infuriatingly, on a cliffhanger. The last thing the Monstruo Uncle wrote was that she was planning to escape the Twelve Towns somehow, to outrun her death sentence. But Seven hadn't been able to find out if she'd succeeded or if they really had killed her. And she might never find out.

Thorn's phone pinged. "Poppy said to turn the telecast on!"

It was what they had been waiting for, an announcement about the Spare rights bill.

Tiordan Whisperbrew came on the screen, their face somber, and Seven's stomach dropped. She looked at Thorn, who scrambled closer to Seven, and took her hand as they watched.

"Today is a sad day in Ravenskill history. By a slim margin, the anti-Spare legislation has passed in a rare community-wide vote just this afternoon."

After everything had happened with Thorn's cloak, there had been a call from the Hill Society for a community vote. Except according to some old rules, not everyone was *allowed* to vote, only representatives from each neighborhood, and it was overwhelmingly stacked with Hill Society sympathizers and anti-Spare witches. It had been a sham, but Seven had hoped that the good witches would outweigh the bad. She had been wrong.

Seven shook her head. They couldn't do this, could they? Just take away what little rights Spares had?

"Spurred on by outrage at the win of the capable champion Thorn Laroux, and the Uncle-ship of Seven Salazar, certain members of our community have banded together to bring us back to the days when things were much, much worse for Spares. But the legislation is in for a fight, as pro-Spare groups have already raised strong objections. I, as your faithful reporter, try to remain impartial, but there are some situations that are just right and wrong, and this is wrong. To any Spare who is watching this today, know that I am on your side. They won't win this without a fight. And they cannot beat us if we are united."

Then the broadcast was cut out completely, and the telecast screen went dark.

Late that night, a raven came to Seven's window. It knocked on the glass with its beak. Seven thought of Thorn's hands being burnt and opened the window with caution, one hand up as a warning. She searched the black bird's leg for any notes or scrolls attached, but there were none.

"I mean no harm, Uncle Seven," the raven said. "I have a message for you."

"All right, let's hear it," Seven said.

"Look for the lost one," said the crow.

"The lost one?"

The crow nodded.

"The lost what?"

"I do not know; that is the only message I was given."

"And who gave it to you?"

"A squirrel, a small brown squirrel from another town."

A squirrel, Seven thought as the crow flew away into the night.

She did not know any squirrels well, but she would ask the raccoons in the morning. As she lay down to rest that night, all she could think about was "the lost one" and what in the Twelve Towns it could mean.

EPILOGUE

SEVEN HAD BEEN PLAGUED with dreams of the Nightbeast for weeks. It was a baby, and Seven held it in her arms, rocking it to sleep.

"It's just like the dream you used to have," she told Thorn as they walked to school one morning.

"Not used to," Thorn said. "I've been having it for the past few weeks too."

Just then, Seven heard a piercing cry. It was the Nightbeast, and Seven could tell that it was hurt.

"Thorn, I have to go. Tell them I got sick at school." Seven began to run in the direction of the enchanted forest.

"Seven! I heard it too!" Thorn cried out, and Seven stopped dead in her tracks.

"What?" Seven turned around slowly.

"I . . . heard the Nightbeast crying too," Thorn said,

tears streaming down her face. It was just like the moment Valley had confessed that she too had been hearing the Nightbeast. The memory of her friend made Seven's chest tighten with grief, grief that was still fresh and painful and sour.

Seven held one hand out for Thorn and raised an eyebrow, and Thorn took hold, then together they ran to the enchanted part of the forest. When they reached the Nightbeast, it was panting on the ground, lying on its side. A sharp pang hit Seven right in the heart, the same way it did every time she'd seen the Nightbeast hurt or upset. The two witches rounded the monstruo carefully, slowly, but nothing could've prepared them for what they saw.

Three Nightbeast cubs, cuddled up with the Nightbeast. With their mother.

"Oh my goats." Thorn held her hands up to her mouth. "It had babies?"

"Seven," the Nightbeast said weakly, "come closer."

Seven walked closer to the monstruo, and the pull she felt toward it had grown so strong in just one moment, she felt her heart might burst.

"These are my babies. Please, you cannot tell a soul," the Nightbeast said. "If you do, they will hunt them. But they are not dangerous."

Seven knew it was not lying to her and nodded. "I promise. But won't the Gran notice when she brings you food?"

"She does not come in, only enchants the food to appear here," the Nightbeast said.

"Good." Seven smiled down at the babies. They were small but still big, kinda like Beefy.

"You may carry one, if they allow you," the Nightbeast said.

Seven's eyes shone with excitement. "Can Thorn carry one too?"

"Oh my goats, oh my goats," Thorn said.

"Yes. She may." The Nightbeast nodded. "I am tired."

Seven and Thorn picked up two of the Nightbeast cubs as the third slept soundly next to its mother. Seven could not help but think of Valley.

The moment she held the cub to her chest, Seven understood so many things, and yet she could not easily put words to it. She felt a deep love for the creature, she felt a connection to it, an immense pull, and Seven knew she would do anything to protect these cubs. She would give her life for them and somehow she knew they would do the same for her.

"This is just . . . like my dreams. The ones I used to have about a Nightbeast baby," Thorn said. There were tears streaming down her face now. "Except I'm not afraid this time." She looked up at Seven. "All I feel is love."

"Me too," Seven said as she looked at the Nightbeast and its cubs. "That's all I feel too."

ACKNOWLEDGMENTS

First, I'd like to thank my incredible, incredible readers. There is some contention over what you're calling yourselves . . . Toad-heads, Witchlings, goats? You should probably hold a meeting to decide, but until then I will call you all my raccoons. Thank you for reading Witchlings book one, for all the fan art, the cosplay, the letters, the messages—I read every single thing, and I can't tell you how HAPPY it makes me that you love this story and world as much as I do. From the bottom of my heart, thank you for taking a chance on this series, Valley, Seven, Thorn, and me. I will keep writing these stories as long as you keep reading them. Hope you weren't too upset by the ending of this book, and I'm sending you strength for the book-three wait. I promise it will be worth it.

To *my* champion and agent, Suzie Townsend, an enormous thank-you. I would never be able to do half of what I do without you. Thank you for keeping me on track, encouraging me, and always knowing what to say. You are the absolute best at what you do, and I am incredibly lucky and grateful to have you on my side.

A Beefy-sized thank-you to Emily Seife, my amazing editor. Witchlings would be a Goose House–sized mess without your guidance, thoughtful notes, and patience. Thank you for continuing to make me a better writer and for caring so much about this world and these characters. I am so lucky to have you as an editor and hope we get to work together for a long, long time.

Sophia, you are honest to goose the MVW. Thank you for always having my back and being a Witchlings fan in your own right. I appreciate you so much, and the Oracle told me they envision great things for your future. You really bring joy to my job every day.

To the Scholastic Committee on Magical Misdeeds—Kassy Lopez for your Oracle-level notes and assistance; Rachel Feld for your marketing sorcery and enthusiasm worthy of any Witches of Heartbreak Cove book launch; Seale Ballenger for being a publicity wizard and for the best Edgar Allan Toad cosplay to date; Lizette Serrano, Emily Heddleson, and Maisha Johnson for being my own personal Miss Deweys and going to bat for me in the educational and library market; Christopher Stengel for designing a stunning cover and jacket that any aesthetic-obsessed House of Stars witch would approve of;

Constance Gibbs and Katie Dutton for making Witchlings look so good on the witchernet (and for making that Edgar Allan Toad replica; I love him!); my production team Janell Harris and Elizabeth Krych for doing a job Jonafren and Alaric would be proud of; and copy editor Priscilla Eakeley and proofreaders Lara Kennedy, Jessica White, and Kristine Scheiner for Frog House–level attention to detail—I appreciate you so much! You are ALL toadally awesome. Thank you for your hard work, dedication, love, and care for this series!

To Lissy Marlin for the enchanting illustrations and artwork, you really created something magical, and I am grateful for you! And to all the authors, bloggers, and reviewers who supported me online and beyond the Cursed Forest of Twitter, thank you so much!

To my own coven, Kat, Phil, Ryan, and Peter—thank you for always being by my side, listening to me panic over what turns out to actually be a good thing, and letting me beat you at *Just Dance* (Ryan only). I love you guys more than you will ever, ever know, and I am the luckiest person in the world to have such talented, loyal, kind, and most importantly (for me as a House of Stars witch) beautiful friends. Let's go ride the Nightbeast to karaoke!

To David, Pancho, and my whole family of Spares, thank you for supporting me (all of you) and for reading my books (some of you). I love you all so much and appreciate you putting up with me as the weird but most famous one.

ABOUT THE AUTHOR

Claribel A. Ortega, *New York Times* bestselling author of *Ghost Squad* and *Witchlings*, is a former reporter who writes middle grade and young adult fantasy inspired by her Dominican heritage. When she's not busy turning her obsession with eighties pop culture, magic, and video games into books, she's cohosting her podcast, *Bad Author Book Club*. Claribel has been featured on BuzzFeed, NPR, *Good Morning America*, and *Deadline*.

You can find her on Twitter, Instagram, and TikTok at @Claribel_Ortega and on her website at claribelortega.com.